MW01713652

The Water Buffalo That Shed Her Girdle

A Novel By

Reva Leah Stern

BookLand press

TORONTO, CANADA

This book is a work of fiction. Names, characters, places and incidents are either the product of the author's imagination or are used fictitiously, and any resemblance to actual persons living or dead, events or locales is entirely coincidental.

Published by:
Bookland Press Inc.
6021 Yonge Street, Suite 1010
Toronto, Ontario M2M 3W2
www.booklandpress.com

Printed and bound in Canada

Text editor: Stacey Balakofsky
Front cover illustration by Kandy Stern

Library and Archives Canada Cataloguing in Publication

Stern, Reva Leah
The water buffalo that shed her girdle / a novel by Reva Leah Stern.

ISBN 978-0-9783793-5-3

I. Title.

PS8637.T483W38 2008 C813'.6 C2008-902813-9

For Mom and Dad who exemplified their titles.
Their love for their children was not loudly proclaimed,
it was just graciously given.

"The high minded person does not bear grudges, for it is not the mark of a great soul to remember injuries, but to forget them."

~ *Aristotle* 384-322 BCE

CHAPTER ONE

I am contemplating the perfect suicide.

High Jumping... I live in a hermetically sealed high-rise condominium... on the second floor. If I could somehow squeeze through the window's five-inch opening, I'd most certainly land on the grassy knoll below where I would become, at best, a paraplegic.

A Sleeping Pill Cocktail... I hate drugs that do anything other than annihilate putrid infections, so I've never accumulated a home pharmacy... but I do have a half bottle of stale-dated Advil and a litre of Metamucil, which if combined could succeed in turning me into a runny vegetable stew.

Wrist Dissection... I don't have any razor blades (at least none that aren't clogged with armpit stubble). Besides, I hate the smell of blood and I couldn't tolerate leaving behind a mess of permanent stains on my pristine ivory carpets.

Death by Stench... If only I still had my beautiful solid brick home with its airtight garage. My new condominium's multi-level parking facility with its space age ventilation system can do nothing more than turn carbon monoxide into foul-smelling smog.

At seven a.m. my phone rings. I let Bell answer. At seven-fifteen Bell is busy at it again.

Before the hour is up Bell has wait-listed nine calls for me, four of which are from my friend Madeleine. I could call her back and tell her that everything is fine. Or I could admit to her that since my twenty-four-year-old baby son is getting married in six days… without me… I actually feel like shit.

I stare blankly at the ivory silk evening gown I've left hanging on the closet door; and once again I begin to leak streams of bitter tears. I have repeated this exhausting exercise throughout most of the night. I begin to contemplate how many gallons of the salty liquid can be stored in my body before I drown in my own personal "Dead Sea."

The incessant ringing is wearing me down but I manage to keep myself from answering. I wait and listen to the annoyingly cheery voice of my friend Madeleine resonating through her message:

"Hi, Rachel. It's me. How ya doin'? Did you sleep all right? Call me okay?"

A match has been ignited and smoke signals are billowing across the phone lines. My support system has been called in to squelch the fire.

I start to play back the rest of my messages, but they all seem to smack of compassionate conspiracy; all, but one. The cheerful confident request from my six-year-old grandson Gabriel sings through the earpiece: "Saftah, mommy just bought me new shoes for Uncle Aaron's wedding. She says they're dancing shoes and ya know what? They're really comfortable, so I'll be able to dance with you better than when I'm wearing my sneakers. So, you know what? You better wear comfortable shoes too so we can both dance better, okay?"

Tears slide along my temples and puddle up in my ears as his ardent "I love you, Saftah" reverberates in my head. Then a final click and the hollow silence sets in once again. A tissue soaks up the evidence of the pain that has continued to leak all over my pillow. I have an urgent need to fill my mind with less daunting information.

I listen hazily to my sister's team-motivating message: "Hi, Rach. It's me. Look, we all know the big day is coming... but we're all trying to pretend it's not to make it easier for you to pretend it's not. So, why are you making this so damned difficult for us? Why can't you just rant and swear like a drunken biker and get it out of your system?"

"Just remember you have three other kids who love you and let it go at that!"

There is no point in calling back to remind her that I have four kids and that I'd like them all in my life. She will just remind me once again: "Speaking of your three 'normal' kids, I will never understand why in hell they agreed to march at Aaron's faccactah wedding?"

In an attempt to avoid my single sister Rebecca's lecture on child rearing, I opt to return Madeleine's call instead. By now her cheerfulness has clearly subsided.

"Okay, Rachel. Let's cut the crap!" Madeleine barks in her most robust, shit-kicking voice.

"We all know you're going to have a miserable week, so what can we do to make it better, one day at a time? Do you want to go out for lunch...or do you want company at your place? Which is it going to be, huh?"

"Thanks, Madeleine, but I really just want to be left alone for now."

"Alone is a dumb idea, Rachel. This is the worst time to be

alone."

"Why? What in hell do you think I'm gonna do, off myself?"

"Oh yeah. I'm really worried. Come on. Get real. Aaron's a selfish, spoiled brat and if that ex-husband of yours had half a brain, he wouldn't be rewarding the little shit by throwing him a lavish wedding without the mother-of-the-groom."

"Maddy, he's still my son, little shit or not!"

"Yeah, and his big shit father is helping him freeze you out of the wedding .... So, Kiddo, wake up and feel the icicles!"

"Look, reminding me of what my bloody ex may or may not have done doesn't change the fact that Aaron hasn't spoken to me in two years and doesn't want me at his wedding!"

"Rachel, Aaron waited until he was twenty-two and through needing you to support him before he suddenly decided to reject you. You, on the other hand, have retaliated by sending him greeting cards and food packages. How dare you abuse him with good wishes and homemade pies?"

"Come on, Madeleine. What? I wasn't supposed to try to connect? Anyway I stopped sending stuff at least five months ago... after I found out that he was dumping my unopened cards into the trash."

"Good for you. And now it's time to put it behind you and move on, okay?"

"Move on huh? ... Do you know what I did last night? I pulled my mother-of-the-bride gown from Wendy's wedding out of the closet and tried it on. I wanted to see if it still fit... just in case Aaron has a last minute change of heart."

"Ah-ha! So you might contemplate suicide if the gown doesn't fit?"

"Madeleine, don't call the men in white coats, but yesterday ... I called the banquet hall and asked if it was possible for me to hide in the kitchen to watch the ceremony."

"Are you out of your mind? Why would you even think of doing such a stupid thing?"

"So that some day, I could tell him that I was there. I was a witness. Anyway, it doesn't matter because it turns out that the only thing I'd see from the kitchen is the garbage dumpster."

"Ya know what Rachel? I actually think you'd stand under that wedding canopy if he called and asked you today."

"Hell, I'd stand under it if he called from a cell phone while he's marching down the aisle!"

"Are you a Pollyanna, an idiot, or a sadist? Sometimes, I just can't figure you out!"

"If you do, call me, then we'll have lunch. In the meantime I'll be right here in bed where I do my best thinking."

I listen for the hollow buzz of the disconnected line before I press the off button. I've had enough conversation for now. The other messages will remain on hold until I feel ready to ward off all well-meaning offers and pseudo-therapeutic suggestions.

I slither out of bed and stagger to the bathroom with the notion that emptying my bladder might clear my head. It doesn't. I methodically wash my hands while gawking at my unsightly reflection as if it alone is to blame for the pale, puffy image that glares back at me.

I stare blankly into the sparse medicine cabinet once again before heading back to the asylum of my queen-sized bed. En route I take a peek out my second floor window to glimpse what lies below. I heave a sardonic sigh as I estimate the height of the fresh snow bank that seems to be rising to my windowsill.

As I settle myself under the heavy cotton quilt, I begin to chant a newly created mantra: "I will not think about the wedding, I will think of other things. I will not think about the wedding, I will think..."

I've done a lot of thinking since my youngest child Aaron walked out of my life, but I don't feel any the wiser for it. I'm still baffled by this child that I thought had been given so much and who believes he received nothing at all. I, on the other hand, grew up thinking that I was born into aristocracy, only to discover that the stale white bread and gravy we dined on at our rusty chrome dinette was not the entrée of choice at the prime minister's Duncan Fife table.

Of late my history has proven to be kinder on my heart than my present. But perhaps I can make today easier if I just concentrate on remembering the past. I'll close my eyes, clench my teeth, and brace my mind against any fallout I might experience as I carefully recall how I got to this place. I didn't cruise along smoothly. In fact it was a rather perplexing and often turbulent voyage.

I think my troubles may have originated with my limited history of dating that began in high school and continued a few years later with the meeting of my future husband.

CHAPTER TWO

In the process of my evolution from childhood to adult, I became uncomfortably aware that there are definite drawbacks to skipping grades in elementary school.

By the time I entered high school and realized that my new girlfriends were the norm for first-year students, it became perfectly clear that I was a misfit. They were mostly three inches taller, two years older, and twenty pounds heavier than me. I felt like a female Mickey Rooney. To help me conform I needed very specific attributes, like, for instance, breasts. How could I ever get any high school guy to be anything but a brother figure to me without a pair of first rate knockers?

Every girl in my class had some reasonable manifestation of a bosom, except me. So I spent an entire weekend building one out of an old brassiere of my mother's and some two-ply Kleenex. I had to work discreetly so that my brothers, David and Adam, wouldn't get wise and cause me serious heartache.

I secretly cut and pinned, tucked and stitched, until I was so pleased with my handiwork I could barely contain my joy. But

I had to wait all weekend before I could try out my new bosom on the class.

Monday morning finally arrived and I was up with the rooster, preening and stuffing my chest `a la Kimberly Clark. I examined every angle of my mounds in the mirror before shrouding them with a skimpy Banlon sweater.

Bravado aside, I started out a little self-conscious about my overnight blooms. But by the time I reached the schoolhouse, I was pumped and ready. I removed my jacket, placed it in my locker, and headed for class and the premier unveiling of my womanhood.

As I reached the sunlit room, I became aware of an added bonus that I hadn't bargained on: the bright September sun. Its megawatt spotlight penetrated my baby pink pullover and outlined the straps and criss-cross plunge of my reconstituted brassiere. My plan was going better than I could have ever imagined.

It took a little time, but eventually I became aware that the boys were starting to sneak a peek. Even my balding, beady-eyed history teacher seemed preoccupied with my miraculous growth spurt. All through elementary school I had to watch as my girlfriends blossomed, seemingly overnight. Well, now it was my turn and I wanted to enjoy every minute of it.

The teacher asked me to step forward and read a chapter from *The History of the New World*. I bounded up to the front of the class, raised my book, and began to read. A few pages into the chapter I detected a low muffled rumble travelling through the room, which I ignored. I was used to the lack of concentration by my fellow classmates who were not a bookish crowd to say the least. Within minutes, a more intense murmur riffled throughout the class. The riffle was soon followed by a loud titter. It wasn't long before I could hear all of the male voices in the room humming an indiscernible tune that rapidly developed into a full-out testosterone sing-song: *O-o-oh... yes... she's the great... prete-en-der... oo-oo-oo-o...*

I could feel the sweat hurtling out of every pore in my body. I could also feel one two-ply "falsie" soaking up the moisture in front of my right nipple, while the other "falsie" defected to the middle of my chest causing me to look like a mammalian Cyclops. The song continued unabated, and even though my history teacher seemed every bit as amused by my misery as was the rest of his breed, I remained resolute. I would never allow those cretins to win. But I did consider how much more comfortable I might have been if only *The History of the New World* had been a much larger book.

That experience did clearly help to alter my path to wisdom because, after that dreadful day, I discarded the idea of ever aiding and abetting Mother Nature again. I lived without my blossoming womanhood for yet another year. But, eventually, she gave me more than my share of bosom for which I have alternately blessed and cursed her.

My next brush along the road to my dating destiny happened long after the Kleenex incident was all but forgotten. It was at least twelve months later, and in teenage years, that's like a decade. Your pals don't bother to remember the humiliation of yesterday when there are so many new and present opportunities to shame and debase you.

My dad was aptly dubbed "The Warden" by my pals, who were forced to come up with every ridiculous excuse in the handbook of teenaged excuses to get me out of my house for an evening. Perhaps it was the fact that I was younger than most of my friends, or perhaps it was my dad's fear that any y-chromosomed member of the species that crossed my path would ravage me on the spot. I suppose I should have felt flattered that he thought I was such a catch, but the truth is, I was a little slow in development when it came to attracting boys. Hell, I was smart, compassionate, insightful, popular, and patient. I was the perfect platonic pal.

My mom would discreetly reassure me: "Be patient dear, 'cause one day you'll grow up to be a beautiful swan just like in the fairy tale, but for now you're just that anxious duckling."

"Thanks mom. But it's 'ugly duckling'."

During that school year, I watched my friends pair off one by one. It was like being chosen last for the baseball team. Whenever I joined them, I felt like parsley on a dinner plate. So, for a little while, I opted for the uncomplicated company of my books and records.

As the year developed so did my body, but I barely noticed. It was too gradual for me.

I was also totally oblivious to the fact that my platonic guy pals had begun to act self-conscious and stupid around me, and that they had become less interested in my brain size and more interested in my bra size. My girlfriends started dropping hints that this buddy or that buddy liked me, but I was too sharp to fall for that trap. They tried to get me all worked up about Tom, Dick or… Hunter.

Hunter was the blue-eyed cool cat with the perfect body, teeth, and hair. But I was sure that if I fell for it, I'd soon discover it was all just a harmless joke… on me.

I took great care to avoid any eye contact whatsoever with Hunter and his chums for fear they would humiliate me. For months, my friends kept nagging at me, telling me that he really, really liked me and wanted to ask me out. But I kept sending them away with one of my smart-assed defensive assault tactics. Eventually they broke me down.

To get us together, Hunter's buddies told my girlfriends to make sure that I showed up at the next tea dance. I had never been allowed to go to a nighttime school dance, even though most of my girlfriends had been going since grade school. But tea dances were right after the final class of the day, so my dad would never even have to know. The only important factors left to consider were that Hunter was going to be there... and (oh my God) he wanted me!

The big day finally arrived and I was as fidgety as a toddler in a wedding procession. All of the "what ifs" that I could invent kept creeping through my mind. My girlfriends tried to convince me that there were no valid "what ifs" to worry about, but I was really more comfortable worrying. So I smiled bravely, told them I was fine, and then privately went right on worrying.

On the big day, when the final school bell rang, all the girls ran to their lockers, grabbed their makeup kits, and headed for the washroom where they transformed themselves from fresh-faced school girls to femmes fatales. I, on the other hand, looked the same coming out as going in.

In the gymnasium, the hi-fi blasted dreamy Elvis tunes as the girls gathered at one end, leaving the boys to congregate at the other. It was a Mexican standoff.

Finally, one brave man broke rank. It was Hunter.

He seemed to be moving across the gym floor in animated slow motion. Everyone gasped as he continued on a diagonal path directly toward me. The girls tried to gulp back their squeals of joy as he moved ever closer. Megan leaned in and whispered enthusiastically:

"Holy Shit. He's coming right to you!"

As he got closer, I could hear him humming along with Elvis:

"Don't be cru-u-u-uel to a heart so true...I don't want no other love...baby it's just you I'm thinkin' of..."

My heart was revving like a souped-up engine. I cast my

eyes downward in a demure affectation.

It was the longest walk in history, but now, finally, I could see his blue suede shoes right in front of me. It was time to slowly raise my eyes to meet his.

There he stood in his tight Levis and sky blue Banlon v-neck, staring at me with those sapphire eyes. I waited… the romance magazines tell you that you can't rush these things… until at long last he spoke:

"Would you like to dance?"

Oh my God. There it was. The moment I had dreamed of. The envy of all men and the desire of all women... Hunter… was asking me!

I looked up and calmly replied: "Sure. I'd love to."

I saw a twinkle in his eye as he continued:

"Well... maybe somebody'll ask ya!"

By the time I turned sixteen I'd forgotten all about Hunter and had been seeing Clark for almost a year.

Clark was all that Hunter had been… only doubled. He was tall, dark, and definitely handsome. He was the perfect athlete, student, and human being. At six-feet, four inches he was a natural basketball star and a dynamic competitive swimmer as well.

The fact is Clark was almost perfect, except for one thorny little flaw. We didn't share the same religion.

Now that didn't seem to bother his parents, who were devout, church-going Protestants, but if my Jewish atheist father had detected even a hint of such a match, I would have been banished to some earthly purgatory.

The first time that Clark and I actually spoke was on the night my three girlfriends and I got stuck twelve miles away from home without a ride back from the skating rink. He swooped in to the rescue like a caped crusader. As my friends pulled and shoved each other to get into the front seat beside him, Clark calmly walked over to the passenger side, asked the girls to jump out and asked me to slide in beside him. I obeyed.

It took Clark several tries before I would agree to even have a Coke with him. The Hunter incident had left me pretty suspicious of anyone who would dare to show an interest in me.

Even while we shared several Cokes over several days, I continued to listen for the crushing punch line that would send me into therapy. But it never came. Instead I grew to know Clark as kind, intelligent, humorous, and honest.

One night, after weeks of secret dating, I dredged up the courage to ask Clark why he was interested in me and without hesitation he answered: "That first night at the rink when I saw you shake your head and smile as you watched your friends cat fighting over who would sit in the front seat, I was sold. When you refused to go out with me five times, I guess I should've given up but it just made me even more determined. We haven't had a boring minute together since we met. You're smart, you're a good listener, you're patient and kind…"

The flow was interrupted by my silent stinging prediction that the inevitable next line would be "and I think we can be great buddies." I managed to keep my thoughts to myself, thus allowing him to complete his own farewell speech.

"… and the fact that you are the best looking girl with the best body in the entire school counts for something too, you know. And, Rachel, I really hope you feel the same way about me."

The verdict was in. Having mirrored my sentiments toward him word for word, I knew that he was the soul mate of my life and that we were meant to be together. The question was:

Could I give up my blood for love?

I knew that if my father were ever to find out about us,

I would either be disowned or dismembered, and living in the small town of Prescott with less than 4,000 inhabitants, it was very likely that our secret would inevitably leak out

My mother knew about us intuitively, as mothers usually do, but she took the whole thing in her stride. She was probably confident that our puppy love would grow up to become, at best, a platonic old hound or, at worst, rabid. Either way, I'm certain she was convinced that in time it would expire; but she couldn't have been more wrong because we were hopelessly and irrevocably in love.

One evening while my dad was busy downstairs in our dry goods store, my Mom looked up from the mittens she was knitting and mumbled:

"Your dad's going to Toronto next week to help your brothers arrange loans for their tuition. He's taking Rebecca along, so it'll be just you and me... all on our own... for two or three days."

"M-m-hmm," I mumbled back with obvious disinterest. After all, how was a couple of days alone with my mother, in the middle of a school week, going to change my life?

"I suppose you'd like to invite that Clark fellow over for dinner," she continued.

As I began to pledge my undying gratitude, she resounded with, "Just don't let your father find out that you invited him over here behind his back or you'll be in big trouble young lady!"

During that forbidden dinner, it became evident to me that in spite of her aching conscience, my mother liked Clark.

What a terrible burden I had placed on her.

I don't think that she had ever been dishonest with my father about anything in their entire marriage before this and I was terrified that uncovering our little liaison could jeopardize their lives as much as it would mine. I could be held responsible for their inevitable divorce. With that in mind, I bravely declined the next opportunity to bring Clark to another clandestine dinner with mom. Thus I single-handedly saved my parents' marriage.

After that, Clark and I withdrew into the shadows once again and soon mom stopped asking about him.

One star-drenched night, Clark slipped an eye-popping diamond on the appropriate finger of my left hand and proposed that ancient and sacred question. I was speechless. He waited patiently for my answer, but I was incoherent for the rest of the evening.

At sixteen, after a year and a half with the only real boyfriend I had ever known, it was clear to me that I needed to put some distance between us so that I could weigh the risks of the lifetime commitment he was asking of me. Choosing Clark the Gentile would surely mean permanent exile from my family and I wasn't sure if I could face that sentence. Clark and I talked it over and we agreed to give ourselves a year apart to prepare for whatever decision would come.

I begged my parents to send me to Toronto to finish my education. Of course I was careful not to mention my undying love for Clark or the fact that I wanted to get away from them. My dad's rigid decrees were beginning to wear on my patience and I needed to rebel, with his blessings of course. I was also dreading the idea of being left behind in Prescott when my two best friends in the world were escaping to Montreal and Toronto. Esther Levy was heading off to study in Montreal, while Megan O'Connor was hoping to retreat to Loreto Abbey, a Catholic boarding school in Toronto for lost girls. Oh, she wasn't actually lost, but she had lost her father when she was barely a toddler, and her mother had died from a brain tumour just as Megan entered high school.

Megan lived under the spell of her wicked Aunt, *Poison Apple* while I lived at home with my dad, *Attila the Hun*. Megan loved to spend time at my house where she could temporarily escape from the exhausting Cinderella duties that were heaped on her. I, on the other hand, envied the freedom that allowed her to leave her house any time of the day without fear of enemy interrogation on her return. She and I spent many joyous sleepovers plotting our revenge. They say that one man's meat is another man's poison... but most of the time Megan and I fought over how "Grade A special" we thought the other's hind o' beef was.

After months of listening to my exhaustive nagging and whining, my father finally acquiesced to try the experiment for a year. He would allow me to continue my studies in Toronto as long as I lived with my brother David and his new bride. I thought it was a great idea. After all, how tough could that be? David was only twenty-one and his bride was nineteen. They were practically my contemporaries.

That summer, Megan and I headed for Toronto and our exciting new lives. But by the end of that first school year, things had definitely changed. My sister-in-law had insisted that I move out of their apartment and into my grandmother's attic because she needed tranquillity and harmony while she suffered through her first pregnancy. Meanwhile, Megan had left the evil convent and returned to her loving Aunt. (It's amazing how exposure to real tyranny can alter your perspective.)

During my trial separation from Clark, I came to accept that blood does take precedence over love when you fear losing a few pints of the stuff. I had to face the fact that my father would never accept my chosen one if he weren't one of our Chosen Ones. So, by the end of the school year, my relationship with Clark had become broken-hearted history.

Like Megan, I had also become disenchanted with life in Toronto, but I didn't want to go back to Prescott a beaten woman.

I decided to take a little time off to consider some life altering options. I had to determine whether to forge ahead toward law school or take a unique and special path, which actually meant that I had no idea what I wanted to do.

I knew that I didn't want to go home for the summer to work in my parents store because I'd be living in a prison compound where, under duress, the Warden could force me to squeal that I had no plans for the next semester.

In an act of self-preservation, I took a summer job at a bank in Toronto, a decision that made me a two-time winner. First, it gave me the freedom to come and go as I pleased and second it impressed the hell out of my parents who suspected that I took the job in the stifling hot city just to help lift the financial burden from them. Actually that second point infused me with my first real bout of Jewish guilt.

The real truth is, I wasn't eager to go home and find out that Clark might already be cuddling up to some new one and only.

In spite of the fact that I was the breakor and he was the breakee, I needed to believe that his broken heart was a chronic condition that would take decades to heal.

Even though I have to admit to some ugly romantic encounters that may sully my memoirs, I can still bravely reflect on the highlights of my limited experiences with men. It's true that Clark was my first real boyfriend, but he didn't give me my first real kiss. That happened on another momentous occasion that took place before I ever knew there was to be a Clark in my life.

Along the banks of the St. Lawrence River between Johnstown and Prescott stood dozens of broken down, historical monuments that the locals held in high esteem. Those beacons were tributes to the noble British soldiers who fought the good fight to keep Canada out of the hands of those greedy Yanks. At least that's what the locals used to say after they had chugged back a few dozen beers.

"Beware of the bold, ravenous old Eagle who's ready to gobble up our innocent, tender, young Beaver!"

Nevertheless, on any Saturday night you could find our noble protesters across the border gobbling up American beer and haggling for American bargains with our Canadian money. Then, to the delight of their families and the utter frustration of our local merchants, those noble men would smuggle their cut-rate stash across the border and back to town.

One of those shoreline monuments was The Windmill. No one seemed to have any idea why it was called The Windmill because it was in fact a lighthouse.

The Windmill was situated on a hill that overlooked the serene and stately St. Lawrence River. For many years that remote and majestic mound was the gathering place for all the hormonally over-developed kids in the area. It was the place where weird and wonderful rites of passage transpired… and it was where I experienced my first kiss.

On the ridge below the funnel-shaped obelisk lay a long expanse of rocky shore that was rife with secret hiding places. The choice spot was tucked away in the elbow of an inlet where you couldn't be spotted by a casual passer-by. On that site, the big kids built a glorious fire pit where the finest bonfires ever crafted illuminated our innocence. During those hot summer evenings the boys would set out with their bows and arrows on hunting expeditions while the girls stayed behind. We just didn't have the stomach for the kill.

Once the hunters returned victorious, the "women" generally vacated the area while the "men" cleaned and carved their prey. The women would return on cue to dredge and fry the delicacies in a huge iron skillet over the open pit fire. There is nothing today that can compare with the crackling crunch of those pan-fried frogs legs. The closest I've come is the Colonel's extra crispy fingers".

After our succulent snack, it was always time for the games to begin ... but only for the big kids. The little ones would be told: "You mosquitoes have a very important job to do for your Generals. It's your duty to stay at the top of the hill and watch out for the enemy."

So in the dark of night, while the big kids dabbled in their special undercover investigations, we minors sat out on the wet grass guarding against the enemy and watching out for the infestation of cooties they warned would attack if we moved from the spot.

The summer I turned eight I decided that I had taken enough of this class system, so I jumped up and firmly objected: "I'm not sitting up on the hill watching for anybody tonight. Either I get to play or I go right home and tell mommy and daddy what you're doing, and then they'll tell everybody else's parents and you'll all be in big trouble!"

With that, I plopped myself down by the bonfire, while my brothers and their friends retreated to a more isolated spot on the beach for a pow-wow.

It must have been a unanimous vote because they returned promptly with the answer I wanted to hear: "Alright, you kids can play."

Of course I hadn't asked if any of the other little kids wanted to join in. But I was speaking for those underdogs whether they liked it or not.

It seemed that every time it was my turn to spin the bottle, my attention was somehow averted so I'd always find the bottle pointing at an open space. Spin-the-bottle just didn't seem to be my game. The group moved on to post-office, a game I felt confident I could master. But alas, it still seemed that I was never in the right place at the right time. A growing suspicion motivated me to stand firm and demand my rights. The group, now eager to grant my request, suggested that we play a new game that offered me a really good chance of winning. I was blindfolded and seated in the middle of their circle. I was told to pucker up for a kiss and they would remove the blindfold on the count of three.

"One. Two." I sucked my lips together. "Three." I opened my eyes wide and there in front of my face was little Johnny Biccum's bare bum.

"Kith thith," he defiantly lisped.

My feelings had definitely been pricked, but I wouldn't let them get the best of me. I leaned forward and smacked the air voraciously, pretending to kiss his peachy little four-year-old tush. Soon the entire campsite became raucous with laughter. I had risen to the occasion.

As we began to disburse, the cutest ten-year-old in our whole school sidled up to me, looked deeply into my eyes, then gently touched his full soft lips to mine. It only lasted for an instant but I'll always remember it as the most tender and special kiss I ever received.

There was one other who tasted my lips before Clark and he was the surprise of my life.

My friend Megan had been hinting to me for several weeks. "One of the guys really likes you. Honest, Rachel. It's true. He's dying to ask you to go to the movies but he's really afraid you'll refuse …"

"Oh, Christ. Who is this ballsy romantic?"

"I can't tell you his name."

"So how would this work, Megan? You lead me to the movie blindfolded or do I meet this spineless jerk with a bag over his head?"

I became even more doubtful after Megan pleaded that we double date. I deduced that since she needed me to get out of Saturday cleaning at Aunt Poison Apple's house, she'd be prepared to set me up with an orangutan. In spite of my scepticism, I agreed to go along with the plan if she told me who the lucky guy was.

She was cornered. If she wanted my help so she could sit at the back of the theatre and neck with Mitch, she would have to own up.

She looked at me sheepishly and whispered, "It's Hunter."

"Hunter? The 'maybe someone will ask you' Hunter? Are you out of your mind? After what he did to me, you actually think I'd go out with him?"

Megan smiled saucily and replied:

"Uh-huh."

I hadn't seen Hunter for more than a year. His dad had been transferred to the next town and the whole family had moved the summer after the school dance incident.

Megan forged ahead: "I told you a million times that everybody got on Hunter's case for that smart-assed stunt he pulled. But, Rachel, he really did like you. The problem was that you were constantly embarrassing him in front of all his buddies because you wouldn't say hi or even look at him when you passed him in the hall; so he got you back."

I knew that Megan wouldn't have suggested the date if she had any doubt about his story. So I made up my mind that I needed closure on the issue. I needed to rejoice in the spirit of this glorious revelation and accept the fact that my no-nonsense attitude and terrific boobs would just knock his socks off.

Since I was still struggling in vain for evening-out rights at the advanced age of fourteen, it was a relief to hear that sixteen-year-old Hunter would be happy to settle for a Saturday matinee with me instead.

Megan and her boyfriend Mitch were also game. After all, what time of day they necked at the back of a dark theatre made little difference to them.

Aunt Poison Apple suggested that I sleep over at Megan's the night before the movie. She had a list of chores that had to be finished before she'd let her niece out of the tower and of course dear auntie knew that I was just the person to help get them done. We split up the duties and raced through them, leaving ample time to partake in some homemade beauty treatments before bed.

By the time we arrived at the movie theatre the next afternoon, the line-up was all the way down the block. We were late, but we looked fabulous: scrubbed, shiny, stylish, and fragrant. We had it all going for us.

We spotted Mitch and headed to the front of the line to meet our prince charmings.

Megan led the way, barely able to control her erupting hormones as she zeroed in on macho Mitch. As for Hunter, I saw no sign of him. A sense of dread washed over me as the thought raced through my mind that I was likely the brunt of another cruel joke. But before I could wind up for a punch, Megan dodged the blow.

"Hunter, stop holding up the wall and join us," Megan quipped. My elusive date had been hidden from view by the masses of impatient teenyboppers who were pushing and shoving in line. "Hey, Hunter, how've you been?" I said, without looking up.

"Cool man, real cool," he eloquently replied.

That was the extent of our initial exchange. In the silence, I slowly raised my eyes to sneak a glance. I was mesmerized by the herd of wild zits that now grazed all over Hunter's once perfect face.

We took our seats and waited the obligatory thirty minutes for the lights to go down. There was a lot of social networking to be done in those priceless minutes. It was a time to catch up on the latest gossip or for the town bully to scare some unsuspecting kid out of his candy or for the loud mouth brat who saw the movie the night before to yell out the ending.

I don't remember what movie we saw that afternoon, but in my mind's eye I still see a vivid Picasso portrait of that day.

Hunter had certainly changed. You might accurately say he had grown. I'm sure that his new Pillsbury doughboy look was a direct result of the high academic and low athletic opportunities offered at his new school. I didn't care. There was history at stake here. After all those years of actively dreaming about this hunk, he was finally there in my reality and I wasn't about to let him go because of a few dozen Twinkies.

The romantic interlude began when Hunter's hand slithered lightly across the back of my seat and finally rested tentatively on my shoulder. I can still recall the faint fragrance of tobacco on his fingers as he clumsily raked them through my hair. He rubbed his Clearasil-coated cheek against mine and then slowly turned my face toward his. In the glow of the projection light I watched as he voraciously licked his lips as if to remove any telltale luncheon leftovers before firmly pressing them against mine. I suddenly felt light-headed and shaky, but, since I had read a lot on the subject, I was sure that this was what I was to expect from romance. I didn't want to seem like a loose woman, so I remained passive, wondering what would come next and how much more light-headed I would become before I reached bliss. It didn't take long before I felt his sticky tongue exploring my ear while his chubby fingers began an inchworm crawl toward my breasts. That was it!

My light-headedness exploded into full-blown nausea and what I really craved was cool, fresh air. I trampled over the melded bodies of Mitch and Megan as I headed for the exit. I reached the alley just as my breakfast reached the pavement. I braced myself against the brick wall and prayed that no one had witnessed my outrageous commentary. But Cupid was not kind. I looked up to find Hunter standing beside me, looking red-faced and worried. So, in my best Susan Hayward bravado, I stiffened my lip, smiled weakly, and assured him that I would not require an ambulance. I then babbled something about Aunt Poison Apple's mock meat loaf and my barfing spell before begging him to forget the ugly scene he had just witnessed. I always suspected that he might have been more concerned that his buddies would find out about his failed attempt to deflower me, than whether or not I needed medical assistance.

The following weekend we all double dated again. After all I couldn't let Aunt Poison Apple's Shepherd's pie ruin my love life. We skipped the movie and headed to the town fair instead. We went a few rounds on the Ferris wheel and ate every variety of junk food known to man and child, and I left the fair grounds feeling fine.

Mitch drove us all to lover's cove and parked. It took less than five minutes before Megan and Mitch were exploring the nooks and crannies of each other's throats, while Hunter and I quietly enjoyed the simple pleasure of sighting the first star of the evening. As the windows became opaque with the passionate vapours that drifted toward us from the front seat, Hunter seemed compelled to take full advantage of the privacy the fog provided. In his best Clark Gable move, he slid his arm around my waist and pulled me close to him. A sly, crooked smile flashed across his face as he moved in for a close up. I could feel his heart racing against mine as his warm breath brushed my cheek. His eager mouth finally found mine and for an instant I thought, "This is good." As his tongue penetrated my lips, the familiar scent of Clearasil penetrated my brain and I soon found myself heaving up the day's menu on the dewy grass of lover's cove.

Many years later on a rare visit to my hometown, I was enjoying dinner in a favourite old Chinese restaurant along with my husband, my children, and my parents when I caught a glimpse of the Clearasil kid. He was probably thirty-five by then and he was movie star stunning. I made every effort to avoid eye contact with my old beau in case he might be prompted to recall our brief dynamic courtship and seek some kind of revenge.

I'm sure that anyone could imagine my gripping horror as I watched my father get up and head directly over to Hunter's table.

Why were they greeting each other like old friends? How in the world did this back slapping relationship ever blossom? Maybe my dad had hired my old secret beau to fix his car or his plumbing or whatever trade it was that Hunter had mastered. My father soon returned to the table with Hunter, his wife, and their three kids in tow. To my mortification, but with great fatherly pride, my dad introduced us all around.

Mrs. Hunter and their kiddies shyly murmured their hellos then quickly returned to their table, but my dad would not release his grasp on his prey. So, for an interminable five minutes, Hunter and I cautiously exchanged a few innocent stories about the good old teachers at Prescott High while everyone continued eating. Everyone, of course, except my father who still clung relentlessly to Hunter's arm until finally, with both pride and cynicism, he proclaimed:

"You know, dear, Hunter's a gastroenterologist. I went to him for my heartburn problem and he fixed me right up. He's a terrific doctor."

He then proudly turned to my husband and asked:

"Did you know that this guy Hunter was after your wife when she was a little pisher? Of course at the time I wasn't supposed to know anything about it. But you don't have to be jealous. Hunter told me the romance never ripened 'cause whenever he came near her, she heaved up meat loaf."

CHAPTER THREE

Before I knew it, the summer of my discontent had come and gone. Clark and I were still past history and I was still living in Toronto and still gainfully employed at the bank.

It hadn't been difficult to convince my boss that I was a capable employee. For a start, I merely needed to arrive early and leave late. He particularly liked the fact that I listened well, learned quickly, and rejected the popular union work ethic of "never do more than you absolutely have to." Those brown-nose practices kept me at the top of his staff advancement list. Practically overnight I went from gofer to file clerk to teller, advancements that didn't sit very well with the rest of the staff. While promoting me once again to the prestigious position of head teller, my boss, Mr. Hendrix, told me on the Q.T.: "I'm almost certain that you're probably the first *Jewess* ever to hold down a full-time job in our bank."

My staking that claim didn't sit too well with most of the Waspish bank staff either.

Mr. Hendrix was a wonderful old guy and a keen observer of human behaviour. He had taken special notice of a young man who came into the bank every week to cash a cheque. He told me that for some reason, this young man always seemed to hang around until I was available to serve him. I had never noticed such a person, but the boss said that next time, he would point him out to my colleague, Lynn, whose wicket was closer to the entrance than mine and she could signal me.

One busy Friday afternoon, I was seated at my desk basking in my newest promotion as "management trainee" when Lynn came rushing over.

"Rachel. He's here!" she whispered enthusiastically.

I looked up to see a kind of scruffy looking character leaning against the wicket that had formerly been mine. I recognized him as someone that I had served several times before. But I had never taken any particular notice of him in his well-worn, oversized tweed coat, thick woolly muffler and bad James Dean sneer. He looked like any of the young construction workers who rushed through the doors on Friday afternoons anxious to turn their muscle-earned paycheques into weekend-dreams cash.

When Lynn approached him to ask if she could help, he raised his hand and pointed his thumb and finger in pistol-like fashion directly at me and bluntly answered, "No. But she can."

Just at that moment my boss sauntered by my desk mumbling a strong suggestion that I help the gentleman. I obediently approached the counter.

"Good afternoon. What can I do for you?" I asked in a voice as crisp as frozen celery.

"I wanna cash this cheque," was his brusque reply.

"Sir, this is a government cheque. Any of the tellers can do that for you."

"But I'm not asking them. I'm asking you," he said

defiantly.

"Fine, but I'll need identification."

Suddenly, like the Scarlet Pimpernel, Mr. Hendrix appeared from out of nowhere. He placed his initials on the back of the cheque to okay it and then immediately disappeared again. I looked at the cheque to confirm the name. It was made out to Mr. H. Krup. No first name. Just H.

I briefly challenged Mr. H. Krup over the spelling of his last name, which I was very certain should have two p's! I told him that Krup without the second "p" should be pronounced *Croup,* like the cough. He stood fast on the pronunciation, so I reluctantly allowed him to win the argument. I now knew his last name, but his signature was so illegible I couldn't decipher the first one. I was pretty sure there were six letters in it, but other than that it was just monkey scratchings.

I counted out the money twice and placed it in his hand. As I handed over the last bill I looked up in time to catch a sly sexy smile flash across the handsome face that I had never noticed before. I quickly looked away, hoping to hide the evidence displayed in my beet-coloured cheeks, but I couldn't keep myself from sneaking another peek. His deep brown eyes penetrated to the back of my skull as he folded his bills, flipped up his collar, and abruptly turned on his heel and left.

What could the "H" stand for I wondered? Herbert? Too nerdy for such an arrogant guy. Harley? Possibly. He had the muscle macho thing happening all right. What about Hercules? No. That's eight letters and, anyway, what kind of sick mother would stick that label on a child?

A week later "H" returned. But this time he stepped right up and asked for me. Again I cashed his cheque, but this time he didn't turn and leave. Instead he pulled a little notebook from his pocket and pushed it toward me while commanding in a wellprojected stage whisper: "Write your home number down there, okay?"

"Sorry, but this is a place of business!" I indignantly sputtered.

He moved in a little closer and repeated in a clear basso profundo voice, "Are you gonna put your number down here or not?"

As my boss strolled casually by, he muttered, "I suggest you write down your number before he pulls out a megaphone."

I quickly scribbled down my number and pushed the book back across the counter.

"Why in the world would you want my number anyway?" I asked defiantly. He cracked a smug grin and replied:

"Maybe I'll give you a call sometime!"

Oh God. I was experiencing my own personal haunting: An ultimately humiliating invitation, six letters beginning with "H", and it wasn't Hunter.

By the time I arrived home from work that day, panic had set in and I was duly nauseous. Out there some pushy alien from the planet déjà vu had my name and number and I had no idea who he was.

Those were the days when I dated my brothers' friends or my friends' brothers, but to date a stranger I met in a bank would be completely unacceptable to my family.

I knew nothing about him. Was he educated? Was he honest? Was he a serial killer? But most important of all... was he Jewish? The questions haunted me over the entire weekend.

Finally, in an act of desperation, I called my brothers to see if either of them had ever heard his name in their travels. I had wisely jotted down the name off the cheque, so, just in case he called, I'd know to whom I was refusing to speak.

Adam suggested that if this guy appeared at my door

unannounced, I should sic our stern, intimidating eighty-year-old grandmother on him.

It was with David and my sister-in-law Lila that I finally had some success in my covert investigation. Having moved from Montreal after her mother passed away, Lila had lived in Toronto for only a few years. Nevertheless, she was concerned that "H" might be one of the three Krup brothers that used to hang out with her black sheep cousin who "ran with a pretty tough high school crowd." But more important than a possible rap sheet was her niggling fear that they weren't Jewish. She strongly suggested that I forget about him before she handed the phone to David who seemed to support her concern. "I knew those Krup boys from the YMHA and, Rachel, you know what? It was really scary how abusive they were." He whispered before adding: "They used to take a defenceless old basketball and heave it right across the gym floor!"

My heavy silence must have freaked David out because he instantly relented.

"They're Jewish. They're Jewish!" he confessed. "Relax, for God's sake. Oh and just for the record, I think one of the brothers used to lifeguard at the Y and teach swimming to public school kids. Maybe it's him and maybe he's using those government cheques to help his family out or maybe to pay his way through university. Anyway, stop worrying; he's not Krup the Ripper. I heard the guy worships his mother, is buddies with Elvis, and mends broken pigeon wings in his spare time. So, when are you going out with him, huh?"

"Maybe I should wait until he calls and asks me, don't you think?"

"Sure. But I've got you very interested now, don't I?" he teased.

"David, why wouldn't I be interested in a hard working,

educated, Jewish guy who loves his mother, hangs out with "The King," and cares for handicapped pigeons?"

"Ra-ach, there is one thing," he interjected. I didn't like the sound of that Ra-ach because it was my family's practice to use the intimate, two-syllable inflection of the abbreviated Rach over the more formal Rachel when introducing exceptionally good or exceptionally bad news.

"Ra-ach, there is one thing. None of the Krup brothers I knew had a first name that started with H. He could be the dark family secret, the bad apple, a psycho…"

I hung up the phone and prayed: "Oh dear God, if you listen to daughters of atheists, please don't let this Krup thing turn out to be another tasteless joke on me!"

I finally worked up the nerve to call a school chum and ask if her brother had ever heard of a Krup whose first name started with H. He claimed to know everyone that played basketball at the Y and he insisted that there was no H six-letter Krup.

A few days later the mysterious Mr. Krup finally called. He explained that he had intended to call sooner, but he was cramming for his university midterms.

"It wouldn't have been fair to have to cut our date short because I had to run home to study," he confessed. "Especially if you're still willing to go out with me after my sorta rude behaviour at the bank."

I was impressed by the glimmer of humility that I never would have imagined he possessed. As for me, the burning unasked question was soon answered:

"By the way Rachel… may I call you Rachel?"

"Uh-huh."

"Good. Then you can call me Spinner."

"Spinner? That's not spelled with an H!"

"Uh... yeah. You noticed, huh? I have two brothers: Moishe

and Itsak and I'm Harvey, but our friends know us as Mickey, Lenny and Spinner. We used nicknames so we'd fit in better."

"Why would you do that?"

"Going to school in Cabbage Town, it was safer for us to have more Canadian sounding names."

I quickly dove onto my soapbox: "You know, Harvey, in my little town where I grew up I rarely set eyes on another Jew, other than the five I was related to. And Rachel Tzippora Morganstein is a very Jewish name of which I am very proud. Anyway, I had to put up with all kinds of name-calling and teasing and worse because of it, and I never would have lied or apologized for who I was!"

"Yeah, well, you also never met the Borden Street bullies. Eight, six-foot strapping Pollock brothers and their dozen or so Ukrainian cousins who'd all had fathers in the army… and I don't mean ours."

He was right. I'd never had the pleasure.

On our first date Harvey Spinner Krup took me to see a rerun of "Seven Brides for Seven Brothers."

On the phone, he gave me a ballpark time of arrival: "I'll pick you up somewhere between six-thirty and seven o'clock. Got that?"

"Uh-huh. Between six-thirty and seven o'clock."

I was ready for six-fifteen just to be safe.

Harvey arrived at six. He waited in the vestibule for fifteen minutes while my grandmother dragged her ample self up three flights of stairs to deliver his message that I was fifteen minutes late.

All decked out in my new navy princess line dress and carrying my Jackie-O styled winter coat, I scampered down the steps, curious to see how that scruffy frog prince would look all cleaned up. I guess he wasn't thinking the same of me because he barely glanced at me before turning toward the door and shouting over his shoulder: "We're late! Let's go or we'll miss the previews."

I've often wondered what possessed me to follow him out the door that night. He was intimidating, insensitive, and downright rude...but he was also handsome, confident, and punctual... so follow I did. Without a murmur, I struggled to pull on my coat as I headed out the door after him. The icy street shimmered like a crystal pond and I, ignoring my own personal peril, had insisted on wearing four-inch spike heels to complete my ensemble. Luckily I made it to his car without an embarrassing slip. I closed the car door and lit up a cigarette to establish my sophisticated, independent image. He reached over, grabbed the cigarette out of my hand, and flicked it out his window. "Nobody smokes in my car," he proclaimed as he handed me a stick of Doublemint gum along with the following declaration: "Cigarettes smell like crap!" I was speechless.

He threw me a self-satisfied grin, revved up his pseudo antique '52 Plymouth, and skated all the way to the theatre on bald tires.

After the movie, he was gracious enough to ask if I was hungry. When I nodded eagerly, he headed his "autosleigh" in the direction of his favourite deli.

He was talkative and animated en route while I remained disturbingly silent. I discovered that he was humorous and sexy. I just didn't know what to make of this good-looking diamond in the rough. He was a unique blend of Bowery boys' crudeness and Bobby Darren cool. They say that girls usually gravitate toward men that remind them of their fathers, but Harvey was as different from my father as a coyote is from a lion.

Before we got out of the car at the deli, he asked me if I would do him a favour.

"Su-re, if I can," I nervously offered.

"Good," he said. "I'd really like you to take your hair down."

I was incredibly flattered. At the bank, he generally saw me with my waist length hair fanned out over my shoulders in true bohemian fashion. It was obvious that he found that more appealing than the more structured look of the French twist I was sporting for the occasion.

In a Rita Hayworth kind of moment, I quickly pulled out the pins that constrained my golden mane. Then I demurely asked, "Is that better?"

"It sure is!" he replied enthusiastically. "Ya know, with your hair pulled back like that and those pieces sticking out at the sides, you looked like a water buffalo."

The manager met us at the deli door to let us know that they were closing and the only thing they hadn't locked up or dumped out was a couple of cups of coffee still left in the pot.

"That's fine," my gracious date opined. "That's all we wanted anyway."

By now I was getting pretty nervous about just how forceful this macho character might become when we got to my front door. So over our mugs of muddy coffee, I began a propaganda campaign: "Ya know, I think it's pathetic that some people don't even have the courtesy to wait a couple of weeks before sharing their first goodnight kiss, don't you?" There was no reply. He simply sat quietly and listened as I turned into a long-playing album on high speed. I continued my accelerated dissertation all the way back to my grandmother's house. I caught a fleeting glimpse of gallantry when he insisted on opening the car door for me and helping me out. I was enjoying the sensation of his hand on mine and the reassuring feel of his arm around my waist as we slowly made our way to my front steps. When we finally arrived, he asked me if I was all right, to which I nervously but sincerely replied: "Yes. Thanks for helping me make it through the evening without breaking something. I was a real idiot to wear high heels on a night like this."

"Why? I think you were brave to wear those shoes in this rotten weather. Besides, they look good on you."

What a rebound.

"Well, anyway, thanks for the movie, Harvey … It was a really nice evening..."

He was standing face to face with me now and I saw something in his sultry dark eyes that I liked a lot. I blushed. He smiled softly. Then he reached out, gripped my hand, and shook it perfunctorily.

Forget his boorish remarks and rude behaviour. There was something about H. Krup that made me feel warm all over and I liked it.

"You're welcome." he replied. "Well, maybe I'll see you around sometime. Bye." And with that he walked away without looking back.

Another terrifying Hunter flashback zipped through my mind.

My God, what had I done?

Time crawled by and there wasn't a trace of Harvey anywhere. There was no sign of him for the entire week.

On Monday morning I dragged my sad self into the bank and kept a one-eyed vigil on the door until noon. Finally I made my way next door to the greasy spoon to heal my bludgeoned heart over a hot beef sandwich smothered in gravy. I was raising the first glistening forkful of mashed potatoes to my mouth when Lynn came rushing up to the table.

"He's here! He's in the bank asking for you right now," she bubbled, while I casually slid the fork into my mouth.

"Well?" she urged.

I was unmoved, except of course for my jaws.

"Oh, don't give me that I-couldn't-care-less crap. You've been praying for this!" Lynn declared.

"You're wrong," I said flatly. "If that guy is dumb enough to think I sat around waiting for him, well... he's got another think coming."

"But you did just sit around waiting for him," Lynn candidly reminded me.

"Yeah, well if I did, then I must have been crazy but I'm fully recovered now!"

Of course I returned to the bank and without hesitation accepted his apology for his absence and his invitation. "If you go out with me Saturday night, I'll make it up to you."

He called me on Friday night to ask, "By the way, did I mention that we're going to the Dental Black Tie Ball tomorrow night?" That was how I found out that he was studying to be a dentist.

Needless to say I didn't own a gown or even a black tie, so Harvey opted instead to forego the ball the next night and drive us out to High Park to drink foaming hot chocolate at a drive-in burger joint while we watched the ducks slide across the frozen pond on their tail feathers. It was one of the most romantic nights of my life and we never even touched.

But, a dentist? He actually wanted to be a dentist? Why oh God ... anything... but a dentist?

Growing up, I always wanted to be someone who would make a difference. Someone people would want around because of my talent or skill such as a lawyer, doctor, social worker, teacher, or artist who all work to make a positive difference in the lives of those they serve and are paid anywhere from handsomely to barely for their efforts.

I excluded dentists from my potential list because, through my excruciating childhood experiences with those lords of pain, I was certain that they served no useful purpose and I was appalled to discover that they actually got paid for the torture they inflicted on unsuspecting victims. My experiences with dentists were traumatic. As intellectually astute as my father was, he was completely ignorant of the benefits of good dental health. His rules for dental hygiene were, "stay away from taffy, brush your teeth with salt twice a day, and have a dentist pull them out if they hurt."

We had two dentists in our little town: Dr. Nutall and Dr. Dopeeh, and though their names seemed plagiarized from The Seven Dwarfs, they still managed to evoke fear and insecurity in every small child. I suspect that one ivory butcher would have been enough to serve our town if he didn't need another to fill in for him whenever he was wasted. One sadistic dentist inhabited an eerie vine smothered hut and the other lived in a gin bottle.

I can honestly say that while growing up, I never thought of dentistry as a noble or lucrative profession. So discovering that Harvey's chosen occupation was dentistry did disturb me at first, but when I fell in love with the man behind the white coat, I tried not to think about him being up to his knuckles in pyorrhoea, halitosis and tooth decay. Anyway, women adore their obstetricians and it's best not to think of what they're up to their wrists in.

For two weeks after that second date, it seemed that Harvey and I were inevitably bound together forever. But by the middle of the third week, it seemed as if the ties that bound were fraying. I hadn't heard from Harvey in three days and I was becoming fearful that the coarse and insensitive Harvey I met on our first date had repossessed the wise and compassionate Harvey I had begun to get hooked on.

As the still silent week loomed closer to its end, my heart

sank lower with each passing minute. On Thursday evening I sat in my grandmother's front vestibule by the phone, gritting my teeth and willing it to ring. By now days of tooth grinding had started an electrical storm in my mouth. My jaw ached and my teeth pulsed until my brain finally cottoned on to the idea that I needed a dentist.

It was sheer luck that Harvey answered on the first ring because I had made a deal with myself that I would hang up if he didn't. I barely had time to tell him that I had a toothache before he was at my door and whisking me off to his newly graduated friend's clinic for a look-see.

Marvin was a very conscientious or maybe a very naive dentist, but he bought my story without reservation.

Maybe it was due to the kind of dental care Doctors Dopeeh and Nutall had bestowed on me for all those many years, but whatever the reason, I left the clinic that night with one less tooth and two less cavities and Harvey. At the time, that seemed a small price to pay for love.

It was ironic to find my grandmother greeting me at the door and telling me that she had forgotten to give me a message from my friend Harvey, who had called earlier in the week to say that he was studying for a big exam, and he would call on Friday the minute it was over.

On our next date, Harvey explained why he didn't see me during that week.

"The truth is, Rachel, the way I feel about you, I'd never have gotten any studying done if I dropped by or called. So I had to bite the bullet and stay away. But I don't ever want to do that again."

We were engaged two months later.

It was Harvey's last year of university, and we had to study the pros and cons of working for someone else or going it on our own. I say we, because I had been conscripted to become his dental assistant. I knew that going it on our own would be a tougher road at first, but the comfort of knowing that no one could steal his practice made it all seem worthwhile. His parents were not, and therefore he was not, convinced. But I had a powerful weapon with which to persuade him.

As a child, I always knew that my Uncle Saul was Dr. Saul Gordon, a medical practitioner, but it was Harvey that told me my uncle also had a degree in dentistry and was highly respected at the dental college.

It only took a strategic little push from my wise Uncle Saul to steer Harvey in the direction to, "Be your own boss!"

There I was, about to marry the Jewish man I'd dreamed of and my parents had hoped for. But really, did he have to be a dentist?

Looking back on my life, I'm perpetually surprised by the detours I've had to take that led me to where I am. Most of the simple blueprints I sketched for my future were erased and replaced by more enhanced and complex designs along the way.

There was a great debate over whether I was a virgin when we were married. Well perhaps it wasn't as huge an issue as the trial of the Rosenbergs, but it is an important page in my history book.

It all began over a cup of coffee in my brother Adam's kitchen.

My sister-in-law Miriam had called me over to have a chat about the birds and the bees. Or as I see it now, the vultures and the scorpions.

She was concerned that with my country girl naiveté, I would not be prepared for the possible trauma of the big night. It took her thirty minutes to raise the topic of s-e-x and another forty-five to ask if I had made an appointment for my premarital check-up yet.

Not wanting to look unworldly I pretended that I knew what she was talking about and responded immediately:

"Uh-huh."

"Oh-h," she whined. "I was just going to recommend that you see my gynaecologist."

"Umm... Actually, I'm seeing someone else," I announced, as I tried to get my mind around what in hell a GYNAECOLOGIST might be.

She pushed again. "Who are you going to?"

"I hope you don't mind, Miriam, but, umm... that's kind of personal. I'd rather not say anything more about it right now."

"Oh, sure. As long as you're going to see someone, it really doesn't matter to me who it is. I just know that the first glimpse of your husband's... umm... thing... can be pretty terrifying if you're unprepared."

How could I tell her that I'd been glimpsing his thing for weeks and I didn't find it the least bit scary?

"Rachel, it's kind of like entering a dark cave without a flashlight."

"Well then, Miriam, I'll just ask Harvey to bring along a big torch before he sets out to explore my cave."

Her spontaneous giggle over my inference that we hadn't really done it yet seemed to relieve some of the tension.

I was sure that my brother had influenced Miriam's invitation to talk to me about sex and I was equally sure that he felt it was important for me to have a premarital check-up. And since he was my big brother and a doctor, how could I ignore him?

The minute I got back to my room, I looked up gynaecologist in the dictionary. Then I looked it up in the yellow pages and found a medical clinic just two blocks from my grandmother's house, which made it a perfect choice.

I sat in the reception area obediently waiting while dozens of groaning women with large swollen bellies shuffled back and forth to the washroom. From some of the more talkative patients I shared the couch with, I learned that there were six doctors in the clinic, five of whom were partners and that my doctor was the exception. He was so new to the clinic that none of the women I spoke to had ever met him. I desperately wanted to ask one of these experienced women what to expect but I was much too shy.

It will be fine! I repeated this over and over in my head. I would simply have to act like a grown-up and trust the doctor.

A frumpy, middle-aged nurse led me into the examining room and handed me a faded cotton gown.

"Remove all your clothing, including your underwear, and put on this gown. The doctor will be in to see you in a few minutes. Any questions?"

I had a million of them swirling around in my brain, but at that moment, I couldn't latch on to even one.

Since I had never been completely naked, in broad daylight, in front of another human being since I was about three years old, I could only pray that the gown was bigger than it looked.

As I sat on the cold leather table in my skimpy shroud waiting for a stranger to peer into my private orifices, I began to reconsider. Then, just as I decided to attempt a get-away, the doctor entered.

He was tall, balding, somewhat rotund, and probably no more than thirty-five.

"Good afternoon, Rachel. I'm Dr. Karnalk."

"Uh-huh. Hi," I barely whispered.

"Is this your first time?"

"Uh-huh."

"Good. The first time is always the best."

"I mean... uh... it's my first time having a check-up... uh... like this... uh... down there," I stammered.

"Well, enjoy yourself. Now come on, Rachel, you're very tense and that won't do. You're going to have to relax before I can examine you, okay?"

"Uh-huh."

"Are you a virgin?"

"Uh-huh."

"Good. Do you have a boyfriend?"

"Uh-huh, I'm engaged."

"I see. Okay. I want you to spread your legs and slip your bare toes into those stirrups. Just like you were riding a horse... bareback. Can you do that?"

"Uh-huh. I'll try."

"Good girl. That's all I ask. Give it a try now."

I closed my eyes, as if to shut myself out of his sight, and I slid. I felt a sudden, faint gust of air between my legs that pricked my curiosity. I raised my head and slowly opened my eyes. I saw Dr. Karnalk with his lips pursed and cheeks bulging suddenly exhale a puff of wind directly at my crotch.

"I'm just checking your reflexes. Are you okay?"

"Uh-huh," I nervously replied.

"Alright, Rachel, I want you to relax while I grab my instrument."

With my legs up and locked in the stirrups, Dr. Karnalk approached carrying an object that resembled a shoehorn. Using my stomach as a utility table he rested the cold steel instrument there. He then placed his bare fingers between my legs and uttered, "Coochy, coochy coo," before plunging a digit into my secret cave.

He stopped suddenly and proclaimed: "I can't continue with this examination, Rachel, because the area is thick and swollen and you're pregnant!"

Now I always understood that unless I'd had intercourse I hadn't... you know...done it. So to be told by a doctor that I was pregnant came as a shattering surprise since I wasn't married yet and we hadn't done it. After I explained that little fact to Dr. Karnalk, he qualified his statement by declaring that I was "pregnant by association." Of course if I had ever had a gynaecological examination before that day, I would have known that there was something very wrong with the entire scenario. Even Harvey, who considered himself an astute man of science, was downed by the news that his army of sperm had somehow left their penile post, travelled stealthily through his underwear and along the sofa, where it had set up camp in my forbidden territory. He was as shocked as I, but he would not question the qualified word of a specialist either.

Harvey and I wandered aimlessly for hours through the streets of Cabbage Town, hoping that some miraculous vision might appear before us to guide us down the right path.

Finally, when no spirit came forward, we decided to confide in one of Harvey's brothers, who unilaterally decided the next day to discuss our secret with the other brother without our knowledge; and together they determined that they had a responsibility to bring our intimate issue up for discussion with their entire family.

This breach of loyalty resulted in the *Krup family inquisition.* Over the next several days, I was forced to endure repeated insults and accusations about my character, my history and my integrity from any and all of the Krup clan. I was so naive; I actually never questioned their right to destroy my privacy and dignity. If only I could have called on my mother's profound sexual advice to comfort me.

When I was just a teen-ager, my mother and I had engaged

in two deeply meaningful talks about s-e-x.

The first discussion happened soon after I had blossomed into womanhood at the advanced age of fourteen and a half.

I had just completed my third menstrual cycle and was too terrified and embarrassed by the entire event to talk about it to anyone other than my girlfriend Megan who was old hat at the "curse," having been visited by hers at the tender age of eleven.

I was excited by the phenomenon of mother's intuition, when my mother was inspired to approach me and ask:

"Rachel, are you using the uh… white…uh… things in that light blue box on the top shelf of my closet?"

"Uh-huh!"

"Oh… Okay."

I knew from that day on how in tune my mother was with my intimate concerns. That enlightening talk was soon followed by a more in-depth exchange when I was fifteen:

"Mom, Trudy Smythe is going all the way with Slick Jackson and all the girls are saying she's a slut 'cause it's not the right time. So, what is the right time? When are you allowed to go all the way with a guy, huh?"

"Where did you learn that kind of language, young lady?"

"Mo-om, come on. I just wanna know."

"Fine! The right time to…um…you know…go … is on your wedding night," she defensively replied.

I persisted. "How come not 'til then?"

She sucked in a head-spinning gulp of oxygen and continued.

"Because, if you save your special gift for the right man, then your wedding night will be the most beautiful, enjoyable experience you can imagine. But with the wrong man at the wrong time, it'll be a miserable, living hell! Just look at your Auntie Min.

Or you can wait and ask Trudy Smythe in a couple of years."

I should have asked if the special gift included necking and petting, but at the time that impudent question would have probably gotten me grounded for a year.

The Krup interrogation provoked long buried memories to rise up once again and haunt the graveyard of my thoughts.

I was jolted back to the summer of 1952, when new neighbours moved into the farmhouse by the gully. I had liked the old neighbours, so it was natural to expect that I'd also like the new ones.

I kept myself visible by hanging around my father's flower boxes, sluggardly pretending to pull off the dead pansy blossoms that had withered there in the sweltering heat.

After several long, sweaty days of waiting, one of the new kids finally noticed me lolling about at the edge of her property and invited me over to meet the rest of her family. As far as I could tell, the rest of the Doucet family consisted of nine children and a mother. I had never heard of so many children in one family before. I always thought that mothers could only lay so many eggs and that was it.

Toward the end of that summer I had become best friends with Marie Doucet, who was only a year and a half older than I. She had long copper-pipe ringlets, haunting grey eyes and skin as smooth as rolled pastry dough.

I was beside myself with joy when Marie invited me to her eighth birthday party. It was my first-ever-real-friend's birthday party and I could barely contain my bliss. Saturday couldn't come quickly enough. Even when Friday finally arrived, the big day still seemed months away.

Knowing that, at long last I could fit into my cousin Myra's beautiful, white hand-me-down pinafore that I so loved made the prospect of the entire event a dream come true and worth waiting for.

"Let me take a gander at ya," Mrs. Hough commanded.

Mrs. Hough was an old semi-homeless woman our parents kind of adopted around the time my brothers and I found out we would soon be sharing our claustrophobic bedroom with a newly filled bassinette. We were almost as poor as Mrs. Hough, but she paid her room and board by babysitting my baby sister while our parents worked some eighteen-hour days. Like a gerbil on a wheel they were locked into the relentless running of an inn and cabins. It was barely a living, but for my brothers and I there were real advantages, such as limited supervision. It meant we were free to play with whomever we liked; sneak out to swim in the forbidden quarry; steal strawberries from the nearest farmer; and collect tips for running secret errands for cabin guests. Of course that was all contingent on our not getting caught in the act of committing any of these punishable crimes.

We were pretty safe with Mrs. Hough as our ally. She was a sweet, gentle woman who I thought was ancient but was probably no more than fifty. She was white-haired, pink-cheeked and perfectly cherubic. It was love at first sight for all of us. She told wonderful stories, baked great cookies and generally kept my baby sister Rebecca out of my way. What more could any six-year old want? She also tended to my father's flower boxes filled with their array of pansies that adorned our house and cabins. I did love those pansies with their little pixie faces. A garden of them used to remind me of an innocent children's choir. I always expected that any minute those spunky little blossoms were going to break into a Shirley Temple medley.

After Mrs. Hough had put the finishing touches on my pigtails, she stood back and proclaimed: "Well don't you look like a little doll today?" I loved when she noticed me.

She tucked Marie Doucet's gift under my arm; I waved

goodbye and headed out on my great adventure. I ran through the farmer's field and skipped along the shoulder of the old river road that led to the Doucets' house.

Mrs. Doucet was in the kitchen and all of the nine children were milling about when I came bounding through the door. I was immediately drawn to the delicious looking party treats that were spread out on the table. I could hardly wait to taste them. I set my best hungry urchin gaze on Mrs. Doucet, who didn't seem to be reacting to my usual tantalizing charms. Somehow she seemed different today. Her slight frame seemed bent and weary, and she was definitely quieter and more sullen than I had seen her on any of my other visits. I thought it was strange that of all the days she could pick to be sad, she had chosen Marie's birthday.

As I stood pondering her mood, I sniffed an acrid odour seeping into the house. I wanted to ask about it, but Mrs. Hough's last words to me before I left home were: "Now ya remember, there, Rachel: Behave yerself, young lady. Stay clean. And be polite, eh?"

Suddenly a tall lanky man entered and moved toward Mrs. Doucet. I watched her flinch as he placed his thin, knobbly hands firmly on her bottom. He guffawed like a donkey before releasing her. He then leaned into the icebox, grabbed a couple of tall green bottles, and headed outside with them.

Marie explained that the man was her father and that he liked to have a bottle or two of beer to help him relax whenever he was at home, which was approximately one weekend a month. I guessed that his infrequent visits accounted for the reason we had never met.

Once the other young guests arrived, we all headed outside, where we discovered Mr. Doucet spread out on an old cot snoring like a jackhammer. Every few minutes he would open his red-rimmed eyes and shout for one of his kids to run inside and get him another beer.

"Hey you rotten little brats," he would holler, "bring me another God Damn beer before I die o' thirst out here." And as quickly as his kids could say, "I'll go daddy," there would be a cold new bottle in his hot sweaty hand and a shiny penny in the hand that brought it.

With no organized games planned, we young natives were getting restless and whiney. Marie and I sat down on a shaded rock near the throng of empty beer bottles and proceeded to line them up and pitch pebbles into them. I was ahead by two pebbles and on my way to winning the four pennies Marie had scored from her beer deliveries when suddenly Mr. Doucet rose to his feet as steady as a rock. Wearing a gaping brown-toothed grin, he grandly announced: "Alright ya brats, we're gonna have a game o' hide and seek... and the winner gits a jumbo-sized Hershey bar."

Marie and I abruptly stopped pitching pebbles, the boys threw aside their freshly dug worms, and the rest of the kids stopped torturing the Doucets' mangy three-legged dog. We all jumped up and down with joy as the master-of-the-house sprung into action. He laid down the rules, assigned someone to be *it*, and whistled through his fingers for the games to begin. His enthusiasm was euphoria to us.

As the hiders were being uncovered one by one, squeals of "I found you" resounded from every corner of the yard. But I was still safely in the game. "They'll never find me," I thought. I was spurred on by the powerful fantasy of doling out a small square of my own huge chocolate bar to each of my brothers and then devouring the major portion myself, right before their eyes.

There were only two more hidden kids to go before I would be declared the winner.

I was crouched down in the bushes against the south wall

of the barn when I heard a "psst," followed by another "psst." Then I saw Mr. Doucet peeking around the far end of the barn, waving me toward him. I followed his lead. When I reached him, he discreetly opened up the barn door and ushered me inside, chuckling all the while.

"They'll never find ya up there in the loft.... and fer sure you'll win the prize. I'll stand guard while ya git up the ladder. Go on, whatcha waitin' fer, eh? Ya want that candy bar, don'tcha? Hurry now, they're gonna find ya in a minute if ya don't git up there!"

With a swirling sense of excitement and trepidation I started up the seemingly insurmountable ladder. With each step, the rungs seemed to move further apart while my six-and-a-half-year-old legs seemed to grow shorter. But it didn't matter how tall that ladder grew... the image of that huge Hershey bar propelled me toward victory.

I had almost reached the top rung when I caught a whiff of the same putrid odour that had soured my stomach when I first entered the Doucets' kitchen. I suddenly felt Mr. Doucet breathing against the back of my neck. The noxious stench quashed my urge for chocolate. The voices of my playmates suddenly disappeared. The only sound remaining was my heart pounding like a bongo in my throat. I tried to squeeze by him to head back down the ladder but he pushed me up the last rung and I tumbled onto the loft.

With one quick tug, Mr. Doucet threw me onto my back and placed his long spindly hand over my mouth. He thrust his sharp bony knee into my tender thigh, swiftly putting a halt to my squirming. As the nauseating blend of sour beer and stale tobacco wafted through my brain, Marie's father reached up under my beautiful white pinafore and ripped my best panties right off my bottom. The next sound I heard was the swift buzz of his zipper.

As he struggled with one hand, to remove his trousers, I managed to grasp a little air that leaked in through a gap in his palm. I inhaled as deeply as I could, then, without forethought, I bit down on his hand as hard as my baby teeth would allow. In an instant he let go and rolled away groping at his injury and howling like a speared boar.

I leaped from the loft and landed in a musty haystack below. Images of fang-toothed monsters propelled me toward home faster than Supergirl in flight.

Outside our kitchen window I curled up beneath my father's precious flower box and sobbed my heart out under the watchful eyes of those ever-grinning pansies.

I'd been spanked before for biting my brothers when they'd picked on me, so I knew I was in real trouble for biting a grown-up. But what terrified me more (because I knew some secret grown-up stuff about men and women) was that I was sure if a man was anywhere near a woman's private parts she could grow a baby in her stomach. I didn't want to have a baby. I had enough trouble with Rebecca. And how did you get them out of you anyway? Did they have to cut you open or did you just squeeze it out through your bottom like doo-doo? That's the way our dog Brownie did it and it was really gross.

I felt suddenly heartened at the sound of Mrs. Hough singing to my little sister:

> *"If you go down to the woods today, you better go in disguise.*
> *If you go down to the woods today beware of a big surprise..."*

Cautiously I went around to the side of the cottage, climbed up the trellis, and sneaked in through my parents' window. I removed my filthy pinafore, pulled on my mother's soft chenille bed jacket and tripped past the kitchen shouting to Mrs. Hough en route that I was in need of a bath. She was momentarily taken aback by my unsightly condition, which I instantly tried to explain away by lying… badly.

"I fell into a … um … a … bramble bush Mrs. Hough… um …a … just like in the story of Brer Fox and Brer Rabbit."

"I see. So is that where ya lost yer front tooth young lady? Bitin' that mean old Brer Fox?"

I jumped up onto the edge of the tub and lurched toward the mirror. I was stunned by my reflection. My tooth was gone. It was lost forever in that drunken old fox's mangy paw.

"Uh-huh!" I replied.

Although I could see the look of doubt on Mrs. Hough's face, I was relieved that she didn't press me for an answer.

Of one thing I was certain: The awful thing that had just happened in that loft was my fault, and I was sure that if my dad ever found out, I'd be deprived of friends and chocolate for the rest of my life.

Later that night when my mother asked how the party was… I lied again.

"Oh, it was okay I guess, but I decided I'm not going to be friends with Marie anymore!"

She never asked why. Neither did my father. It wasn't in their nature.

On this singular issue they trusted my judgement. But when I think back now on the numerous times that I worried that every tummy ache and every gas pain might turn out to be a baby in my belly, I dearly wish they had been more curious.

They did wonder, however, why I hadn't taken more care to save my tooth for the tooth fairy's magical visit. But I simply told them, "a monster has it and I can't get it back."

I was pretty certain they bought the story because the next morning there was a nickel in my water glass and a note:

Dear Rachel

I found that old monster and forced him to give up the tooth.

Love, the Tooth Fairy.

P.S. I promise he'll never bother you again.

Soon after the birthday party, the Doucets moved away, and a new family moved in; but I never bothered to make their acquaintance.

Just three days after the nightmare of the cruel Krup interrogations, I was visited by a glowing miracle. It was my menstrual period in all its crimson glory.

When I called Dr. Karnalk to tell him the wonderful news, he suggested that I come in for a look-see to make sure that everything was all right. I'm still amazed at the gross naiveté I fostered toward the medical profession that would have prompted me to return to that office.

This time I was instinctively more suspicious though. This time I was to learn the great difference between naiveté and stupidity.

It was one particular question that left me pretty certain that this was not proper medical conduct. With my legs once again in the stirrups, Dr. Karnalk smiled crudely as he asked:

"I have eleven digits. Which one would you prefer I put inside you?"

I jumped down from the table holding the sheet between my legs and ran to the door calling for the nurse. I told her my examination was finished, and I would like her to stay while I got dressed.

"I'm feeling a little woozy," I said. She looked over at the doctor, then back at me and mumbled dryly, "Uh-huh. I'm not surprised."

The doctor remained completely unruffled, even as he signed off in front of the nurse:

"Well, Rachel. I'm pretty sure you're fit as a fiddle and ready for your big night. I look forward to delivering your first baby nine months after!"

In frantic desperation I finally called my brother Adam, who was interning at the Mt. Sinai Hospital, and told him the whole sordid story. He suggested that I forget Dr. Karnalk ever existed, but recommended that I see Miriam's specialist to find out if I had any real female problems we should know about before my wedding night.

Dr. Shaw examined me with a nurse present at all times and a look of serious concentration on his face. After I dressed the nurse escorted me into the doctor's office, where he shared his diagnosis with me.

"Before you embark on your honeymoon, Miss Morganstein, I would like to schedule you for some weekly treatments to prepare your vaginal opening, 'cause as it stands my dear, you can barely fit a Q-tip up there. I presume your intended is larger than that?"

A couple of years later, I heard that Dr. Karnalk was stripped of his medical licence after multiple complaints of sexual assault were lodged against him. I often fantasized that the courts would sentence the miscreant to scrubbing toilets on the maternity ward.

I am lucky that my psyche was left intact though. Except for the fact that, to this very day, I can't chortle *coochy, coochy coo* when I tickle a baby under its chin!

After the pregnancy scare, it was clear that my future in-laws had little use for me. They were still determined to believe that the doctor could never have made such a diagnosis if I wasn't a loose woman. And they were further convinced that a good girl with any crumb of self-respect would never let any male, not even a doctor, look at her naked body.

The ugliness that was revealed in that crisis was something I thought I might never get over. But time -- and "Holy" intervention -- helped to heal the wound.

One afternoon, about three months before our scheduled wedding, Harvey came rushing over to my flat to whisk me away to his parents' home for a meeting.

"Oh please God. Not again," I silently whimpered before bravely standing my ground.

"Harvey...I... uh... I'm not going!"

"Honey," he said, "trust me. You won't be sorry... I promise."

I had rarely set foot in his parents' house since "the inquisition," and when I did manage to get invited for the odd dinner, rarely a word passed my way during the entire meal.

Of course I succumbed to his request and went along. I loved Harvey "Spinner" Krup and I knew that this cold war was hurting him as much as it was hurting me, so how could I resist any opportunity to resolve it?

I crossed the threshold of his parents' home and flinched as his father approached. Without warning, Mr. Krup threw his arms around me and hugged... hard. Then Mrs. Krup reached for me. She was crying real tears and smiling all the while.

"Come in, come in, *darlink*. It's okay. We want to talk to you about the wedding. We want you to know how happy we are about it!"

My fear that I had just entered the Twilight Zone was soon abated as the "New Order of Krup's World Peace" unfolded.

It seemed that soon after the Karnalk faux pregnancy incident, my future father-in-law had sent a letter (along with a generous donation) to a very special kind of Rabbi in New York City who I got the feeling dealt with the edification of confused relations. My concerned future father-in-law had asked the Rabbi for his wisdom and guidance in dealing with the errant choice of would-be-wife his son had made.

And now, several months later, they had finally received a reply (and a receipt). The Holy Rabbi told them that I was a "**Gitte Neshuma*" (*A good and pure soul), and that our marriage would be a blessed event that would produce wonderful offspring. He even suggested: "It's a marriage made in heaven." Well, what more was there to say? That Rabbi was obviously a brilliant scholar and a man of many gifts.

CHAPTER FOUR

As a child I had definite dreams about a future with my Prince Charming that involved romance on exotic beaches, singing folk songs with our brood of kids at backyard barbecues, and when we got old, travelling the world on goodwill missions. Unlike my friends and later even my daughters, I had never chiselled in stone any plans for my eventual wedding ceremony. Illustrated story books had helped to nurture my childhood fantasies about what beautiful fairy tale weddings could look like, but I had no idea how to wrap my mind around the kind of wedding that poor Polish Jewish mothers of spoiled city sons expected.

I was completely overwhelmed by Mama Krup's strange old-country etiquette and family politics.

1. "Auntie so-and-so won't sit with cousin so-and-so because uncle so-and-so once loaned brother so-and-so's father five dollars... and neither one ever paid it back, which makes them all crooks. But it's not nice if you don't invite them... and anyway they give cash gifts."

2. "You must have a luncheon, a tea, and a shower because the other relatives did and it's their turn to pay us back for all the expensive gifts we gave them!"

3. "No! No! No! Candlelight, shmandle light! You definitely cannot have a candlelight ceremony because it would be dangerous and also... no one we know has ever done it, so it must be **paast nicht*!" *[*Not appropriate.]*

4. "What do you mean you're not buying twin beds! ***Gottennu*! *[**Oh my God]* What kind of good Jewish wife sleeps in the same bed as her husband? It's *paast nicht* Rachel, I'm telling you."

5. "Absolutely No! The bridesmaids can't wear black because black is for mourning and it's *paast nicht*. Don't worry, Rachel, you'll have plenty of time to wear black after you're married."

On the other hand, my parents stayed boarded up in their little town, wrote the necessary cheques, and quietly remained three hundred miles away until the nuptials.

Since I had no point of reference for weddings except those old childhood fairy tales, I was reluctant to dispute the word of my in-laws, who had lived in the city for decades and had attended dozens of those Polish parades.

It wasn't that I didn't have unique and thrilling ideas. It was simply that I lived in fear that my unusual vision might incense Harvey's family yet again.

By the time our wedding date drew near, Harvey and I had attended a number of his friends' nuptials and it had become clear to me that the major difference between their weddings and the one we were planning was money. Many of his buddies married well, as they say. So if I'd been planning one of their weddings, I could have drawn on the fantasies from all those grand old fairy tales. But instead our wedding was a revelation in the ordinary.

The bridesmaids wore hot pink taffeta, the bride wore virginal white upholstery fabric and the groom wore shiny black polyester. The cornucopia of food was bland, the floral centrepieces were uninspiring, and the middle-aged band played loud, bouncy music. What more could Mama Krup want in a perfect Polish Jewish wedding?

I was able to surprise the Krup family by adding some of my own unique touches to the event: We hired a nine-year-old singer who performed a Judy Garland medley along with some popular Yiddish favourites before launching into her personal rendition of hot hit parade tunes. Some of the guests seemed a little offended by the child prodigy's surprise rendition of the "Gotta Have a Gimmick" stripper number from Gypsy.

I took great pains to carefully package little gifts of chocolate for each of the guests to take home (I copied the idea from an Italian wedding). I put the fancy little treat packets into a huge basket and hid it under the head table to be given out as the guests left the party. But by the end of the evening there were only a handful of treats left under the table and a room full of furious parents who weren't aware that there was liquor in the chocolate bon-bons they'd been stealing for their children all night. The parents had used the treats as a diversion to keep the kids out of their hair while they enjoyed themselves on the dance floor. It worked until almost the stroke of midnight, when the children began to throw up all over their expensive wedding outfits.

As an added innovation, I also instructed the caterer to serve crepes Suzettes. I thought that crepes would lend a touch of class to a rather déclassé event. Since most of the Krups' guests thought it was stupidly strange to serve pancakes at night, they avoided them completely.

Harvey reassured me that he loved them and that "crepes Suzettes were a damned good idea." He was sweet not to mention the fact that we could have built a bungalow with the stacks of crepes that were left over.

Actually everything was going off without too much pain until our first dance.

The wedding singer announced the blessed event, closed his eyes, and began to croon our Everley Brothers favourite...

Darl-in' you can cou-nt on me, 'ti-il the su-un dries u-up the sea, un-til then I'll al-ways be...de-vo-oted to you!

Unfortunately I ended up sharing the bride and groom's dance with my Uncle Albert in lieu of my groom who was nowhere to be found. In mid-dip I heard a roar of applause from the crowd as Harvey sheepishly cut in. My uncle offered a relieved smile as he graciously restored me to an upright position and handed me over to my groom. The crowd shouted warm fuzzy affirmations such as: "Hey, Rachel, ya better cuff 'im if ya want ta keep 'im," or, "Hey, way ta go, Spinner. You just keep her guessing." Large unwelcome tears of humiliation began to crawl down my cheeks. Harvey pulled a hanky from his pocket and gently wiped away the salty crystals, while offering up the warm, melting smile that had won me over on our first date. This time he held me tight and kissed me tenderly on the forehead and for that fleeting moment I forgot how hurt and angry I was.

"Where were you?" I finally whimpered.

"I was outside with the guys. We were just talking about... ya know...stuff. Honest to God, I didn't know they'd started our dance. Why didn't you come and get me?"

"In the first place, I didn't have a clue where you were and in the second place, 'out with the guys' on our wedding day is not where you should be in the first place."

"You're right, honey. I love you and I'm so sorry if I upset you. I'll never do that again. I promise." He followed that soul grabbing Harlequin cliché with a most inappropriate, passionate and public kiss. With the exquisite music of Benny Berlbaum and his Royal Flush swelling in the background, we floated across the dance floor, our virtuous lips locked in pious matrimony. I think I caught sight of Mama Krup clutching her heart in mortal shame as we danced by.

It was traditional at modern Jewish weddings during the sixties, for the bride to change out of her gown before throwing the bouquet and bidding adieu to the guests. A lot of money was spent on a brand new honeymoon suit that the bride was to wear for all of seventeen minutes, after which the couple was expected to rush off to an expensive hotel suite where she would immediately strip it off and they would get down to doing their duty so that three months later they could announce an impending birth. Harvey and I, on the other hand, dragged ourselves away from the festivities at 2 a.m. and back to our attic flat. We stayed up the rest of the night opening our gifts while still wearing our honeymoon suits. We took great pleasure in counting and recounting our wedding money until the taxi arrived at 4 a.m. to whisk us away to the airport.

Since we were married on a frosty Christmas day, we had decided to splurge with our wedding money and honeymoon on the warm, tropical island of Nassau. Neither of us had ever been on an airplane before, so that in itself was sure to be an adventure.

By the time we arrived in the Bahamas we were exhausted.

No one had told me that it's common on an airplane for your body to bloat up like The Hindenberg. But there was clearly more of me getting off the plane than had gotten on. By now I wished that I had not listened to my mother who insisted on buying me a girdle to wear under my honeymoon suit.

As we disembarked at the airport, we took our first

languishing look at Nassau. It was just the way we imagined it would be. We tingled at the sight of the waving palm trees that stood in perpetual ovation to the majesty of the turquoise Caribbean Sea, and we gloried in the warmth of the pink sunlight.

We were greeted at the luggage bay by the smiling face of our Bahamian chauffeur who whisked us into a beat-up station wagon and off to our hotel.

As we drove along the scenic country road, the temperature in the car reached medium-well on the thermometer. While my body continued to inflate, my thoughts drifted back to our mother/daughter talk...

"Do I think you're fat? Rachel, you're a size seven, you're downright scrawny. It's not a matter of whether you're slim enough; it's just that it's not lady-like to wear a form-fitting knitted suit without a girdle. It's really kind of s-s-slutty!"

How could I argue against that logic? Besides my mother so rarely offered me intimate advice. I had to believe it was a religious dictum. So, consequently, I ended up harnessed in that rubber compression chamber for over twenty-four hours.

By the time we arrived at our hotel, I virtually oozed out of the stifling car and hobbled into the lobby bathroom desperate to remove the elastic garment that now seemed permanently bonded to my body. I pulled and tugged to no avail. I peeked around the ladies' room door and beckoned for Harvey to find me a scissors. He offered a curious look but asked no questions before running off to find the weapon. I cut and flayed that rubbery casing from my buttocks just in time. There were deep, red gashes across my thighs where the metal garters had worked their way into my skin. I threw the shreds of rubber into the trash, soothed my wounds with cold water, and stuffed my stockings into my handbag. I attempted to slip into my shoes but my size 7AA feet had blossomed into size 9 DDDs. The swelling was relentless. As

I walked out of the ladies room wearing my charcoal grey double knit Chanel knock-off and bare feet, Harvey informed me that the hotel didn't know who we were and that we didn't have a room. It crossed my mind that they may have refused to accommodate us because they knew I wasn't wearing a girdle. We soon discovered to our relief that they had simply made a mistake and our room would be ready by morning. In the meantime, we were assigned a temporary room for the night and a bellboy to escort us.

The elevator carried us down one stop before we exited. Our personal valet then hurriedly led us along a dark hallway past a machine room to a tiny cubicle with an eight-inch vine-covered window. The cubby was furnished with a single bed tented in yellowed cheesecloth, a wooden chair with no seat, a closet with no doors, and a toilet. Not a washroom... just a toilet. No tub, no sink and no shower.

After a brief medley of my husband's loud demands and my wailing cries, the front desk offered us temporary lodgings at another private five-star hotel for the night. Our relief instantly vanished when we asked that our luggage be sent over. That was when the manager stammered out his admission that the hotel driver had somehow missed some of our bags at the airport. But he guaranteed that he would have them picked them up and delivered to our new hotel within the hour.

The small, elegant lodge we'd been sent to was even more exquisite than the huge mega hotel we'd originally booked. Harvey was impressed that we were taken directly to our room without even a check-in stop at the front desk. He was sure that the swift service was due to the fact he had informed them that he was a "Doctor." I didn't want to disturb his ego but I was pretty sure it was the sight of my swollen bare feet and wilted suit that prompted the bell captain into swift service.

I showered before dinner and then, since only Harvey's

bag had managed to follow us, I dressed in one of his T-shirts and pyjama bottoms. The dining room was filled with well-dressed couples enjoying the romantic mood while I, on the other hand, looked like an overgrown street urchin. As I strode barefoot behind the tuxedoed maitre d', we heard one long communal gasp.

By morning, however, everything looked brighter. The swelling had gone down, our luggage had arrived, and we had been on the most wonderful nighttime expedition of our lives. Harvey was an extraordinary explorer. He had no fear of dark caves. He visited some of the most mysterious places known to the human body. As for me, I was a quick learning Sherpa. That morning, my mother's sexual wisdom drifted through my thoughts: "*If you save it for the person you intend to spend the rest of your life with, your wedding night will be the most beautiful and enjoyable experience you can imagine.*"

Mother knows best!

Of course I also owe some of that gratitude to the gynaecologist who made sure that my intended would be able to manoeuvre his way into the cave.

That morning, we enjoyed breakfast on the terrace before setting out on a walking tour of the old town. By the time we returned to our room later that afternoon, my leg was throbbing with pain. I concluded that this wrinkle was prompted by the infamous girdle constriction.

As evening approached my leg became numb, but it didn't diminish the intense pain I was feeling. The hotel doctor told us that I had been bitten in the tendon sheath by some parasitic fly that caused temporary paralysis. He gave me some pills and a shot that knocked me out for hours. Harvey was so kind throughout the ordeal. He attended to me like an RN, placing cold compresses on my forehead and making sure that I took my pills every three hours as prescribed.

By the next day my leg was fine but my stomach was erupting like Mt. Etna. I was doubled over in agony when the hotel doctor made his return visit. It didn't take long before he was writing me another prescription to clear up the problems caused by the first. It wasn't that there was anything wrong with the pills he had prescribed. It's just that Harvey hadn't noticed the sign posted inside the medicine cabinet that warned guests not to drink the water "because it could cause gastro-enteritis or worms." I was living proof that it was possible to achieve both.

We had gotten off to a bad start, but we made up for it after we returned to Toronto and our cosy flat in my grandmother's old house on Palmerston Avenue. If there were any ghosts in the attic, they might have been spooked by all the activity that went on up there...in our double bed.

Soon after Harvey graduated, we were able to move up, so to speak.

"Up" was a tiny 5th floor apartment in an unfinished high-rise on the busiest street in the city.

I loved my role as part-time homemaker and part-time Nurse Friday. As for Harvey, he was a dental virtuoso. He loved the difference he could make in the look and confidence of his patients, and he loved the generous fees they paid him as well.

My turn as a dental assistant was relatively short-lived, when the nauseating odour of a patient's trench mouth sent me heaving into his spittoon.

Just days after that humiliating event, I found out that Harvey and I were going to have our first child. From then on I was pretty much destined to be a stay-at-home mom, at least until our children were safely cloistered in school.

I had an idyllic life with Harvey in those early years. Our joy was bolstered by the fact that our family eventually grew from the two of us to six of us, with an equal number of adorable little guys and dolls.

We shared our domestic bliss with our own siblings and their growing families. There was usually some reason for us all to get together and celebrate. It was always somebody's birthday or anniversary or just our simple need to laugh. The Krup brothers were notorious for their great gift of joke telling. It's not that they were good at it. On the contrary, they were dreadful at it. It's just that they would giggle so much during the telling, everyone within earshot was contaminated by their contagious laughter, and before long we would all be holding our stomachs and begging for relief. I don't think the brothers ever finished a punch line in one sitting.

Unlike most of our friends, who at the very hint of pending motherhood were eager to move into new square brick homes, in sterile, natureless, subdivisions. I wanted a breezy wooden summer cottage in the country. I had erased all of the more negative aspects of country living from my mind, and I was determined to offer my first child, and those that would follow, nothing but pure Canadian summers. I wanted our kids to share in the fresh air and clean rural living that I had been so fortunate to experience in my youth.

Well, Harvey finally agreed to buy a cottage after I persuaded him that it would be cheaper than eventually sending our kids to sleepover camp. So our first major investment was a lumbering, two-story summerhouse that we purchased for a mere $8,000.

Our old wood-framed cottage quickly became a beehive of activity. Besides a rich supply of relatives, our good friends and even uninvited acquaintances were all welcomed with great vats of food and grand Southern (Ontario) hospitality. Harvey would take one and all for a tour around the grounds of Balsam Beach and then off for a ride in his prized police boat, while I would stay behind playing Betty Crocker. I was known to bake two dozen fresh fruit pies in one day for a special beach party or to skewer over 50 rods of shish kabob for some event or other. I just needed a pat on the back for encouragement and then off I would go to stuff another hundred mushrooms. It was a good way to be acknowledged by Harvey's friends and family. It hadn't been easy for most of them to accept me at first. I was an *artsy type*, so I didn't fit their profile of a typical Toronto Jewish Princess. I claimed interest in very different quests, such as folk music, reading, painting, and my fellow man. I liked to think of myself as a bohemian with deep thoughts and lofty dreams, while they seemed to prefer to think of me as an eccentric Jewish farmer with hayseed up my butt. I didn't want to be tossed into the royal pit of upper middle class excesses, so to hang on to my eccentricities I rebelled. To our husbands' weekly poker games, I brought my easel and paints along to give me something meaningful to do while the other wives dabbled in their own pedestrian hobbies. I didn't like mah jongg, I didn't know any gossip, I didn't own designer labelled clothes, and I didn't measure the depth of my husband's love by the size of the diamond he bestowed on me. I was an outcast.

In our social circle we were blessed to have an abundance of children who shared their own collective ideas about what was meaningful to their parents. Eventually I learned the joy of attiring my kids in designer jeans, as well as providing them with Tonkas and Barbies they required to feel truly fulfilled. Of course over time I also recanted the dramatic fantasy that I was the "shunned artist" and accepted the fact that perhaps the wives were right. Perhaps I was just an "eccentric Jewish hayseed" after all.

Whenever I think back on our crazy days of summer, I get giddy. Harvey and I were young, daring, and sexually charged. It didn't much matter where or when, we were usually game to show each other the best of ourselves... unless of course we had to contend with visitors sleeping against the thin wall that separated our bedroom from their guestroom. During those times we would simply escape to a more remote location and carry on.

One of our more memorable encounters was erupting on the floor of our little boat while we were afloat in the middle of the lake. We had set aside our fishing gear and were in the wild throws of suntan-scented love-making when we were interrupted by the shouts of one of our more obnoxious neighbours who was out cruising in his monster ship.

Harvey engineered an Olympic somersault across the deck. He fumbled in the fish pail for his missing swimsuit, while tossing me a beach towel that landed on our windshield. Harvey located his trunks under the picnic basket but seemed to have trouble getting his legs into them. In the meantime I became the fabled "deer in the head lights." Our pesky neighbour had obviously sucked up just a beer or two short of a vat and was attempting to pull his double-decked cruiser alongside our glorified rowboat. At least we had a ten second warning. Harvey pulled the towel free from the glass and I covered myself just in time to look the picture of innocence as the cruiser arrived at our threshold.

By the look of the motley crew on board, we had little to worry about since they were all so piss-eyed drunk they would never have remembered anything by the next day anyway. We exchanged a few comments about the weather and the enviable size of Harvey's rainbow trout before the sotted captain raised his hand to his forehead in a mock military salute and knocked himself over. His wife took over the wheel, shouted "land ho," and they resumed their ride... as did we.

The rest of that week I was busy preparing for our bi-monthly Saturday Night Social. That summer I had been re-appointed Entertainment Director of Balsam Beach. Each social event required a great deal of planning, creativity, and hard work; a kind of theatrical experience in its own strange way. I ran around for days before each production, pulling together the music, food, décor, and all the special touches that made it worth my effort.

At the Saturday "hoe-down" Harvey and I were relaxing on a bale of hay in the middle of the recreation hall when I spotted the loud-mouthed captain swaggering in our direction. If I'd been heading toward Iraq in a balloon I'd have felt more hopeful we'd return unscathed. The captain slapped Harvey on the back, gave me a wet cheek kiss, and stepped back exclaiming as loudly as he could: "My God, Rachel, you never cease to amaze me. Every single party this summer has been even better than last year's parade of hits, and tonight is really outstanding. Well done!"

The captain never mentioned bumping into us in the middle of the lake. We joyously exhaled because we had nothing more to worry about. We were still buoyed and sailing.

Minutes later, the captain's wife looking rather lobsteresque sauntered stiffly our way.

"O-o-o, Helen, that burn looks painful," I empathized. "I guess beer and sunbathing don't mix too well, huh?"

"You know, Rachel, I'm surprised that you didn't get burned to a crisp the other day. We all saw parts of you that I'll bet no one but Spinner has seen since you were a baby."

There we were, exposed and deflated.

We tried to be more vigilant in our future endeavours: at the drive-in theatre, on sandy beaches, in front of the fireplace, in the shower, at romantic dinners on exotic islands...

I don't mean to pretend as if all of our sexual activities were so satisfying... not for a minute. That would be a familial myth. No, there were times when our sex life was inhibited by such mundane foreplay as watching Harvey clip his toenails in bed.

But since those times weren't particularly fun back then,

they're not particularly fun to recall now either.

The summer our first child turned one, my mom and dad came to visit us at our country cottage. The weather had been exquisite throughout the month, so we all spent a lot of time together enjoying the benefits of country living as we sun-bathed, barbecued, fished, and picnicked. I was blessed that my husband had such affection for my parents. I had friends who almost ended their marriages because of battles over in-laws. One weekend during their stay Harvey and I went into the city for a friend's wedding while my parents stayed in the country to babysit our daughter, Wendy. They had insisted that we stay in town overnight and enjoy the freedom while we had it. We obliged. A night of unmuffled sex was pretty tempting to us after two weeks of sharing a membrane-like wall with my parents.

The morning after the wedding, as we were getting ready to return to the country, the phone rang. It was a cottage neighbour who was calling to let us know that she had our baby daughter with her. She explained that my dad had collapsed and was being rushed by ambulance to a Toronto hospital.

For five weeks we clung to a feeble hope that he would pull through. My brother was a resident in the same hospital and the cardiologist suggested to him that we get my father's affairs in order because it was doubtful that he would ever recover from such a massive coronary.

Fortunately, God wasn't expecting our dad to join him (or her) up there just yet. So after a harrowing three-month stay in the hospital, he was finally released with an excellent prognosis.

During those months, my sixteen-year-old sister was pretty much left behind in Prescott. Since she still lived there with my parents, Rebecca was the only one my mother could depend on to keep an eye on things.

My parents' old friend Eddie Girard managed the

business whenever they were away, but since they didn't have a staff, Eddie needed someone standing by so that he could take a lunch or bathroom break. Rebecca was the chosen one. According to the letters and phone calls we all received from Eddie, things seemed to be going along smoothly back home. We reassured our mother, who remained at the hospital wedged between guilt and our father's bedside that it was okay for her to stay in Toronto and stand by her man. We insisted that she leave the immediate business worries to Eddie and Rebecca, who were doing a sensational job.

During those long, lonely weeks of our father's recuperation, Rebecca and her forbidden boyfriend John had the golden opportunity to spend the kind of time alone together that teens dream of… and father's dread.

That ironic opportunity resulted in the inevitable advent of our father's worst fear, Rebecca's pregnancy. We were all sure that when my father discovered the secret, it would send him right back into intensive care.

When the deed was finally revealed, dad gave a pretty good imitation of a pressure cooker exploding, but it must speak to the extraordinary quality of treatment he received that the shock triggered neither a twinge of angina nor even the runs.

There was no book or website on how to handle this pregnancy crisis, so we all bumbled our way through it, making clumsy mistakes along the way. We discussed Rebecca's choices as if we were all so evolved and liberal minded: abortion, unwed motherhood or adoption? But the truth is, none of us was really comfortable deciding on any of her options. In the end it was my sister who decided, saving us all a lifetime of guilt.

Rebecca decided to give baby Loreli up for adoption through a reputable, private Jewish agency.

I admit it. We all breathed a sigh of relief as we praised

her decision and rationalized her choice.

"Look, abortion is incredibly risky. Why should a skinny little sixteen-year-old have to give up her entire future? What could she possibly be expected to know about raising a child anyway? She's barely one herself."

Hell I was mature, experienced, and responsible. I was married, with a child and another on the way.... and I was almost twenty-one.

After that traumatic event Rebecca never allowed herself to settle down long enough to get married and have other children, but she always maintained a discreet and enviable loyalty to the child she knew only for an instant.

I've always believed that Rebecca did the right thing; but every year on July second, she would try to hide the tears that insisted on appearing uninvited to the party she held in her mind.

Because my second child Sophie was born just months after Loreli, Rebecca developed a very special connection to her and for a time it was obvious that Sophie was her favourite. But as the Morganstein population exploded, Rebecca's Auntie Mame status moved from one child to another as her whimsy dictated.

Rebecca eventually moved to Los Angeles where, on the silver anniversary of Loreli's birth, she received an answer to her lifelong prayer when she was located by her daughter.

It is a strange irony that Rebecca and Loreli look and sound more like each other than any of my four children look and sound like me.

Shortly after their reunion, my sister was offered a career opportunity back in Toronto and without hesitation she left her adopted State of California and returned to Canada and her only child.

For many years before Loreli re-entered her world, my sister led a life that was so different from mine we could have been raised on separate planets. She travelled to all of the fashion centres of the world as a buyer for a major retailer. She lived big, moved in fast circles, and had little patience for my white picket fence lifestyle. We were always polite and respectful to each other, but we remained as outside of each other's lives as Republicans and Democrats on election day. Now, over leisurely lunches we faun over our treasury of gemstones that is our children and grandchildren, evading the fact that one day without warning, our joy could suddenly shatter like flawed crystal.

I'm still delicately picking fine shards of glass out of my own psyche.

CHAPTER FIVE

During my fruitful marriage, Dr. Shaw often joked that I had gone from being diagnosed as the "woman who was going to have a tough time getting pregnant, to the woman who got pregnant if her husband merely winked at her."

When our first son came along after the birth of our two daughters, we felt so incredibly blessed to have brought three exquisite and interesting beings into this world that we had to try at least one more time. Perhaps we could even have another son. So when the hands on the menstrual clock said "you're late," we ran to Dr. Shaw once again giggling with delight.

Our good fortune was quickly bankrupted when the gynaecologist announced: "You will have to abort this pregnancy, immediately!"

What made Dr. Shaw's order even more traumatizing was the fact that my husband and I were both pro-choice but were not being offered a choice.

The doctor hurriedly explained the urgency: "The pain and swelling you had in your leg last year was phlebitis, a condition that puts you at a great risk of dying from a blood clot during pregnancy. Rachel, you were supposed to be on the pill. Why would you go off it without discussing it with me first? You could have avoided this whole terrible mess!"

My husband and I were stunned by the intensity of the doctor's rebuke, but we bowed to his divine wisdom and passively agreed to obey his instructions.

"Time is of the essence!" he insisted. "Here in Toronto, the red tape can hold you up for months, but in Buffalo they can operate immediately. Every day you procrastinate you will be increasing the threat to your life. My office can arrange an appointment for you at an abortion clinic there. So, do I call Buffalo or not?"

"Yes," Harvey whispered, "please call."

It was the Victoria Day weekend and my parents had no idea why they had been asked to come all the way from Prescott to Toronto just to babysit. It was completely out of character for us to go away on a long weekend without our children. But as always, they didn't ask.

That Sunday night we checked into a bleak room at the Holiday Inn in Buffalo, where we spent our time trying to reassure each other that everything would be okay. We sat on the bed, picking at a bucket of greasy chicken and wondering if we would ever escape this nightmare.

Harvey had always been a sympathetic caregiver. He was the kind of person who was eagerly committed to be by your side if you were ill. Perhaps if I had been a hypochondriac we might still be together.

I gradually became concerned over his propensity to diagnose every slight cough, twinge, or bruise as a life-threatening situation, which required us to immediately rush our children to their paediatrician or the nearest hospital. I, on the other hand, believed that a high fever, an open wound, or intense pain were the only reasons to hightail it for help. I often worried that the overwhelming sympathy and attention that he showered on the children whenever they so much as sneezed might be sending them a dangerous message.

I don't know if either of us slept that night in Buffalo, but it wouldn't have mattered because our thoughts were no less terrifying than our nightmares would have been. The next morning we picked up the scrap of paper with our "directions to hell" scratched on it and headed out to have our dream cancelled.

We plodded up the clinic steps with shaky knees. We entered and stood there dumbfounded at the paradox of sights before us. The clinic itself was spotlessly clean and cheerfully decorated, but the people seated around us looked like they had been sent from central casting for the Jerry Springer Show. Any moment I expected to see a floor director hop into the reception area to begin the audience warm-up.

Leather, tattoos, and micro-minis dominated the visual images of the more conservative members of the group. All of the ladies and their insignificant others seemed anxious to get on with it and get back to whatever it was that got them there in the first place. And then there was me: depressed, embarrassed, and frightened to death ... and in no hurry to confront my fate.

It seemed as if we had only just arrived when the nurse came out to lead me into the operatory. (Where are those overcrowded waiting rooms and understaffed operatories when you want them?)

I dutifully followed the perky young nurse while Harvey remained in the waiting room, alone.

The chubby, middle-aged doctor was pleasant enough, but innately clinical. He had been through this a zillion times, and it was really nothing... for him.

Horrific images rushed through my brain as I watched the

nurse and doctor stroll back and forth between the stirrups, going about their Monday morning business. I watched the needle disappear into my vein, I heard the nurse tell me to relax as she placed a plastic mask over my nose and mouth, and then, minutes later, it was all over. My fantasy of giving my husband another son had been surgically removed and was now lying in a covered Petri dish. I was told to stay very still and they would come back to release me when they felt I was ready. I lay there staring at the covered metal dish, imagining what that little organism might have become. I wondered whether I should think of it as the little boy or the little girl that I might have given birth to by late autumn.

When the doctor returned to check on me, I timidly asked: "Doctor, is there any way of knowing what sex…it… it might have been?"

He studied me for a few seconds and then inquired: "Why? Would you have had a preference if you'd gone to term?"

Since I sensed something leading in his question, I responded on a hunch.

"Oh no, not at all. I was just curious, that's all. It wouldn't have mattered one way or the other."

"Well," he offered, "I wouldn't repeat this in a court room, but it was a boy."

I choked back the scream that threatened to give me away. I thanked the doctor for his candour. He nodded, picked up the remains, and exited. As the impact of his words continued to bore into my heart like a silver bullet, I closed my eyes and vowed that I would never tell my husband. I could at least save him from sharing the devastating impact of the same bullet.

We returned to the city in virtual silence. My parents asked why I looked so pale, and whatever my answer was, it satisfied them. As always, they didn't want to pursue a private issue... and that was where we left it.

The summer arrived in all its reborn splendour, but for the first time in my life, I had no passion for it. I had little passion for anything. I believed that our simple crime of fertilization had condemned our unborn child to the guillotine. I couldn't get past the fact that I had sacrificed his life for mine without even getting a second opinion.

We had moved out to our glorious country home, but my heart was back in the operatory in Buffalo.

I was learning that while Harvey had boundless sympathy for physical pain, he had little compassion for an ailing psyche. His advice? "Relax! Get over it! You're not the first woman to have an abortion ya know. Why are you making such a big deal about it?"

By mid July I had pretty much become a recluse. I rarely went down by the lake except to watch my children romping in the water with their fellow campers when no one else was around. During the week, when my husband was in the city working, I preferred to sit on my veranda painting or writing. It was a lonely endeavour, but not nearly as lonely as I had begun to feel when I was with my husband, who had already "gotten over it."

I often thought of running to my family for comfort, but something always stopped me. I'm still not sure why I hid the secret from them. Perhaps I was afraid that they would tell me I screwed up. Or even worse, they might show pure compassion and understanding for my loss; and I wasn't ready to receive that from my parents or siblings when I couldn't get it from my husband.

The summer was winding down when my brother Adam arrived in Toronto to direct a film. He managed to get a few days off to come and relax at our summerhouse. During a leisurely stroll down a country road, the floodgates finally opened. As the two of us rambled along, I confessed every detail of the chilling events that led to my traumatic visit to Buffalo.

He was stunned by it all and offended that I hadn't confided in him before the fact when he might have been able to offer some useful advice.

"I'm getting a little tired of you coming to me after the horse is out of the barn, Rach. When are you going to learn to let me in before you have to clean the horse shit up by yourself?"

When I shared my perception that something about the whole experience felt very wrong, my brother insisted that I go to see his friend Dr. Berman who was a cardiovascular specialist. Adam armed me with a series of pertinent questions about phlebitis. I was confident now that returning to the beginning of this terrible odyssey was the only way to heal myself. I was comforted by the idea that I would soon understand the seriousness of the condition that Dr. Shaw had previously diagnosed and how lucky I was that he was able to protect us from a fate worse than abortion.

Dr. Berman put me through an exhaustive series of tests before finally reaching the conclusion that sent shivers down my back:

"Rachel, if you had phlebitis, then you've had a recovery of Biblical proportions. There isn't a trace of scar tissue or any other indication that you have ever suffered from phlebitis! So come on, smile and be happy. You're just fine."

I stumbled out of his office, stung by the swarm of doubts that buzzed through my thoughts.

If there was no phlebitis, why did the gynaecologist insist I had to abort? Why didn't I call on my brother for advice in the first place? What have I done?

My husband was lying out in the sun waiting for me when I arrived back at the cottage. I didn't know what to say to him. He looked up at me from his lounge chair and asked,

"So, how did it go? Everything okay?"

"Uh-huh, I guess so," I replied.

"So? He doesn't think you had phlebitis, does he?"

He didn't even flinch as he flippantly posed that grotesque yet rhetorical question.

I was stunned. I had never doubted that I'd had phlebitis until the specialist broke the news. If Harvey had doubts, he had never mentioned them to me.

"No!" I snapped. "He doesn't and I didn't!"

"So, what are you so upset about?" he countered. "That pain in your leg last year was probably just a pulled ligament or something. You should be relieved that it wasn't phlebitis."

"Relieved because I never had phlebitis? Harvey, don't you get it? The doctor was dead wrong. It means that there was no reason to abort our baby!"

"Look, it's no big deal. What's done is done. Get over it already. Maybe now we can get back to some…you know…more pressing issues," he said with a wink.

When I was a little girl, I vaguely remember seeing an old June Alison movie that went something like this:

Dick Powell comes home to find his demure little wife looking up at him with tear-filled eyes. The music fades out while in a hushed whisper, she tells him that they're going to have a baby. He cries, she cries... they are so-o-o happy. They hug and kiss then Dick Powell stops, looks at her, his eyes brimming with love and coyly asks, "When?" She breathlessly answers, "In the spring." The music fades in and the director cuts to a little white cottage surrounded by burgeoning spring gardens. At the bedside sits the proud papa, smiling as he gazes at his baby son. The mother lies there joyfully absorbing the beautiful family portrait.

And that's the way I dreamed it happens. But then I grew

up to realize that from the time you miss your first menstrual period, your husband is pretty much in on the secret; so, no surprises, unless of course you're intensely determined.

Well, Harvey had "winked" and for the next three months I made a poor but valiant attempt to withhold the surprise `a la June Allison. Since the first six months of my previous pregnancies started out as a sentence to hard nausea without hope of reprieve, this time I cunningly alleged to have a chronic case of the Asian flu.

After I discovered I was pregnant again, following the dreaded abortion experience, I found Dr. Silverberg, a new gynaecologist, who assured me that he would do everything possible to deliver a healthy baby and mother.

Around the end of my fifth month, I had a haemorrhaging incident that sent me into the hospital where Dr. Silverberg discovered that I had a placenta privia, which is a Latin way of saying that the placenta was below the baby instead of vice versa (a condition that isn't unheard of, but isn't all that common either). My choices were bed rest in the hospital for the remainder of my pregnancy or lose the baby. I opted for the bed rest.

The most difficult part of my exile was not seeing my children for the next few months.

On two occasions the doctor allowed my husband to wheel me downstairs so that I could sit outside in the garden with them. But both visits ended in medical crises for me, so there were no more visits. There were a couple of times when my husband managed to sneak the kids up the five flights of stairs, past the nurse's station, and into my room. Those brief but sweet moments always ended with their immediate eviction. Periodically, friends would bring my children to the hospital grounds so that I could catch a glimpse of the tops of their heads from my fifth-floor window. They would try to look up and offer a tentative wave toward one of the dingy window panes hoping it might be mine and hoping to catch a glimpse of their mother.

As time passed, I started to panic over the gnawing possibility that they might fear I'd deserted them. So to remind them that I was still in their lives and thinking of them, I devised a plan. I collected all of the candies, flowers, ribbons, and ornaments that friends sent me, and every day I created miniature gift baskets filled with treats for each of the children. Whoever came to visit was pressed into courier service because the gifts had to arrive before morning. I knew that the children would worry if they opened their eyes and there was no surprise from mom waiting for them on their night tables. Ironically, it was my children who helped to keep me focused during this long lonely ordeal.

Dr. Silverberg also worked hard at keeping up my morale. He dropped by every day to assure me that I was doing well and to tell me how brave he thought I was.

One night, I confided in him about my greatest angst, which was the safety and health of the three children everyone assumed were secure and happy at home.

"Dr. Silverberg, just days after I landed in the hospital, Harvey pulled the children out of summer camp and brought them into the city so that he wouldn't have to commute each night. Then he put an ad in the paper for a nanny and he hired the first person that showed up for the interview. All my friends and relatives have inadvertently told me that the woman is not only incapable but also appears to be mentally unstable. I've told Harvey how overwhelmed I am with worry and anxiety over these stories I'm hearing."

"Well good that you've told him, Rachel. Now I'm sure Harvey will take care of everything and you'll get some peace of mind."

"Dr. Silverberg, Harvey took care of it by asking my

friends to spare me any further phone calls that weren't filled with happy stories. So now my friends are afraid to call me or if they do, they'll talk about anything but my children. So I just sit here and imagine all sorts of awful things."

"The kids are probably having a great summer, Rachel. It's an opportunity for them to have fun with their dad."

"No chance. Almost every night after he visits me, he goes out to a movie with a friend or to play cards with his buddies to take his mind off his worries for a while. I keep pleading with him, to return the children to our country place where they have so many friends and relatives to help out but he just ignores me. Consequently, they're spending the summer hanging around our house with nothing to do and no one watching over them except some incompetent, unstable stranger."

Dr. Silverberg set up a meeting to explain to Harvey how his visits seem to spark new rounds of arguments between us that inevitably result in another health crisis for me.

"Harvey, it's so important to the baby and to Rachel that you do what she asks," the doctor patiently explained. Harvey nodded sincerely. But he never got the message. The children remained in the city.

In the meantime, I was getting weaker and weaker and no one could really figure out why. The doctor asked me daily if I was ready to be induced, but I couldn't give in. This little determined soul growing inside me had fought too hard and been through too much to be foiled again by reckless fear.

Late one night I encountered new and unusual symptoms: I felt as if I were floating on helium while tethered inside a vacuum container, dreaming chapter after chapter of strange and vivid events.

Dr. Silverberg arrived in the morning looking sombre. "Rachel, last night you had the nurses in a panic again. Your blood pressure hit rock bottom for the third time in the last two weeks. You're here this morning, thanks to luck and the nurses, but you are clearly getting weaker. I feel that if we wait any longer it will seriously jeopardize you and your baby."

I quietly whispered, "Its okay," but he didn't hear me. He continued, "If we're going to have any hope of saving the baby, we must induce you tomorrow."

"Dr. Silverberg, that's what I was going to tell you. I'm ready if you are."

His confused expression prompted a giggle from me that even I didn't expect.

"You sure changed your attitude in the past twenty-four hours. Did you receive a special message from God while you were out cold?"

"If he sends them in the form of a dream then maybe I did."

"A dream?" he repeated with definite curiosity.

"Uh-huh. Last night I dreamed a whole book of amazing dreams but here's the one that really changed my mind: I was floating peacefully above my bed watching this beautiful little red-headed baby boy come riding toward me on a huge red wave.

"The vision was like a composite of Moses in the bull rushes, the red sea parting, and a trip to Niagara Falls. All I know is that gorgeous little guy was smiling and enjoying the ride. So, we're both ready if you are."

The doctor patted my hand and crinkled his face in a brave, beguiling smile: "Let's go in first thing tomorrow morning and get little Moses out of there ... Okay?"

"Okay."

He had taken me this far and I had no reason to distrust him now.

The delivery room looked like a factory assembly line. It

seemed as if every doctor and nurse in the entire city was gathered in that room for the "miracle child's" coming out party.

After months of dramatic foreshadowing, it turned out that my labour was relatively brief and comparatively painless, thanks to modern medicine and the gentle hand of the anaesthetist.

By mid morning I had given birth, relatively uneventfully, to a healthy redheaded baby boy. The wave of euphoria that saturated the maternity floor was palpable. My husband and I cried tears of relief and overwhelming joy for our new son who we named Aaron Baruch.

That hot August day seemed to be a popular one for new births. And since all of the recovery rooms were occupied, I was stockpiled on a gurney in the hallway to wait my turn. I insisted that Harvey rush to the nearest phone to let our families and the immediate world hear the messianic news.

I'm sure that it's cabalistic blasphemy to say this, but I will always believe that the determined little soul that had been so wrongly deprived of life in that Buffalo abortion clinic had finally been given the perfect body in which to dwell.

Some time later Harvey returned for my grilling and I didn't disappoint: "Are the kids excited? Who said what? How did they sound? Were they surprised it was a boy?" Patiently he began to reel off whatever notable comments he could remember. Harvey gazed at me in utter astonishment when I suddenly interrupted him in mid quote screaming, "The gurney's falling, my God, the gurney's falling." He made a desperate attempt to convince me that it was perfectly steady but I could feel myself tumbling toward the ground. He shouted for a nurse who came racing down the hallway. She glanced at me and moaned, "Oh my sweet Jesus!" Then she shouted, "Someone find Dr. Silverberg, stat! Tell him we have a code blue!"

I opened my eyes and found myself lying in a dark hollow room. I tried to raise myself up, but I weighed in like a Volkswagen. As someone lifted my head to tuck a pillow underneath it, I caught a glimpse of my massive belly. I had just given birth prematurely to the smallest baby of my four litters and I looked as if I were fifteen months pregnant. I tried to turn my head to look for my husband, but the mechanism just wouldn't work. Then, through a maze of disconnected sounds, I could hear his voice straining desperately to reassure me.

"You just hang in there, honey. Dr. Silverberg's right here and everything's gonna be okay."

The doctor leaned in and smiled feebly. Through a veritable haze I watched a glossy tear roll down his cheek. His voice quivered: "We need to talk, okay?"

"Dr. Silverberg?" I whispered. "What's happening to me? Where's my baby?"

His throat crackled: "Please don't worry about your son. He's perfectly alright... but we need you to sign a consent form so that we can make sure you're alright too."

"What do you mean? What's wrong with me?" I murmured.

"Rachel, your uterus has ruptured and your abdomen is filling with blood. We're transfusing you, but we can't keep up with the blood loss. We need to do a hysterectomy and we need your permission... now!"

The next face I saw was that of my friendly anaesthetist who was slapping my hand and asking me if I knew where I was and what my name was and other such inane questions.

I was surrounded by flowers and gift packages. Directly in front of me was an enormous bouquet of the most breathtaking, long-stemmed peach coloured roses I had ever seen.

"Am I dead?" I mumbled.

"Not unless I am too," the sleep doctor chuckled. A jolly looking nurse rose from a chair by the side of my bed and asked if I would like anything.

"My baby. Please, can I see him?"

The nurse patted my hand and offered one of those reassuring grandmotherly smiles:

"Of course you can dear. The nursery staff will be bringing your little miracle child in shortly. In the meantime you just rest up. You're gonna need your strength."

"When are they going to operate on me?"

A naughty grin spread across the nurse's gentle face: "That would be yesterday my dear. By the way, your doctor stayed here for hours waiting for you to wake up but he finally had to call off the vigil so that he could get some rest. He said to tell you he'll be back first thing in the morning... you can count on it. Your husband will be back soon, he just stepped out to get a bite to eat, he's been here all night as well. In the meantime why don't I read you some of these beautiful gift cards?"

The peach roses were from my doctor, with a note that said:

"Congratulations and welcome back, we missed you!

With respect and admiration,

Dr. Jack Silverberg."

"Welcome back" was just what I needed to talk to him about. I wanted to know if he really understood where I had been.

In the seventies, children were not welcome as visitors in any hospital maternity ward in Toronto, which meant that baby Aaron's siblings didn't get to see him until he was finally welcomed into their home.

After Aaron's dynamic birth, and my traumatic rebirth it took almost two more weeks before the doctors allowed us to go home. I had been gone for almost three months and I was terrified that my children would no longer know me. I was desperate for, and fearful of, our homecoming.

The children stayed behind with the housekeeper that their father had hired during my tenure in the maternity ward. But Harvey brought along Mrs. Gerhardt, the no-nonsense Austrian baby nurse who had escorted all of my other infants from hospital to home.

With our other babies she had been hired to help out for the better part of a week, but since I had not been upright for almost three months prior to the delivery, it was decided that this time Mrs. Gerhardt would stay on for three weeks. Her job was to closely attend to the new baby, a responsibility she took quite literally. She made it clear on the way home from the hospital that if the other children needed anything, she would not be available to help. Harvey reassured her that anything that I couldn't do that needed to be done would be done by the person he described as our live-in nanny.

As the car rolled down our street, I marvelled at how lush the landscape was and how the tree branches, locked in a welcoming embrace, formed a brilliant green canopy over our driveway.

I had barely opened my car door before all three children were on top of me, gifting me with hugs and kisses. I revelled in the outpouring of affection and blindly returned the love. My fear of rejection had subsided, but my senses quickly shifted to some glaring concerns. My olfactory sense had suddenly zeroed in on an odour unlike anything I had ever smelled before: simultaneously, my vision was equally assaulted. This disturbing blitz on my senses was emanating from my three darling children.

Four-year-old Brandon had long, stringy hair that hid his eyes and skirted his shoulders. His fingernails were as long as his nail-beds and under each one was a reservoir of black pasty muck.

His t-shirt and shorts were faded, stained, and filthy, and the only thing on his feet was about a half-inch of grime. The girls didn't fair much better. With one glance it was clear to me that they had all become the neighbourhood ragamuffins. For that instant I was almost pleased with the Gestapo-style tactics of Mrs. Gerhardt who had swiftly scooped the baby out of my arms and took him straight into the house barely giving Aaron's siblings much of a chance to even catch a glimpse of their new baby brother.

As soon as I was able to get myself out of the car, Harvey headed off to the mall with a long list of necessities that the nurse and I had compiled.

I slowly headed into the house accompanied by my three luscious children who were in dire need of cleaning and possibly sterilizing. They walked me through the house, watching as I absorbed every room, basking in the comfort of familiarity. The main floor looked just as I had left it: neat, clean and homey. When I pulled myself up the stairs, I came upon a very different habitat. Each of the children's rooms was unkempt, smelly, and dusty. Articles of clothing lay wherever they had been dropped, and food leftovers were everywhere. Even the flies and ants were informed of the disaster and had come rushing to the crash site. I wasn't sure where to begin, so I closed the doors and turned to face the children, all three of whom had remained as far away from their rooms as the staircase would allow. To their relief, I reassured them that we would play, read stories, and sing songs very soon, but we had to take care of a couple of things first.

I limped stealthily down the two flights of stairs to the housekeeper's room.

I introduced myself to the woman who was caught lying on the couch in the recreation room watching TV. I asked her how it was that the main floor and my bedroom were so clean and well kept, while the children's rooms were a virtual health hazard. She confidently replied:

"Dr. Krup told me that I was to treat this house as if it were my home and to treat the children as if they were my own too. So I told those kids that they had to clean up their own rooms. If they want to live like pigs, that's their choice. I don't spoil brats. If you want to spoil them, that's your choice. But Dr. Krup told me he'd be here so I could have today and tomorrow off, so if you want something done, it'll have to wait until I'm back upstairs after the weekend."

My response was brief and so was the time it took her to pack up and leave our house.

To Harvey's credit, he did drive her all the way down to the train station.

Harvey's good deed allowed me time to scrub, lather, shear, manicure, and powder each child in turn until they all looked and smelled quite human. As I administered loving spa treatments, they regaled me with nightmarish stories about the banished housekeeper and her beastly ways.

Once the children were returned to normalcy, they each hovered over their new baby brother, waiting their turn to hold, hug and kiss him until his hungry tummy or the Gestapo nurse interrupted their pleasure.

Aaron was the only one of my four children that was not nursed. The doctors had forbidden me to even attempt breast-feeding after his birth. There were so many traumas before and after the delivery that they feared it would endanger me, hinder my recuperation, and further prolong my hospital stay. I argued to no avail, but since I was barely conscious for days on end after his birth, it seemed only right that I should acquiesce to the pleas of the doctors and nurses who assured me that in a contest, Enfilac would run neck and neck with breast milk any day. It never occurred to me that that decision could one day contribute to my son's inconceivable wrath toward me.

It's a funny thing about knowing that this is your last child. There is a need to protect and coddle that particular one much more than you ever intended. It's not about more love or more things or even more time. It's really about fear. He is "the" baby, the last and the ultimate baby. There will never be another so you need to hang on just a little longer. There are also more people to help you do it. With three siblings surrounding him at all times, there was little opportunity for Aaron to ever feel unattended, especially since two of them were mothers in training. The girls catered to his every need, or at the very least, they made sure that I did. If he sucked his fingers they worried that he was starving. If he cooed they were sure that he would be talking by three months. And if he dirtied his diaper they would shriek and gasp and shout their e-ew's and yucks as they ran for cover. He never went unnoticed. With his thick mane of glorious red curls and his early, joyful smile, how could he?

CHAPTER SIX

The next four years of Aaron's life were among the most fulfilling of mine. The older children were in school and I was free to mollycoddle the baby.

The year he turned four I knew that we would have to enrol him in Jr. Kindergarten for his sake. It was time for him to spread his wings and meet the rest of the world. The problem now was for Harvey and I to agree on what school would be best for Aaron.

Little did we know that the decision would eventually be made for us and in such a dramatic way.

One could say that I fell into my career as a theatre director through an incidental "Act of God."

When it happened I was a young housewife, married to a Jewish 'doctor', with whom I had two beautiful daughters. By all accounts, we were a fine looking TV family. My husband boasted to all who would listen: "Donna Reed could take lessons in home-making and decorating from my wife."

But I was in desperate need of intellectual nourishment.

So Harvey and I joined a small band of young, passionate Chosen Ones who were about to embark on the creation of "a new synagogue for the thinking class." I was sure that it would be a noble challenge to be a pioneer. Of course we realized that we wouldn't have to dredge swamps, fight for our land, or tangle with snakes. But with the clarity that time inevitably generates, comes the wisdom to acknowledge that we did just that. We caught rainwater in pails as it soaked through the holey tent we erected for High Holiday services. We progressed to the creation of a clapboard portable, which because it was perched in the middle of a swampy field, required us to politely scrape the muck from our shoes before entering. We fought with politicians over our right to build a permanent sanctuary on the land we'd sacrificed so much to acquire. Then, after we finally completed construction on our beautiful synagogue, we had to tangle with our reptilian leadership that was poisoning our spiritual paradise with its ego-driven political venom. We were still wading through mud at the portable while we were auditioning rabbis to head up our newly founded Beth Israel Synagogue.

Since no one could agree on what kind of a spiritual leader it would take to please all of the mighty egos that populated the search committee, a progression of holy men strode confidently through our front door only to be brusquely escorted out the back.

Some of us on the periphery were convinced that nothing less than a man of Biblical magnitude would suffice.

Our Moses finally came to us in the form of a young middle-aged, slightly stooped and balding New Yorker named Ari Cohen, who was not only a rabbi but a cantor as well.

"What a coup," boasted the sanctimonious search committee. "Two pros for the price of one!"

After having successfully passed the committee interview,

Rabbi/Cantor Cohen was invited to attend a Friday night service where he would be scrutinized by the rest of the congregation before a final decision was made. The congregation was asked to come out to meet this modern-day Moses at a special event that was to be planned by the sisterhood. My contribution to this holy night was to be limited to the very things I was noted for at home: planning captivating parties, preparing enticing refreshments, and decorating with verve. This was a feast that once again offered me a chance to dabble in titillating brain candy, but with no intellectual nutrition whatsoever.

I arrived for a social planning meeting of our Beth Israel Sisterhood event aware of a buzz in the air that I couldn't quite grasp. It didn't take long however, before an angst-ridden president approached me about their dilemma. In a pseudo-snobby accent, she whispered through her clenched lower jaw: "Rachel, dear, we have acquired access to a 'sociodramatic' manuscript that I believe is actually *Tony* material, but we need someone who can pull it all together in a performance. And since the girls tell me that you have a knack for anything artsy, we've decided that you should take on the role of ...whatever they call the person who takes on that role. So, what do you think?"

My mind began to sing hymns of joy at the very idea of a challenge. I had no idea what was required of me, but I was determined to find out. Visions of Lady Macbeth and Dorothy Parker stalked my brain as I tried to focus on the wild idea that I was about to embark on an adventure in theatre.

"Sure, I can take on that role," I replied.

"Good. Whatever you need is yours. We just want this to be a hugely successful event, okay, de-ear?"

"Su-ure. But the first thing I'll need to do," as if I really knew "is to read the script."

"Oh, well you see, we don't have it yet because my

husband's cousin in Cleveland is still writing it, but it'll be finished soon, and it's going to be great! Actually, she is in fact going to do it next month with her grade three students."

Oh dear God... what have I done?

Well, the delay gave me a week to call my Uncle Albert who was the head of the Academy of Dramatic Arts in New York to explain my plight, and then I asked him "What have I done?"

Uncle Albert was incredibly supportive. He told me, "I have every faith that you can be a brilliant producer/ director."

So that's what you call it.

Within days I received a carton filled with Uncle Albert's recommended reading material. I poured over every word of every text, making reams of notes as I went along. By the time I attended the next meeting I was semi-fluent in the language of theatre, which is more than I can say for the president's husband's cousin. The script was so primitive that I had to add "writer" to my newfound credits. Thanks to my old high school English teacher, writing was the one related skill that made me comfortable. So I wrote, cast, directed, costumed, stage-managed, and designed the set (a table, two chairs and a plant) for our big performance. Everyone involved in the production was thoroughly enjoying the whole experience. But as for me, I was in love.

The night had come too quickly. Not because we weren't ready, but because it would all be over soon and I couldn't bear the thought. On the other hand, my insides were churning at the prospect that the rabbi might jump up in the middle of the performance and protest the entire event, deeming that theatre is for pagans.

There was absolute silence as the show sailed off like a cruise ship on a calm sea. There wasn't a storm cloud in sight for the entire evening. Harvey sat there glowing with pride, and I warmed myself in his light.

At the curtain call it was our auditioning rabbi/cantor who led the applause... on the Sabbath. I was always given to understand that clapping wasn't allowed in the synagogue on the Sabbath, but I certainly wasn't going to point out the error to "the man of God."

We all waited with childlike anticipation as Rabbi Cohen stepped up to the pulpit to offer up his audition sermon to the congregation. He began his charismatic address by offering praise to the leadership for their obvious commitment to the arts. He admitted that, unsure of his calling, he had majored in both theology and music in college.

"I couldn't decide between God and opera," he quipped, "but then my father pointed out that *Al Jolson had the same dilemma*!" Rabbi Cohen concluded that since God created music, it was logical to assume that his calling was to be both rabbi and cantor."

At the reception he sought me out to tell me how impressed he was with the performance... and then he asked me about my theatre credits.

"Well, this is it," I sheepishly replied.

"Come on now, you don't have to be modest," he proclaimed. I shrugged. He smiled and added, "Well, if this is true then all I can say is, you have definitely found your calling. I'm certain that tonight's presentation will be the first of a long list of glorious theatre credits that are sure to come your way."

For almost ten years our rabbi pushed, challenged, supported, and believed in me, and through all that time I studied with anyone who could teach me anything about theatre.

My uncle arranged for me to sit in on master classes at the academy in New York and Los Angeles, from which I eventually received a diploma in theatre arts.

During those ten years I led a company of fiercely

dedicated amateur thespians who worked long hard hours to create the Beth Israel Drama Group. Some of our members were extraordinarily talented and some were just exceptionally brave, but the mix created a magical brew on stage that dazzled even the most cynical members of the congregation.

The cost of running the company was nominal to the synagogue board whose only responsibility was to allow us to use some nearly unusable basement space to build the shows and the stage on which to present them. We raised the required production dollars by every fundraising means possible. And when that wasn't enough, a few of us would dig into our personal savings to make sure that the show did go on. The group grew in numbers and talent over the years, as well as in our love and respect for each other. There were teachers, housewives, doctors, truckers, salesmen, and even lawyers who came together to act, build sets, sweep the stage, sew costumes, or hand out programmes. Whatever it took to get the show up and running, our members and their families were willing to dig in and do it. Harvey loved "shooting the breeze" with the guys while offering a helping hand.

Our children attended the day school that was housed in the synagogue, so they were always close at hand. I could always count on them asking to use the washroom during class, so that they could slip into the shop area to see what excitement they might be missing. Sophie, who was particularly fascinated by the theatre world, seemed to manage a regularly scheduled stomachache.

Any of the children's plays that I chose to produce were selected on the strength of my own kids' reactions to the story lines that I would casually unfold over dinner.

The group's repertoire ranged in scope from children's fairy tales to Jewish vaudeville show, to legitimate theatre fare, such as *One Flew over the Cuckoo's Nest.*

It was that *Cuckoo* that eventually gave us wings to fly high.

It attracted audiences from hundreds of miles away. There were many nights during that run when our audience looked like a virtual who's who of the theatre. But it was the attention we were receiving from theatre critics that overwhelmed us all. Although we had never dared to fantasize that the Toronto press could ever take us seriously, it came as a welcome reward when they did. There was no doubt that our fame had proven to be a valuable public relations vehicle for the synagogue's board of directors when, after close to ten years, rumours began to abound that they were planning to expand the synagogue. It seemed that the formerly useless space that we had been using to build our sets, props, and costumes was about to be overtaken by toilets. The rumour was supported by the fact that our synagogue membership had grown from several hundred to several thousand bladders.

Over the years the Beth Israel Choir (in which my husband grew from shower singer to pious baritone) had worked together with the drama group on many noble projects. And even though it was the drama group that had always attracted the new members, it was the choir that was favoured by the leadership as the more spiritual endeavour. So, inevitably, it was the drama group that was to be flushed.

Fate proposed that if we were to be plunged down the sewer, we would surface again in the midst of an oasis.

I was standing in my kitchen, preparing a veritable barrel of gefilte fish for our Passover Seder, while attempting to keep my children happily occupied. For Wendy "occupied" simply required that she spend as much time as possible talking her way out of anything that remotely resembled work, while Sophie created her own unnecessary assignment of polishing the stainless steel cutlery to an already reflective finish. Brandon happily accepted the manly job of crushing almonds with a hefty rolling pin and three-year-old Aaron was intent on breaking several eggs for me and dumping them, shell and all, into a bowl where I restrained myself with the belief that I could resurrect them later with the help of a fine sieve. When the phone rang, Sophie interrupted her task to grab the receiver and answer in her finest receptionist's voice.

"Hallu-u-u … Yes she is … Just a moment please. Mo-om, it's for you-ou."

"Honey, find out who it is and tell them I can't take the phone right now 'cause my hands are all yucky, okay?" Sophie did as asked and then relayed the response.

"Mom, it's some lady calling for some man who says he needs to speak to you about something ... just for a minute."

"Okay, honey, can you hold the phone to my ear for a second so I can talk while I mix?"

Sophie attempted to do as she was asked while Aaron tried to wrestle the receiver away from her with his albumin glazed fingers. Sophie won the struggle and the sticky phone was safely cradled between my ear and shoulder.

"Hello ...yes it is... look, I'm really sorry but if you're selling something this is not a good time ... Well … if it's really quick … alright."

The next voice I heard was that of some pushy guy who proceeded to tell me that he was building a new theatre complex to honour his mother's memory, and he wanted to tell me all about it. I figured that he was looking for donations and since we were in no position to help, I made a polite attempt at a fast exit, which was accelerated by Aaron's helpful attempt to add the half dozen or so unfiltered broken eggs directly into Brandon's bowl of crushed nuts. I rescued the nuts, saved the eggs, and still managed to continue to finish the conversation off with a certain amount of restraint: "I'm really sorry, but at the moment I'm up to my elbows in gefilte fish, if you know what that is, and I just don't have time for this right now."

The gentleman would not accept my fish story as an excuse. He insisted that he wasn't looking for a penny from me; he simply wanted to arrange a meeting with a Mr. Charles Sanders who could give me more detailed information on the project he was calling about. I was sensing that if I didn't agree he would only try a new strategy, so, just as Wendy began taunting Aaron over his culinary skills and he began hinting that the eggs might end up on her head, I caved.

I can only presume that Mr. Sanders felt that I had something to offer the project because the day after our meeting I was asked to come on board as a consultant on the building of a dynamic new theatre at the YMHA.

I panicked at the very thought of such an undertaking. I liked my simple, relatively unpressured life, but Harvey was hooked. He felt that it was time that I was finally paid for my services after all those years of hard work in the theatre for no pay. I tried in vain to explain to him that that's what volunteering is all about, but he couldn't grasp the concept. The harder I tried to talk myself out of accepting the job, the more determined he was to talk me into it. Since I was too insecure to see the possibilities, Harvey gathered some of our closest friends together to try to convince me to accept the position. I argued that I was out of my element. "What could I possibly know about building anything?"

Harvey even got my Uncle Albert and my brothers in Los Angeles on the line to encourage me to accept. It seemed that everyone was sure that I could or should do it, except me.

The YMHA, which had been a social landmark for decades, boasted one of the best nursery schools in Toronto. That fact got me thinking that before I made any decision about the offer, I should play the *Bashert game. [**Destiny*]

The Bashert game, in psychobabble, could best be described as an obsessive-compulsive exercise. But since I feel that I invented the game, I prefer to think of it as an intellectual challenge of fate. I simply put a reasonable obstacle at the crossroads of my conflicting paths and then watch to see which one the signs will direct me to follow.

I was aware of the fact that the Y's Jr. Kindergarten had a two-year waiting list. Harvey and I had discussed sending each of our first three children to that Jr. Kindergarten at one time or another but always ended up enrolling them elsewhere.

I had previously avoided any plans to send Aaron anywhere until it was compulsory because he was my baby after all, and I wanted him near me for as long as possible. We began to rationalize that since we trusted our housekeeper to look after Aaron when we went out for an evening, it wasn't such a stretch to entrust him to skilled professionals for a few hours a day. The bonus for me was that he would be down the hall from where my office would be, so I could see him anytime I felt the need. I was now at the crossroads of two convergent courses: Could I bear to put my baby in Jr. Kindergarten at all and could I change my status from volunteer to employee without upsetting the balance in our home and in my head?

It was time to evoke the Bashert game to help me decide. I would put him on the wait list for that overbooked Jr. Kindergarten and see if fate intervened. If he got in then I would take the job; if he didn't then I would return to my life as it was before the phone call.

After a couple of weeks had passed, it was clear that my

son had not made it, so I set up an appointment to decline Mr. Sanders' offer in person.

He greeted me with his grandfatherly charm and asked me to have a seat. Before I could begin, he began complimenting me on some of the suggestions I had made with respect to the theatre and then he reaffirmed his enthusiasm about working with me.

"Something came to my attention at a staff meeting last week, Rachel, which I would like to tell you about." There was a note of conspiracy in his voice.

"When I announced that you would be coming on board in the fall…" I attempted to interrupt.

"… just let me finish my dear. It was brought to my attention that you had applied to get your son into our Jr. Kindergarten program, which was completely full. But I want you to know that I went to the mat for you and arranged a space for your little guy."

I was speechless and terrified.

"You don't have to thank me, young lady. I was happy to do it. Welcome aboard."

This was to be the first performing arts centre of its kind in the country and, since I had no model to follow, I simply threw myself into the project with abounding energy.

My time was spent investigating everything from stage acoustics to the ratio of audience butts to lavatories. There was the anxiety over where rehearsals would be held and what facilities were necessary for building sets, costumes, props, and the like. On the darker side of the business, I had to learn about agents, contracts, budgets and, most hated of all, I had to become a politician. I soon discovered that our YMHA dabbled in the same kind of ego-driven politics as our synagogue. This time, however, I had received a solemn promise that we wouldn't be sold down the sewer for toilets. This time I knew that the chairman, Warren T. Freedman, the pushy guy who had lured me away from my gefilte fish, would fight to protect his interests. Freedman's two brothers were peripherally involved in the fundraising aspect of the project, but I quickly realized that it was the oldest brother, Warren, who was determined to pay homage to the memory of his mother…and it was his ego that was at stake.

Warren Freedman hadn't inherited all of his millions; he had earned most of them the old-fashioned way, through hard work and very, very careful spending. It wasn't that he was cheap, it was just that he seemed to measure his success by the dollar. Every profitable investment was a credit toward his Fortune 500 diploma.

It was several months before I got to meet or even talk to the man who had urged me to take the job in the first place, and oddly, that first eye-to-eye meeting was intended by me to be our last.

Just weeks before I made the decision to take the job, I'd been asked by Mr. Sanders if I could prepare an in-depth report on the proposed use and mission of the theatre.

"Rachel, I believe it's important for you to put all your great ideas on paper to impress those executive and board members who haven't had the pleasure of meeting you yet," Mr. Sanders gushed.

Over the next several months I researched every aspect of theatre and interviewed anyone who could offer a glimmer of enlightenment. I wrote, edited, and bound my prized thesis, which I then proudly dropped on Mr. Sanders' desk for approval. A couple of days later I noticed my beautifully bound report lying in pieces on his secretary's desk. When I asked why it was in such a state, she told me that Mr. Sanders had asked her to rebind it. Then she proudly added, "I've already done it and run off forty copies for the big executive meeting next week."

I picked up a copy and read the cover page, which declared in bold print: "**The Anna Freedman Theatre Prospectus... researched and written by Charles Sanders.**"

Harvey urged me to call and complain to Mr. Freedman, whom he was sure would disapprove of the Sanders fiasco. After many sleepless nights, I finally puffed up the courage to call for an appointment. The secretary asked me to hold while she checked his schedule, but the next voice I heard was that of Warren Freedman. I began to perspire. I regretted having dialled the number. "What will he think? She's a whiner... she's a wimp?" I gathered my courage by simply remembering how furious I was with Charles Sanders. I'm sure that Mr. Freedman could tell by my warbling hysteria that I was on the verge of quitting. He suggested a meeting that very day.

As I entered the stately offices of Warren T. Freedman, the thought rushed through my mind that my pinko commie dad would never have approved of my meeting with this wealthy corporate giant to discuss the plight of the worker. My father's ruddy politics had taught me to be wary of the excessively rich, who were void of basic human compassion.

Contrary to my father's political bias, I found Warren T. Freedman, the distinguished grey-haired-stinking-rich-pushy guy, to be a kind and sympathetic listener.

He reassured me that I wasn't the first to have been robbed of an idea by Charles Sanders. Then he offered me some advice: "Mrs. Krup, if you want to succeed you'll need to learn how to deal with bullies. If it's bothering you that much, then you have to let Sanders know what you've discovered and tell him you want your name put back on the report before the board meeting, and if it's any consolation, I've read the paper and was well aware that you wrote it."

"You were?"

"Of course. Sanders doesn't have a clue what a theatre needs and anyone who knows him knows that. But we are all aware that he's a good leader. He knows if you don't have the ideas yourself, then you have to find the people who do. His problem is that he has a need to take all the credit, which isn't the best way to keep good people happy. Anyway, if you want to talk about this again, just have my secretary set up another appointment, okay?"

"Thanks, Mr. Freedman, but it won't be necessary. I think I can handle this now."

"Okay good, but please feel free to call whenever you run into a problem. This project means a lot to my family. And by the way, your presentation really is terrific."

I was pleased that I chose not to mention a word to Mr. Sanders about the fraud because most of the board members I met after the meeting thanked me for my splendid presentation.

How did they know?

Through every important chapter of my life it seems that I've always found a dedicated mentor. There was my father, my English teacher Miss Evanson, my Uncle Albert, Rabbi Cohen and even my brothers. I guess I never had the self-confidence to believe that I could accomplish any deed without the reinforcement of a strong role model. I quickly learned to count on Warren Freedman's positive encouragement and his keen eye for spotting political and financial potholes.

Seasons of research and planning flew by until two years had passed and the opening of the Anne Freedman Theatre was just a few months away. I continued to produce and direct plays at the Beth Israel Synagogue until just months before the big opening, when the entire company moved into the unheated, unfinished building that, when completed, was to be our new home.

I worked exhaustively, hoping to prove "I did it" to everyone who believed "I could"… and more importantly to myself and anyone else who doubted it. I logged many panicked phone calls to Mr. Freedman, who taught me to look at every disaster as just another challenge. There were so many issues to deal with that we soon formed our own mini-executive made up of some of the best movers and shakers in the community. With a group of five dedicated players, we moved every decision along briskly, avoiding the usual executive bogs that tend to gum up success.

When I look back on all those months of endless problems, I realize that the job I had been given was so mammoth, only someone as naïve as I was could have completed it on time.

I needed the best people I could find, and because money was always in limited supply, they would have to be willing to do their part, simply for the love of it.

I quickly developed a New York minute approach to approaching New Yorkers or even Californians. I would "offer the most prestigious opportunity in the country" to any celebrity I wanted in our theatre and he or she would wisely accept. That was how I enlisted Nobel Literary Prize winner Isaac Bashevis (I. B.) Singer for our theatre's grand opening. I dialled the number I managed to track down, knowing I would get an agent who would transfer me to a manager who would pass it on to a publicist who would tell me I could book an appointment to see him but probably in the next decade; The voice I heard on the other end of the line, however, was that of the genius himself. Once I explained that I was in New York, I. B. insisted that I cab it over immediately and join him and his wife for lunch. And that was the beginning of a deeply rewarding friendship.

Just days before I. B. Singer's play was to open, the couple arrived in Toronto for a mini vacation before the big night.

One evening while waiting for dinner at my home, I. B.

gathered my children together in our library and proceeded to read from his new children's book. Curmudgeon that he was, he claimed he was merely trying to get an honest review from his audience demographic but when I peeked in on them, what I saw looked nothing like a marketing focus group. The older kids were seated on the floor at his feet, but three-year-old Aaron had climbed up on his lap and sat mesmerized by the story, while eight-year-old Brandon made it clear to our guest that he was more intrigued by his belief that when stretched to full stature I.B. and he were almost the same height.

It was a most unusual evening. I. B. regaled us with his glorious stories and to everyone's amusement, Aaron shared some of his own creative tales, which completely delighted the old scribe. The children were so mesmerized they didn't even notice that they had polished off their spinach.

On the big night, I. B. Singer and his wife sat with Harvey and me in the front row waiting anxiously for the curtain to rise on his daring new play, *Yentl*.

Harvey had managed to escape to the lobby before the endless parade of mandatory political speeches began. Every petty bureaucrat who had formerly tried to obstruct our every decision was now prepared to stand up and take full credit for our success.

As the politicians blew their egocentric trumpets, I. B. clearly agitated, leaned over and whispered, "Rachel, you should go up there and tell them that this stage isn't a soap box for village idiots!"

My snickering was suddenly drowned out by the thunderous echo of my name resounding from the speakers. It appeared that I was being resolutely summoned to the stage. This had not been on the programme that I had drawn up. I knew that the last item on the agenda before the curtain went up was the formal dedication of the theatre in memory of the Freedman matriarch.

I wanted to turn to Harvey in the hope he could think of an escape but his seat remained empty and I remained bolted to my chair hoping they would just raise the curtain and let the show begin. But as my name reverberated once again, I.B leaned over and mumbled, "You better get up there, Rachel, or the politicians will grab the mic for an encore and you'll never start the show."

I stumbled awkwardly up the steps, willing myself to breathe deeply and relax. I dared not look out at the ocean of red seats. I had a fixed snapshot in my head of Isaac Bashevis Singer sitting right in front of me, and my LA family sitting proudly in the centre of the house along with my parents and my children, but I really didn't want to raise my eyes to look. If I had, I might have noticed four empty seats because on stage, opposite Mr. Freedman, were the beaming faces of my four children who it seems were surreptitiously and enthusiastically escorted away from my parents and onto the stage. The very sight of them slowed my heart-rate to a survivable level, but as I listened to the kind praise heaped on me by my newest mentor, my cheeks erupted in a lava glow. As he finished my eye was drawn to a little ballerina who came sashaying onto the stage embracing a magnificent bouquet of peach-coloured roses. She handed the flowers to Mr. Freedman who placed them in my arms while whispering a suggestion that I step up to the microphone to say a few words. I approached the mic cautiously, as if it were alive and dangerous. I looked back over my shoulder to make sure that my children and my mentor were standing by in case I keeled over. It was then that I spotted a stagehand darting out from behind Mr. Freedman carrying an easel. Another carrying a large shrouded frame followed him. To my relief, the scene confirmed to me that we had finally reached the last item on the agenda, the unveiling of the Freedman matriarch's portrait. If I could just manage to adlib a few brief and witty anecdotes, I'd be back on the other side of the stage lickety split.

As the ballerina began to exit stage right, her tutu caught the edge of the shroud and pulled it along with her. My eyes were locked on the painting and my mind was spinning out of control as I gazed for the first time at the portrait of the theatre's late patron of the arts. My mind was flooded with vivid images from a dream I had the night before Aaron's birth… three years before anyone had conceived of the Anna Freedman Theatre.

I am standing on a stage, looking out at a sea of plush red velvet chairs that are filled with people bearing warm smiling faces.

A distinguished gentleman steps forward and hands me a huge bouquet of peach roses. On one side of me stands an easel on which is perched a portrait of a handsome white-haired woman wearing a pale blue dress and ivory pearls. On the other side stand my children beaming with pride. Harvey is seated directly in front of me, but hard as I try, all I can see is his back.

CHAPTER SEVEN

When my children were little I used to sing them a song about childhood memories: "Raindrops on roses and whiskers on kittens... silver-white winter that melts into spring... these are a few of my favourite things, I didn't care to sing the part about "when the dog bites" or "when the bee stings," so I usually blended in some of my own lyrics: "Wendy's tall stories and Soph's sassy laughter... Brandon's bold giggle and Aaron's sweet banter ...walks in the forest where every leaf sings... these are a few of my favourite things..."

Through the years I've often replayed that song in my head during my more nostalgic moments, but days before Aaron's wedding, the soundtrack seemed to be stuck on dog bites and bee stings.

Our children grew up very differently from their parents. For Harvey and me as kids, the smell of chicken roasting in the oven signified a special event. The purchase of new shoes meant that the old ones were ragged beyond repair. Home renovations consisted of patching a roof with tarpaper or nailing cheesecloth over a hole in the screen door.

There are so many cheap jokes told by this generation about their parents who lament the good old bad days when kids walked to school through ten-foot snow drifts, shared their bath water with a half dozen siblings, and were lucky to have a piece of meat to eat once a month.

Well, all those jokes might have begun with the history of my family.

I was only three years old when my parents moved from the city of Timmins to a wind-swept, snow-dumped, and somewhat deserted countryside.

The journey really began when my dad got out of the army in serious need of a job. He and my mom considered carting my brothers and me off to Toronto, but his haunting fear of failure in the eyes of his father and sisters pre-empted that move. He was ripe for the picking when his big brother Max came to scatter the seeds of opportunity, proposing that my dad move the family to Prescott, Ontario, where Uncle Max owned a cavernous bus-stop diner off Highway 2.

"Mitchell," he said, "it's a match made in heaven. Sarah's a great little cook and you've got a great head for business... What've you got to lose by gambling that you can turn that old sow's ear into a silk.... uh... money bag for yourselves."

Planting the idea on mom was going to be a hard sell because she just plain didn't like Uncle Max.

"Honey, it could change everything for us," dad crowed. "We'd virtually be running our own business and the kids would grow up breathing fresh country air. Max says we could 'turn a sow's ear into a silk purse' with very little effort. So, whadda ya think?"

Uncle Max was a world-renowned welterweight boxer who had altered the location of a few brain cells during his pugnacious career, but not the ones that made him continually richer. From his Beverly Hillbilly styled mansion in Toronto, Max stammered his way into any deal that anticipated a profit, no matter what the cost. It was one of those clandestine tips that had prompted him to buy acres of sparsely inhabited property along the St. Lawrence River, just five miles east of the metropolis of Prescott (pop. 4,200). The scheme promised that a future seaway project could one day make him the Real Estate Mogul of the Ottawa Valley. His stretch of land was bordered on the east by Johnstown, an isolated area that aspired to one day becoming a dot on the map. South, across the river, stood the dreary town of Ogdensburg, New York. This very area, Uncle Max had been told, was strategically poised for a monumental seaway deal. In the meantime Uncle Max owned fields and fields of ... fields.

There was one exception. The Colonial Inn, as the monstrosity was inappropriately titled, was an architectural blemish on the natural complexion of the St. Lawrence landscape. For many years "The Inn" had been a bus and truck stop along the old road that led to Ottawa. That was before the main traffic was circumvented by a newer four-lane highway that could rush its travellers, on cold grey asphalt, to our country's capital at 40 miles per hour. In summer, however, there were still those stalwart tourists who preferred to cheerfully travel 15 miles per hour through God's green acres.

The elaborate deal between Canada and the United States did eventually make its way into our history books leaving a pleasing irony in its wake: Premium dollars were paid out for any land that was required for the venture, while the remaining property in the area was soon deemed worthless. The boundaries of the new St. Lawrence Seaway enterprise ended less than a hundred yards from my Uncle Max's property line. Unfortunately for my Uncle it was far enough away to leave him entirely out of the land deal but close enough to plunge him into the near depths of madness, which for him was a rather shallow dive.

The seaway was not even a concept when Uncle Max made his offer of a bright future to his kid brother. He simply needed somebody to live on that worthless piece of land so that he could receive a disproportionate tax break; a fact he failed to mention at the time. So, my naive parents packed up our belongings and shipped them on ahead while my uncle arranged to have someone meet the movers at the other end and have everything set up for us when we arrived a few days later.

On a bleak November day, my family left the icy blue winter of Timmins behind and headed by train for the blinding white snow belt of Eastern Ontario.

We arrived at our destination to find a huge old cinder block building in terrible disrepair… and not a sow's ear in sight. What was my dad to do? The night was cold and dark and a hotel was out of the question. There had barely been enough money for the cab ride from the train station.

"At least the key works," I heard my dad optimistically proclaim.

As we entered the icy mausoleum, an old army issue flashlight cast a dim glare on our bleak situation. We waited in the frigid blackness while our dad searched for a fuse box. That welcome first rush of light was as good as it got that night. The impact of that first glimpse of our new home is as vivid to me now as it was at the scant age of three. Within those frozen brick walls we discovered the remains of an art deco styled lunch counter that was partly hidden by stacks of battered wooden chairs and rusted steel-legged tables. Behind the dining room was a huge kitchen that appeared to have been out of commission for centuries. It was equipped with an enormous coal-burning cook-stove that was caked with congealed grease and a wall-to-wall refrigerator that was coated in some revolting dark and sticky substance. In the centre of the kitchen was a short-order counter, the surface of which was made of three-inch maple that was hidden under a thick blanket of frozen rodent droppings. In the middle of the dank, grungy cement floor was a scummy drain that conjured up gruesome images of creatures hidden below that were too terrible for any of us to confront that night.

We made a quick exit out of the kitchen and into the washroom where I stumbled over a heap of old porcelain toilet seats that had been separated from their putrid brown bowls. My whining bladder prompted my parents to make civilizing the bathroom their priority. Dad primed the tanks with our drinking water and soon the elixir was swirling through the system like a spring waterfall. My mother's knuckles were rubbed raw by the time she had scoured the enamel to perfection... and just in time. I rested my bare bottom on the icy rim and sighed as I felt the hot stream of urine trickle into the bowl. While I basked in warm relief, my brothers uncovered a fungus-ridden sink that looked as if it had fallen victim to an alien infection. But with a turn of the corroded knobs we soon discovered that we had both cold and colder running water.

"Well, never you mind," my mother comforted. "With working taps and flush toilets we're in business, and by tomorrow we'll even have hot water."

"Sure we will, if we can find Aladdin's lamp!" nine-year-old David cynically muttered.

Somehow having the toilet and sink in operating mode was an important enough brush with civilization to bolster my Dad's resolve to carry on with our expedition. Together we shuffled through a set of large French doors that led into a cavernous room, which we later learned was the dance hall. There we were relieved to spot our furnishings clustered together at the far end of the space.

With my uncle's promise of a fine place to live and raise children still reverberating in their consciousness, our parents engendered a seemingly immutable optimism. They explained that our miserable bad luck had already surpassed Job's Biblical bout with God, so we could therefore be certain that the worst was now behind us.

Very soon we were snuggled into our pyjamas, sweaters, socks, coats, hats, scarves, and mittens while we anxiously waited to be settled into bed for the night. That was when we all realized that somewhere en route from Timmins to Prescott, our four comfy solid oak framed beds had gone missing and had somehow been replaced with steel army cots. Those heirloom beds had been gifts from my grandparents and they were the only luxuries we possessed.

Although my father was steaming like a probed dragon, he wasted no time at all in finding a solution to our immediate problem. He simply tied three of the cots together to make one big children's bed. The makeshift sleeping barge looked conspicuously out of place in the middle of that vast empty vessel.

I could sense my mother's fear and dread as she piled blankets, towels and clothing on top of our "bed." It was a basic matter of our survival, since there was no heat in the building and it was 20 below outside. She displayed an uncharacteristic sense of humour about the whole experience. "You know what kids? We were lucky that they were such considerate thieves," she said. "After all, they did leave us with something to sleep on. You'd never find a city thief showing concern like that, now would you?"

Our parents piled the one remaining cot high with whatever was left in the boxes and suitcases. At the age of three I couldn't figure out how two grown-ups were ever going to manage to sleep in that one little bed. (Since then, I've shared a berth on a train with my husband and learned the "dirty little secret" of how two grown-ups can sleep in one tiny space and still wake up warm and happy.)

"Okay kids, into bed now," mother chided. "Get some sleep."

"That's right," father agreed, "tomorrow's another day... and things will be much better tomorrow."

"Yeah, right," David muttered under his breath, "only if tomorrow we find that magic lamp or rob a bank!"

The three of us obediently huddled together in our bed listening in terror as the frigid wind screamed through the icy cracks in the windows. Adam encouraged me to hold back the persistent stream of tears that drizzled down my cheeks by terrorizing me with the knowledge that they could freeze and cause my face to break off. I didn't really believe him, but I stopped crying anyway because I wanted to believe he made the story up to help me. I was always vulnerable to anyone who showed me the slightest concern or affection.

It took about a month before other sleeping arrangements could be made, but the truth is, during all that time, I slept soundly.

I don't think I've ever felt quite so safe or secure since.

After that first challenging season at the Colonial Inn, my parents were determined to improve our lot before the next winter solstice.

So it was that in the summer of 1950, armed only with determination and the generous compassion of our new neighbours, my father set about to build us a 1940s style dream house.

Using the primitive blue prints my dad drafted, the team managed to build us a solid, wood cottage with a cubby-hole kitchen, three bedroom nooks and a living room the size of most nineties bathrooms. But we didn't care because there was room for mom's and dad's easy chairs, and floor space in front of our old mahogany radio reserved for the three of us kids to curl up and listen. Every Sunday night throughout the long winter months we had our parents, pan-burnt popcorn, our radio, and each other. What more could any red-blooded Canadian child want except clear reception for all those wonderful American broadcasts.

We loved our tiny dream cottage, but it wasn't long before expansion became necessary when our parents' joy resulted in my baby sister.

Soon our house was a sardine can and she was an irritating little barnacle. There was only one use for such a pest; she would become our guinea pig for any and all curious experiments we might devise.

So, early one morning when everyone was still engrossed in nocturnal bliss, my brother David tiptoed into my room (which I was forced to share with baby Rebecca). We both studied her diligently as she lay there peacefully inhaling her little baby snores.

I don't know if curiosity struck us both at the very same moment or if David had engineered the plan in advance, but in either case the result was the same. We quietly confiscated two small white beans from the kitchen and placed them strategically inside the baby's warm, moist nostrils. We were sure that within minutes they would heat up and sprout; then we could remove them and plant those *besnotted* little seedlings in our back yard. We had learned about the germination of beans at school, and we were anxious to put our education into action. Unfortunately Rebecca foiled our plans with one robust intake of air. We watched in utter amazement as the beans swiftly moved up and out of sight. We tried frantically to retrieve them but it was hopeless. The baby's wailing alerted our parents who grabbed her up and raced her over to the local doctor's house where he performed an emergency *beanectomy.*

That day, David and I discovered that beans in the nose don't heat up instantly, but whipped butts sure do.

After successfully building an entire house, my father and our congenial neighbour Eddy began the task of building a couple of one-room cabins that dad could rent out for the summer.

Over the next two winters the two men completed construction on fourteen little cabins complete with flush toilets and shower stalls. This expansion prompted our parents to change the name of the business from the "Colonial Inn" to the "Colonial Inn and Cabins."

My dad painted a colourful new complexion on the grey neglected gas station that stood a few yards from the inn and then assigned my ten- and eleven-year-old brothers to the chore of pumping gas over the summer break. They balked at the idea at first, but eventually they came to enjoy the responsibility and freedom it offered them. After hours, those juvenile working stiffs sat around with their friends drinking Cokes and telling dirty jokes well into the wee hours. The hut became the meeting place where the local kids entertained themselves with an eclectic variety of musical talents that ranged from playing the comb to strumming a two-stringed banjo. Summer after summer my brother Adam plunked away on an old, splintered guitar that someone had traded him for a gallon of gas.

He took his responsibilities very seriously. He always arrived on time, kept the station clean, and offered every courtesy to the customers... hoping of course to be rewarded with a generous tip. He treated the station like his own personal clubhouse. He even decorated it with posters of his favourite pin-up girl, Canada's own skating sweetheart, Barbara Ann Scott.

One summer evening Adam and I were sitting outside the hut dropping salted peanuts into our Cokes. (The salt makes the cola fizz up into a thick sweet foam, which you devour as it crawls up the neck of the bottle and you can munch on the marinated peanuts later.) It was a perfect evening. The twilight sun made everything around us look rosy. Adam was perched on a three-legged stool, strumming his old guitar and singing a Gene Autrey tune while I tried crooning the harmony.

My reverie soon turned to resentment at the sight of a shiny black Packard pulling up to the pumps. I was annoyed that our song ended abruptly when my brother ran lickety split to "fill 'em up." Judging by Adam's quick reaction, he didn't share my attitude. All he saw was that grand luxury car and the promise of a huge tip. I followed Adam to the pumps as usual, hopeful that I could sneak a peek inside the luxury sedan, but the dazzling purple sunset reflecting off the glass made it impossible.

I always tried to imagine where the travellers came from and what kind of homes they lived in. I wanted to see what they were wearing, especially the children. Suddenly a tall stately gentleman unfolded from the driver's seat and gave my brother his gas order before sprinting into the hut. I followed him inside to keep an eye on him. I liked to do that because it made me feel as if I had a job too. The man picked up a pack of Camels and told me to have the kid add them to his bill. He took a good long look around before heading back out. I surveyed his every move as he sauntered to his car with a suspicious smirk on his face. I watched closely as he approached the passenger side. He knocked on the window and just as the glass began to roll away, he leaned in and blocked my view. He was whispering very softly. (I know it was very softly because I tried very hard to listen from behind the rear bumper.) After a couple of minutes, he opened the car door and out stepped the most beautiful woman I had ever seen. She had long silky blond hair and a perfect smile, and she was all dressed in powder blue, right down to her high heels. My brother gasped at the visual feast before him. But he became dumbstruck when the gentleman asked if he would like to meet Miss Barbara Ann Scott. Since Adam remained speechless, I answered for him in my best, most authoritative voice: "Yes sir, he would. He loves her you know. He has pictures of her all over the hut."

"Yes, I saw that," the gentleman assured me.

Adam remained frozen to the spot while I continued: "There's a million gooey kisses all over those pictures too, 'cause I see him kissing her every single day!"The gentleman chuckled heartily as he pressed a five-dollar bill into Adam's wilted hand.

"That's ninety-three cents for the gas, eighteen for the cigarettes, and the rest is yours… for the great service," he declared.

Miss Scott smiled softly as she sashayed toward Adam.

"I'm very flattered," she gushed. Then without warning she leaned over and placed a soft cherry lipstick kiss right on his forehead.

He wore that crimson tattoo for an eternity… or perhaps it was only until the next morning when my mother insisted that he wash his face.

During those summer months, my mother arose before dawn to scour the restaurant before preparing huge vats of food for the hordes of customers that stayed at the inn. When that was done, she would rush out to scrub the fourteen cabins and change and wash all the linens.

At five I was much too young to understand why my hanging around watching her clean out the cabins made her so tense. It was after she caught me blowing up the novel balloon I found on the bathroom floor that she began to race to the cabins to gather the used sanitary pads, condoms, panties, and other interesting tidbits and dump them in the trash before I arrived. I would watch her slip change, unopened cigarettes packets, romance magazines, and other leftover items into the deep pockets of her smock. We had pounds of orphaned jewellery locked in the office safe for years waiting for their owners' return.

Once the cabins were done, she hauled a rickety wagon filled with a hundred or so pieces of dirty linen across the back-field to the laundry room. Dad had built that big old laundry shack out of scrap wood and equipped it with an antique ringer washer that was intended to make my mother's life a breeze. Whenever she caught her hand in the jaw-clenching wringer of that old machine, it was my job to run for help. In spite of the odd emergency, I loved it when she did the laundry. Watching your mother pinning heavy, wet wash onto a clothesline may not seem like the ideal bonding experience, but it always comforted me to see her standing in the warm, sunny breeze, humming a cheerful tune. In the spring I would sneak underneath the laundry platform to play with the new litter of blush coloured garter snakes that nested there. My mom didn't know about my friends until the day my dad peeked under the landing and found me encompassed by my wiggly little playmates. I think he was enjoying the experience until my mother joined in and caught sight of the reptilian spectacle and fainted right on top of us.

Every summer my elegant Aunt Sophie and my spoiled cousin Myra came by train from Timmins to stay with us. My aunt would immediately don a crisp white uniform and wait tables (the salary was deficient but the tips were enticing). As an only child, Myra's expensive frocks were representative of the spoilage heaped on her by her adoring parents, and since I was the regular recipient of my older cousin's hand-me-downs, I had to endure her habitual tyranny.

Eventually, in spite of my aunt's best waitressing efforts, success was beginning to outgrow our family, and my parents had to hire on a cook, another waitress, and even a gas station attendant. The extra hands never really lessened my parents' burden, but they never complained, they just forged ahead tirelessly working to build their mini-empire.

"The Colonial Inn and Cabins *Resort*," as they again renamed it, had become a beautiful landmark in the area. The grounds were covered in the greenest grass and most bountiful flowers I had ever seen.

My brothers, using their pre-pubescent muscles and our mother's laundry wagon, painstakingly carted dozens of boulders to our property from the stone quarry a mile away. They whitewashed each rock before carefully placing it around the perimeter of the lawn. Our father called it a neighbourly fence. "It defines the property but doesn't exclude anyone."

In the middle of the back yard, my dad had planted a circular plot of seedlings that had just nicely taken root. On one particular summer morning, Mrs. Hough had assigned six-year-old me to keep an eye on Rebecca in the back yard, while she weeded the front window boxes.

From the lazy swaying comfort of a homespun hammock, I watched that eighteen-month-old pogo stick bounce back and forth across the lawn, trying to capture a wayward butterfly. I observed her closely until the warbling songbirds and the whispering breeze lured me into a hazy slumber.

When I awoke, my father was standing over me seething like a blown radiator. It seemed that during my brief respite, "Rebecca of Sunnybrook Farm" had pulled up every seedling in the plot. Then, with sprouts in hand, she had proudly waddled up to the inn to show everyone what she had accomplished. Her trip was somewhat complicated by the fact that she had taken a short cut down the middle of the highway.

It was only the kindness of an astute trucker that saved little Rebecca. He scooped her up and returned her to the nearest sanctuary, which happened to be the Colonial Inn. He explained to my parents in graphic detail: "I been truckin' for over twenty years an' I seen hundreds o' baby animals gettin' squashed to smithereens wanderin' across a busy road… guts splatted everywhere… but I ain't never seen no infant left alone to play 'dodge car' before."

My punishment included replanting every single sprout in the garden. Now, to the average person that may not seem like such a terrible price to pay, but to me it was like working on a chain gang cleaning out latrines. I simply despised having any kind of dirt under my fingernails and my father knew it only too well. So, the punishment did fit the crime. I obediently replanted those damned pansies with their supercilious grins, while keeping the inspirational thought in mind that I might like to leave a little space in the plot to one day plant my baby sister.

Either in spite of or because of the hardships we experienced, my siblings and I were determined to make certain that our children, when we had them, would have as loving a home as we did. I don't recall any of us ever feeling resentment toward our parents for our lack of monetary riches. When we complained or rebelled, it was always against authority. We had a pressing desire for independence.

Harvey on the other hand never cared much for independence; he was far more interested in accumulating wealth

We did give our children most of the niceties we had both lacked, without spoiling them of course. Looking back, I can honestly say that, for the most part, we actually succeeded.

The cultivating and harvesting of any species is philosophically the same in the animal kingdom as it is in the plant world, although I think it's more interesting in humans.

The yield from my five difficult pregnancies was four wonderful little people. Unlike sunflowers or sheep, each little baby bud blossomed into a beautiful, healthy, intelligent child with strong opinions and independent ideas about life. Raising children is much like tending a garden. If you neglect their basic needs you can stunt their growth. The problem is that every generation, believing that it is the enlightened one, will revise the previously revised book on basic needs. It's only when you can look back without bias that you can understand that the basics of good parenting have never changed. Food, shelter, love, support and time still dominate the first, middle, and final chapters.

The basics from my own childhood that gave me the greatest joy were country picnics by the St. Lawrence River, old fashioned town fairs, early morning visits to the farmer's market, apple stealing from nearby orchards, off-key sing-songs on our Sunday drives, or surprise trips to the ice cream shop. Those are some of the rare snapshots of memory that are included in my book of basics. Since my estrangement from Aaron, I have often wondered what snapshots fill the pages of his memory book.

Does he remember the time when, as a redheaded curly-topped Munchkin, he was asked by his Aunt Rebecca (who saw the entire universe reflected in his four-year-old eyes) to model in the "June Bride Fashion Gala?" He jumped all over me with enthusiasm: "Please, mommy, please? I want to do it, please? I can do it. I can do it just like they do it on Sesame Street."

Of course his siblings were certain he would freeze when the lights came up and he realized that I wasn't there to hold his hand, but Aaron wanted a chance to try, and my sister was willing to take a chance on what embarrassment may come of it, so I relented.

We all watched from the wings as the cocky little ring-bearer marched down the runway all decked out in bow tie and tails with a velvet cushion between his hands and a little platinum-haired, flower-bearing angel on his arm. Together, the adorable couple racked up five minutes of enthusiastic applause.

At the reception that followed, a designer groupie gushed over him, "You're quite a little star."

Aaron rebounded authoritatively: "I am not a little star… I'm a huge moon! There are lots of little stars in the sky, but there's only one big moon."

He was such a success that he was asked to model in another even bigger show. He couldn't wait to walk down another runway; and so his siblings begged me until they wore me down. But I was secretly concerned that if I allowed this indulgence, acting might become his destiny.

At the big event he showed his independence when he and the exquisite little flower girl reached the end of the runway and Aaron, instead of taking her hand, began to investigate the far reaches of his right nostril. The delicate little flower girl tempted by his challenge decided to follow suit. The crowd loved it. The producers did not, so that one exploration into a singular nasal passage quickly ended Aaron's modelling career, but made him somewhat of a hero among his siblings. I admit to feeling some relief that now he may be destined for something other than the stage, but in the year following our divorce, Aaron was once again drawn into the entertainment field when a producer friend asked me to bring him out for a screen test for a family television series. He won the role hands down, which made him a very happy "star," a fact which although not true, he touted before his siblings whenever he could.

Unfortunately his fame ended abruptly when he broke the rules … or should I say his father broke the rules. It was a hot summer day, at the end of shooting an episode, and it happened to be on a weekend Aaron and his brother were to spend with their father. When I asked Brandon nonchalantly what the plans were for the weekend, he announced, "Dad is taking us for haircuts." Now this sounds like a responsible thing for a dad to do, except for the fact that it had never happened before because I had always cut their hair. So, it was rather curious that there was a sudden need to take the boys to a barber; especially since the television contract that Harvey had been given to view and I had signed stated that no changes in appearance would be allowed without first consulting with the producers. The reason was clear. If you are in the midst of shooting an episode over a week but the plot all takes place in the same few minutes, then having a brush-cut on a boy who seconds before had curly hair would create havoc. I left an urgent reminder with the two boys to let their dad know that Aaron was not to have a haircut. Of course Aaron arrived on the set that day, shorn like a G.I. and was promptly fired. Harvey thought it was quite funny. Aaron missed the friends he had made on the show, and I felt sick at heart that something that gave Aaron such pleasure and confidence had been taken from him in such a reckless way. He pretty much gave up any aspirations he had for stardom that day. Maybe I should give credit to his father for being such a vengeful contrarian?

Whenever Harvey engineered unnecessary stress on any of the children through some self-serving action, he always justified it by reiterating his philosophy that "children are resilient... they bounce back!"

It took a lot of attention, support, and diversion to help Aaron get over his humiliation at being dropped from that special niche he had carved out for himself which gave him a unique place of respect among his siblings. It's not easy to rally positive attention when you are the youngest of four, but he had done it ... for a few weeks and then it was gone.

I often wonder if Aaron will ever make an honest attempt to look deeply into all of the pitfalls of his childhood and ponder how many times he might have drowned under the lava flow of his parents erupting conflict; and which parent truly dared to climb into the volcano to rescue him.

I don't recall any lava coals in my path on the day I almost drowned.

That's the way my dad always began the story. "I remember the day that Rachel almost drowned." He would say it with an air of mystery. My brothers recalled it with an air of bitterness. "You always managed to ruin everything with your stupid antics," or, "If I were dad I would have let you sink!"

It seemed like a perfect August day, if you didn't work in a windowless kitchen as my parents did. My father trudged out the back door of the inn shouting our names. We quaked in our sandals as each syllable stung our ears. My God, what had we done now? We approached with caution, each eyeing the other, wondering what one had done that we would all be blamed for. How could we defend ourselves against whatever accusations he would dump on us if none of us were prepared to admit we had messed up something, somehow?

"I'm going out to the hut to pump up an inner tube and your mother is making lunch. So you kids need to go right now and get into your bathing suits 'cause we're going to the stone quarry for a picnic."

Those words were as magical to us as; "You've just won a million dollars."

Mom didn't come with us. She said she wanted to try to lie down and take a nap, but we all knew the real reason was that she was afraid of the water, not to mention the fact that my brothers habitually tried to accidentally dunk her whenever they had the chance.

She could tolerate the river because the water was only ankle deep along the shoreline, but it was the bottomless black hole of the fresh water quarry that gave her nightmares.

Since I was only five, I was ordered to stay at the narrow

edge of the quarry, while dad, Adam, and David played water polo in the middle. I didn't mind because my dad would swim over every few minutes and give me a zillion flips off his back.

By the time we dug into our picnic basket, we had worked up quite an appetite. The food was fine but we were disappointed that our mother had neglected to pack dessert. So after lunch my father and Adam hiked to the other side of the quarry to look for wild berries. The cliff at the far side of the quarry stood about fifty feet above the water. Since it was off limits for kids like me, David was stuck babysitting until they returned with a pail full to the brim of succulent fruit. He was supposed to be watching me, but instead he jumped into the quarry to play water tag with his friends. I decided to join in.

I dog-paddled my way toward them as David snarled at me to get back. I wasn't about to listen to him because I knew that he just didn't want me to ruin his fun. I was doing fine until my arms began to feel like putty. I tried to stand up to take a little breather, but there was no bottom beneath my feet. As I sank below the horizon, I could hear Donny Biccum flaccidly announce, "Rachel's goin' down aggin."

I panicked. David screamed for my father, who took a swan dive off the cliff and swam the width of the half-mile quarry in time to rescue me.

He may never have left Canadian soil to win a war medal, but there was no doubt that he was my hero.

Just a couple of years ago, on a visit to L.A., I was telling the drowning story to my nieces when my brother David broke in to the conversation. "First of all Rachel, the cliff was more like fifteen feet high not fifty and the quarry was barely a quarter of a mile wide not half a mile and secondly, it was Bobby Biccum not Donny who said it and he didn't say it softly, it's just that he couldn't get the words out 'cause he was laughing so hard."

Perhaps it was a familial myth, but I still remember that day with great joy. It was a day when my father showed all of us that he had the basics to parenting down pat: love, food, shelter, support, and quality time.

CHAPTER EIGHT

One warm fall day I announced, to my children's delight, that we were all going to have a picnic in the forest.

We cruised along an old country road looking for an opening in the trees. Eventually a welcoming archway of poplars beckoned us. Harvey pulled over and announced that he would wait right there by the side of the road until we came back because he didn't want to leave the car unattended. When seven-year-old Brandon asked if the baseball broadcast on the radio had anything to do with his dad's decision, the crimson blush that frosted Harvey's cheeks was answer enough.

Into the woods we went, leaving Harvey with a bottle of soda, a chicken leg or two, chips and good reception.

"Over the meadow and through the woods to grandmother's house we go..." we chanted as we trekked through the forest collecting treasures for "show and tell."

Aaron chased a butterfly into a hollowed out log from which he emerged victorious with his little pincers clamped onto the monarch's wings. Brandon picked toadstools with his napkin for fear he would get warts. Sophie chose to collect sticky milkweeds, and Wendy gathered buttercups.

As we watched a momma bird drop worms into the open beaks of her little ones, Aaron asked, "Mommy, why do those birdies eat yucky worms wouldn't they like French fries better?"

"They might if they ever tried them, sweetie. But they'd likely get just as sick from eating French fries as you would from eating worms. Besides, too many fried potatoes would make those little birdies too heavy to fly."

"I'd eat worms too, mommy, if it meant I could fly!"

The children wrapped their wild flowers in paper napkins or sealed their woodsy treasures in ventilated jars and set them aside while they helped to lay out our picnic lunch. The fresh air had stimulated their appetite; almost every morsel of food was consumed so there was little left to pack up or leave behind for the wildlife. The children returned to the car anxious to show their daddy what unique gifts the earth had wrought. The ball game was over, and Harvey was sound asleep in the back seat of our station wagon with a large leather- bound book in his lap. The title was spelled out in large gold letters, *Cabala.*

A couple of years before my transition from volunteer /housewife to career woman/homemaker, Harvey had begun a transition of his own. He was rapidly becoming disenchanted with dentistry and increasingly fascinated by the Cabala.

Our rabbi had warned Harvey that it was not healthy for him to delve into this abstruse world on his own. Rabbi Cohen believed that the cryptic data hidden in the mystical text of the Cabala could bring torment to a curiosity seeker if he were to misunderstand or misuse the messages. For the untrained mind, those complex labyrinths of information were potential minefields of explosive misconceptions. Judaic scholars and righteous students of Cabala insist that guidelines be followed when searching for answers in this ancient treasury:

*He must be over forty.

*He must study the Cabala with learned scholars.

*He must be able to study the text in either its original Aramaic or in Hebrew.

Other than being a "he," Harvey was clearly not eligible, but he argued that studying the arcane tome in modern English rendered it harmless.

Friends and family offered a myriad of examples of rabbis and laymen who defied the rules only to end up suffering illness, madness, and even gruesome death. This information prompted me to beg Harvey to wait the five years until he was forty before embarking on this journey. When he dismissed that idea, I tried to convince him to study with a group, or at the very least to confer once more with Rabbi Cohen, but he refused to consider any requests. He continued to pursue unobtainable answers to inconceivable questions.

Eventually his fascination with the Cabala spawned his interest in other mystical pursuits. He read volumes on mythology and the occult and began spouting disturbing notions. His fascination even led him to pour over the musings of L. Ron Hubbard.

Soon he began muttering obscenities, such as "females of our species are as unclean as pigs" and "demon spirits walk alongside of women while angels accompany their husbands."

I tried to be patient, but his unorthodox views were becoming more and more disturbing to me. I had never considered Harvey to be my mentor, but he was my partner. We had always moved in tandem through the successes and struggles of our marriage, always supporting each other's ideas and dreams. It was disquieting to realize that our enthusiasm for one another was relentlessly eroding.

Eventually my required commitment to the theatre project began to suck any remaining ions of energy out of me. I was in a constant state of urgency at work and at home. Often, after a full day of warding off emergencies, I would rush home to make dinner and spend time with my family before running back to the theatre to direct evening rehearsals. Since Harvey was spending less time in the practice of dentistry and more time in the pursuit of an ever-wider variety of obscure concepts, I was probably lucky to be so busy.

As my responsibilities increased, Harvey's support waned. By the time I noticed the elephant in our midst, it had grown into a monster that was filling up every room in the house until it finally got stuck in our bedroom doorway.

The first revolt came during Yom Kippur services one year. On that day coincidentally, I was featured in the *Toronto Star* in a full-page article about my position as artistic director of the Freedman Theatre. Perhaps the rabbi had read the paper that morning, or perhaps someone had mentioned the article to him on his way into services. In any case, when he called out our name from the pulpit to honour us for our annual pledge, he introduced my husband as Dr. Rachel Krup. That did it. Oh, I don't mean to suggest that his slip of the tongue created the bomb. It just detonated it. Everyone chuckled at the Rabbi's faux pas while my husband turned to me with a tight, artificial smile, and through clenched teeth declared in a heaving whisper: "I will never, ever be Dr. Rachel Krup... and don't you ever forget it."

On Thursday nights I generally got a head start on Sabbath dinner preparations, and then I would rush home early Friday afternoons to finish up. On one particular Friday I arrived home midday to find Harvey sitting in the library in his underwear, with his feet up and the Cabala in his lap. I asked if he was feeling all right; he replied, "I never felt better in my life."

I was delighted to hear the words, but since the cynicism in his voice made me suspect that he wasn't being a hundred percent truthful, I lured him into a conversation. Sometimes I wonder if avoidance and denial would have been the wiser plan of action.

I asked again, "Seriously, Harvey, are you sure you're alright?"

He slid forward in his seat before inhaling all of the air in the room. Perhaps it was a lack of oxygen that made me feel woozy or maybe it was a telepathic fear. I sat down opposite him as he began.

"I'm not happy, Rachel."

"You mean today?

"No, Rachel, not just today. I mean every day."

Gulping back the acrid taste of bile that oozed into my throat, I gasped; "You're not happy with me?"

"No, it's not you, it's me. I'm just not sure what I want to do any more."

"What do you mean ... '*do*'?"

"I mean I'm gonna be forty before I know it and I don't know what in hell I want to do with the rest of my life. Maybe I should teach...or go back to University and take a specialty. I don't really give a shit. All I know for sure is that I hate dentistry. I never wanted to go into it in the first place. I could have been a doctor, if I'd have had the marks."

The marks? We'd been married for fifteen years and I never knew that little fact. He had always claimed he went into dentistry because his father pushed him. So why did he lie to me? It wasn't as if I went on safari to find myself a dentist.

I was surprised that such an innocuous secret could make me feel so betrayed, but after a decade and a half of marriage, I figured I should have known that little fact about my husband. I gasped for some of his precious air while I regrouped.

"Honey, this is probably some kind of a mini mid-life crisis," I whispered, trying to disguise my patronizing tone. "If we just get some help we can get through this. Look, I'm sure that many of our friends and relatives have gone through it and they've all survived. Hell, we all go through insecure times."

"Really, Rachel, really? What in hell is insecure about your life? You have it all, everything you want."

I clenched my jaw firmly to hold in my rage, but try as I might, the urge to implode was overwhelming.

"Oh, really, Harvey? I have everything I want? On what planet did you leave your mind?"

"Come on. You've got your career, your kids, your home, everything in one neat little package. I don't see that you're missing a thing."

"Well maybe you should look a little harder 'cause I'm missing plenty, like how about a little comfort and joy from my husband? How about a little support? How about agreeing to go with me to get some professional help for our problems before they become too huge for us to handle?"

"Too huge for *us* to handle? Maybe you need a shrink but I don't have any problems I can't handle."

"So sitting around in a dress shirt and underwear, in the middle of the afternoon, reading the Cabala is normal to you?"

"I don't see anyone else complaining."

"Are you delusional? You don't think the kids realize that tension is growing like a fungus in this house?"

"It's always about the kids, isn't it? Kids are resilient, so don't you worry about the kids. They're just fine. But you're too busy having meetings, doing interviews or rehearsing for the big opening to notice anyway."

"Hey, you wanted me to do this. You keep telling everyone

that you're ecstatic about it. I've asked you over and over if it's okay, and you always gush with reassurance. 'It's great! I'm so proud! I wouldn't have it any other way!' Were you lying about that too?"

"No. The truth is I really don't know what in hell I want. I feel as if I'm drowning. Do you remember I told you about a recurring dream I used to have when I was in high school? The one where I'm in a swimming pool, under the water, and as I look up all I can see is a bowler hat floating above me. The hat follows me wherever I go, keeping me from coming up to the surface. I can't break through, I can't come up for air, and I know I'm going to drown. I always woke up from that nightmare in a panic, gasping for air. I hadn't had that dream for a long time, but it's back and that feeling of panic is now a chronic condition."

"Harvey, just tell me what you need from me and I'll do it. If you want to go back to school then do it. We can sell the house ..."

"We're not selling this house!"

"Look, first you have to decide what you want to do, then somehow we'll manage it."

"Oh really? What the hell would we live on? The pittance they're paying you?"

"Is that what it's all about Harvey? I'm not earning enough? Or is it just that I've come to like my job that has you all worked up? 'Cause if that's what it is then the problem's solved. When I consented to take the damn job, you vowed you'd bear with me for the next few years until I got the theatre up and running. Then I'd be in a better position to determine how much time and energy I'd need to give it in the future. The theatre will open in a couple of months and I thought that we'd decide together where we'd go from there, but if you want me to leave it now, just tell me. Harvey, I don't want this job to hurt us. I told you that when you were pushing me to take it."

"It's not you and it's not your job, Rachel. It's me! It's having responsibility with no rewards. I'm tired of all the demands. My patients whine, the kids whine, everybody wants something from me, and I'm tired of it. You're lucky you've found something you love and you're throwing yourself into it. I envy you. I want to feel that kind of enthusiasm for my work but I don't."

Over the next several months there were many more outbursts, offers of conciliation then more rejections, but we tried not to notice what was happening to us.

It became difficult to ignore the fact that by lunchtime each day, Harvey was heading for home. I would periodically get a phone call from our housekeeper asking if it would be all right to disturb the doctor so that she could vacuum the master bedroom or clean our washroom.

Arriving home one Friday afternoon to prepare for the Sabbath, I headed into our bedroom to change. I was jolted by the sight of Harvey, seated in a wing chair with his feet up on the bed wearing only a skullcap, black socks, and jockey briefs. He was holding the *Cabala* in his hands and watching *As the World Turns.* If the moment weren't so painful it might have been hilarious, a kind of cartoon image that needed no caption.

The same summer the theatre opened, the Beth Israel choir had been invited to attend a choral symposium in Jerusalem. Harvey and I knew it would be impossible for me to go, but I feared that the growing tension between us would escalate if Harvey missed out, so I urged him to go and to take one of our daughters along. He balked at first but gave in when he discovered that many of his choir buddies were also taking kids in lieu of spouses. Since neither of the girls was interested in forfeiting camp and *boys* for three whole weeks, I encouraged Harvey to take Brandon instead. He was only eight years old, but I was sure that he would benefit from quality time with his dad.

I was happy to see them running off to Israel to bond. I would miss them, but it would be an opportunity to stay behind and have my own bonding time with the girls and even more time with four-year-old Aaron.

During that three-week hiatus, Aaron became concerned that I was too lonely for his daddy in that big bed all by myself, so every morning I was treated to a good morning kiss and a very "best story" by my little redheaded superhero. The main character of his stories was an angelfish named Clive who was never afraid to live a life of adventure and heroism. One day Clive could be rescuing a baby from the top of a high-rise and the next he could be protecting a helpless old lady from a mugger.

By the time Aaron was nine, he had actually written down and illustrated his set of Clive stories. He imagined that one day he would create an entire series of Clive comics. There is probably a lot we could learn about Aaron if we only had those stories today. Unfortunately to date no one has ever found those lost volumes of Clive. I think there's a strong possibility that over the years, one of our cleaning ladies dumped the rare fish tales into a trash bin, but Aaron is convinced that I am the culprit who destroyed his place in literary history.

All the time Harvey and Brandon were in Israel, I grew increasingly concerned over the fact that my husband's phone calls home seemed eerily aloof and notably infrequent. We had never been apart for such a long time. I had to travel for my job from time to time, but it was usually overnight, or the odd time if I had to go to California, I took a few extra days and spent some precious hours with my family.

Though we all missed our guys immensely, it was an adventure to live this new family configuration for three weeks. We talked about their daddy and their brother at every opportunity and planned their homecoming with relish.

There was great joy at our summer cottage the night they returned. Our family gathered together to hear all about their experiences. Harvey showed pictures and described some of the highlights of the trip, while Brandon embellished the stories with his own take. It seemed as if "a good time had been had by all" until I playfully cuddled my son in my arms and asked, "So, honey, what was your most favourite part of the trip?" Without hesitation he responded:

"I liked all the places we went, so I don't have any most favourite part... but what I didn't like was the way dad was always looking at all the girls. It was embarrassing. He was always saying to me, 'did ya see that? Did ya see the way those babes were lookin' at me? I could have any one of them if I wanted.' He was always talking to girls and I didn't like that at all."

With that Brandon headed into the kitchen to raid the refrigerator, while I was left to try and conceal my jealousy. I was sure that my worst move would be to make an issue of Brandon's misreading of Harvey's macho bragging. So instead I leaned over and playfully whispered in my husband's ear;

"Thank God I sent my best watch dog along, huh?"

Harvey looked at me with a supercilious sneer and replied: "There'll be other opportunities."

I went to bed that night feeling that in a blink, something significant had been stolen from our lives.

By the following spring I felt some sense of relief that the theatre was up and running. I looked forward to having more control over my time and energy. But Harvey was becoming more and more immersed in those mysteries of obscure thought.

On the lighter side, our household was anticipating Sophie's autumn bat mitzvah. The planning gave us a family activity that we could all get excited about. But during the long hot summer I shivered as the warmth of our family unit continued to cool. Like robots, Harvey and I were propelled through the day, meeting all of our mutual responsibilities with pre-measured effectiveness.

About a month before the big event, I was sitting out in the back yard reading, when Harvey came out in his swimsuit and sunglasses. He was about to stretch out on a lounge chair when Sophie came running out after him crying hysterically. It was clear that she was angry with her father, so I led her inside to calm her down. With tear-filled eyes Sophie sobbed that she didn't want to have a bat mitzvah if her daddy insisted on reading his speech.

Once the hysteria was finally under control, she explained: "Daddy told me to read his speech over and tell him what I think of it so I did and, mom, he mentions practically everybody in the whole entire city except for you. When I told him that he forgot you, he said, 'No I didn't! I don't have to mention her! She can write her own speech!' "

I explained to Sophie that her father was going through a difficult time, and we all needed to show some patience. I assured her that he would do the right thing when the time came.

Having diffused that bomb, I headed back outside to the minefield. I aimed directly at Harvey's ample ego. "I don't know whatever possessed you to do such a stupid thing but it's gonna backfire on you when every single guest at that bat mitzvah realizes that only a gigantic asshole would neglect to thank or, at the very least, mention the mother of his children. Do you think that our kids won't notice? How about our parents or our friends? No matter how much insincere bullshit you dish out, you can't honestly think that they'll buy into it? Your Mr. Sugar'n Nice Guy routine won't save you from yourself if you do this mean and stupid thing!"

On the big night, Harvey delivered his long, self-serving, and rambling speech. He did mention that I looked after the lovely decorative arrangements, adding with a lilt in his voice, "I think everyone here would agree it's what she does best."

That year the poison arrows we'd begun to fling at each other crippled our winter vacation in Barbados. Any thought of torrid romance on the beach was dissipated by the chilling anger that crackled between us as each day wore on.

He sat on his sun cot reading mythology and the *Cabala* while I sat alongside reading Clifford Odets and "Future Shock". Every few minutes he leaned over to enlighten me on my menial status in God's greater scheme of things. How he could glean the most irrational conclusions from such rational teachings was a real puzzlement to me. But if the goal of his negative dissertations on women was pointedly designed to demoralize me, then he was a Machiavellian success.

By the following spring, distrust, jealousy and bitterness were familiar guests in our home. Harvey and I took turns allowing those intruders to dominate our thoughts. Our relationship continued to appear pretty healthy from the outside, while being fiercely cannibalized from within.

We would enjoy periodic spurts of our old selves, but the darkness would always intervene.

When Harvey stopped coming out in the evenings to help in the scene shop, it was clear to me that his enthusiasm for the theatre had all but disappeared. I had always suspected that he enjoyed the camaraderie of the group more than the hobby itself, but it was something that had helped to keep us connected. He had become more deeply immersed in his dark studies and less involved with the family. Everything began to irritate him: the children, the housekeeper, money... but most of all me.

He began to question me about every hour of my time

and every person that I spent it with. Perhaps I should have been buoyed by the discovery that he could still feel jealous. After all wasn't I just a little green around the heart the previous year when I discovered that he had flirted his way through Israel?

CHAPTER NINE

A family trip soon clarified everything for me. The dental fraternity convention that year was to be held in Florida. The children were ecstatic to learn that they were to be included in the plans. Taking the kids on any trip had been the basis of an annual argument since our first child was born. I would plead that we should take the children away during the winter break and go away again later by ourselves, while Harvey tried to reason that our summer cottage was the kids' vacation; so the answer was always no. This year the answer was yes. Not because of anything I said or did, but merely because the convention was being held in Orlando at Christmas time and every couple we knew was taking their children. I also suspect that he didn't want to be alone with me.

By the time we arrived in Orlando, the kids knew that all was not right with our world. The tension between Harvey and me was palpable, although we still tried to put on a vacation face.

By the second day the children chose up sides when

Harvey asked, "Who wants to go on the bus to Disneyworld with me and all the other young boys; and who would rather stay behind with their mother?" The next morning the boys were ready and waiting to head off with their father.

Since the bus wasn't scheduled to leave until mid morning we all had breakfast together then went out to the pool for a quick dip. The sun was dazzling, but we were experiencing a Florida cold wave. There was no way that any of us could take the plunge that morning. We mused over the optimists who sat by the pool wearing winter coats over their bathing suits, but we followed their lead. There were many activities by the pool that could keep kids occupied like table tennis, croquet, ping-pong, pinball, and a variety of coin-operated games. Harvey and I sat around with a group of our friends chatting about any subject that was thrown into the mix. Several new faces joined the conversation and the time seemed to fly. The topic turned to theatre when a couple that introduced themselves as Peter and Jody Lasser joined the group. They wanted me to know that they could be counted among my many satisfied fans at the Freedman Theatre.

When Harvey and the boys left for the bus, the girls and I were still chatting away with the Lassers. I soon discovered that Peter Lasser was not only a dentist but he had played one on TV. It was hard to imagine an aspiring actor wanting to moonlight as a dentist.

The clouds slowly sneaked up on us, chasing the girls and me inside for a hot lunch. Later in the afternoon a clear sky beckoned us all to return to the pool. The girls swam and flirted with the final rays of sunlight while I chatted with the actor /dentist and his wife until she set off for a hair appointment.

The girls were drying off and gathering their things together when the boys came bounding onto the pool deck carrying their towels with Harvey swaggering behind. They appeared to be overly rambunctious, as if they might have been hopped up on candy floss and soda pop. The two boys indulged in a quick dip in the pool before we all fell in line and headed up to our rooms to get ready for our big New Year's Eve bash.

Harvey had barely closed our door before spitting out the most deplorable question he had ever dared to utter: "So, did ya fuck him?"

"Huh?" was about as intelligible a response as I could muster.

"I'm not an idiot, ya know! I don't really care. I'm just curious. Did ya fuck him?"

Vile trash continued to spew from of his mouth while I remained stock-still in a state of disbelief.

"Harvey, if this is some kind of crude joke, then I'm really sorry, but I don't get it."

"Do you think I believe it was a coincidence that I came back to find you still sitting with Peter Lasser? Come on, Rachel, how big an idiot do you think I am?"

Well, since he asked, I told him how big.

The next few hours were a test of my self-control and a trial of my endurance. Getting ready for a formal event when all my body wanted to do was relieve itself of all stored hydrous matter was a challenge. By evening there was nothing left in me to throw up, there were no tears left to lubricate my red eyes, and it seemed as if my kidneys had given up on ever seeing liquid flow through their system again.

That night there was a banquet for the adults to welcome in the New Year and a separate party organized for the kids, so that they could enjoy themselves with controlled abandon while their parents celebrated unencumbered by whining, demanding offspring.

So as soon as I regained control of my bodily functions,

I headed for the adjoining room to get the children showered, primped, and ready for their big night, while in the meantime Harvey was busy getting himself ready. Since he made it to the finish line first, he took the children down to their event as soon I got them properly outfitted. I welcomed the respite.

Just as I finished getting ready, Harvey appeared from the kids' room and suggested, "We should go down together so people don't start asking questions." I nodded my agreement and followed him to the elevator.

The banquet hall looked exquisite all decked out in silver, gold, and crystal, while the bevy of dentists and their spouses that filled the ballroom were all dressed in the requisite black and white theme for the evening.

As we approached our group of friends, I noticed that the Lassers had joined our contingent. I also noticed that Peter and Jody were wearing matching leather outfits that were almost identical to mine. My friend Gloria laughingly joked:

"Hey, you guys, was this providence or did you plan your outfits before you left Toronto?"

Throughout the evening I watched as, two-by-two, all of our friends took to the dance floor. I stood alone, listening to the heart wrenching refrains of The Supremes, Lionel Ritchie and Chicago. Then suddenly I saw Harvey sauntering toward me. I was ready. I could forgive him. All the anger and bitterness could just disappear if we both tried.

"I'm going to check on the kids and see how they're doing," he loudly and nobly declared. "I just want to make sure they're all right," he shouted over the refrain of "*Blue Moon, I saw you standing alone...*"

That was it. I didn't see him for the rest of the evening. I wanted to run up to our room and disappear under the covers for the night, but I was afraid that with my present luck, something would happen to Peter Lasser that would cause him to end up noticeably absent at the same time.

Periodically during the evening, some of my friends would glance quizzically at me, but they were too polite to question my uncoupled state. Instead, one of them would nudge a husband who would twirl me onto the dance floor for a cha-cha or a twist; but the minute a slow song would drift through the speakers, I would make an excuse and head for the washroom.

The old year trudged painfully out of the picture as the drunken refrain of "*Auld Lang Syne*" beckoned 1979 to get started. I stood there humiliated by my loneliness while I peered at the hundreds of couples who were locked in joyous embrace.

From the time I was eighteen years old, Harvey had been my partner, my lover, my cheerleader… and I had been all of those things for him. But now a distorted understanding of mysticism and a bitter paranoia began to control his thinking, and it seemed that no one could set it straight. As for me, I was invigorated and beguiled by the respect and gratification my newfound career was bringing me, and I sought comfort in that. Clearly, we were both too blinded by our mutual resentment and personal agendas to have noticed that the cracks in our marriage had broadened into gullies.

Over the years Harvey's dental buddies consistently signed up for any conference, in or out of town, but he never joined them. He always scoffed that, "it's just an opportunity for those guys to screw around on their wives and I'm not interested." But suddenly he had become interested. He had signed up for a weekend conference on hypnosis. I felt that it was probably safe enough, since it was in town and didn't require him to sleep at a hotel.

On the Friday and Saturday nights of the conference, he was home before the eleven o'clock news, but on Sunday, when he wasn't home by midnight, I was actually getting worried. What if he'd had an accident or been hypnotized, and they couldn't revive him?

I called to find out what time the conference had ended. "Saturday at four in the afternoon?" I repeated.

When Harvey tiptoed into our bedroom, the crude red numbers on the digital clock declared it was 4:25 a.m. Monday morning. In the blackness I whispered, "Is she pretty?"

"What the hell are you talking about?" he sputtered."I was at the conference. It just ended."

"Oh please don't try to make me feel any more stupid than I already do. I called… so I know. Who is she?" He froze and thawed in the same instant.

"I'll tell you who she is. She's my true soul mate. She's everything I've ever wanted in my life, that's who she is!"

After Harvey's declaration of undying love for his new soul mate, I began sleeping in the bathtub. I lay back on my ancestral feather pillow, with my homespun quilt tucked up tightly under my chin, and I waited each night for the defining thud of the front door that had always protected us from the cold, uncaring world outside. My mind was a lint trap of fuzzy thoughts. But when I applied myself, I could imagine a whole slew of clear reasons why the tub was not so bad:

For one thing, I don't have to walk so far to get to the toilet. Hard surfaces are better for your back. If my children tippy-toe into the bedroom in the middle of the night they'll just think that mommy's got the runs. But most of all, I don't have to smell that other woman's body odour on my husband when he slides between the sheets at 4 a.m.

And maybe sleeping in the tub just makes the whole dirty mess feel a little cleaner.

I lay awake night after night planning a thousand different lives I'd live if I could only find the courage to get out of the tub. I entertained thoughts of packing up the kids and driving to Los Angeles. My siblings had all moved to L.A. many years before. Even my parents were living down there part-time. But whenever I had been asked if I would take the plunge toward the Pacific, I always quoted California marriage statistics, and then I would renew my pledge to stay in "Toronto the Good" where life was still "The Donna Reed Show."

In that final year, while Harvey was making himself angrier and angrier at home, I was making myself busier and busier at work. "She" was present somewhere in the background but oddly enough, our lives went on almost as if "she" had never happened.

I told no one. I couldn't. I couldn't even say her name; "she" just remained "she." From the first confrontation it had become my constant nightmare, my secret humiliation. How could I tell anyone about my sleeping arrangements, or the fact that I allowed him to continue to degrade me in public? What could I tell my children or my parents? What could I tell anyone that would make any sense at all? How would they relate to the myriad of obscene scenarios I allowed myself to endure?

Since we had always shared a Mother's Day dinner with my family, Harvey and I had concurred weeks before that we would not break with custom, even though our marriage was rapidly being buried alive.

Just after dawn on that Mother's Day morning, I had wrapped my arms around Harvey's legs in a last ditch effort to prevent him from leaving our bedroom without me. He threw me aside like an Apache dancer and started for the door. He turned and looked at me with noble determination and insisted, "I have every right to spend the day with Susie. She's my soul mate, and one day she could be a mother too ya know!" And with that he stalked out of the house.

Later that day he returned dishevelled but mellow. It was clear how he had spent Mother's Day afternoon.

That evening, to celebrate mothers, we joined several relatives at a lakeside restaurant. My father made a toast, and Harvey, wearing a sardonic grin reached across the table, cupped my face in his hand, and declared, "Aren't I the luckiest guy in the world to have such a beautiful and talented wife?" I yanked my head away and gasped through clenched teeth, "Don't you ever put your hands on me again!"

My parents were mortified by my behaviour, my sister was bewildered, and the rest of the party was no doubt appalled. Fortunately for me, at that moment my children were visiting the restaurant's aquarium checking out the piranha and the guppies, so by the time they returned from their adventure, they found a polite but emotionally catatonic mother.

It was an easy glide through that incident compared to the peril of our next celebration.

I noticed for a couple of weeks after the Mother's Day fiasco that Harvey was staying home every night after dinner. He was also behaving in a contrite and even docile manner. It occurred to me that it was possible that "she" was out of the picture. I actually began to fantasize that our dark dismal nightmare was ending and that we might begin to find our way back into the light.

With that in mind I planned a Father's Day celebration with Harvey and the kids that I hoped would change everything. Early in the week I took the children to the mall to buy their Father's Day gifts. I was committed to stifle each shudder as they carefully chose his favourite colognes and music albums; items that I dreaded he might use to romance "her."

We all spent that glorious June day strolling together along the waterfront, eating lunch at his favourite café, and later sharing dessert with the kids while he opened his presents. After they were all safely asleep, we found ourselves wanting to be alone together for the first time in many months. On that night I abandoned the tub and returned to our bed.

The next morning I awoke feeling confident that Harvey and I would head off to therapy Nirvana together, so that one day we'd be able to laugh at the pathetic marital crisis we had once so bravely weathered.

I returned to work feeling lighter and happier than I had in eons. I was even looking forward to the next weekend. But by the end of that week I was feeling a little under the weather. I realized that the mild discomfort I was feeling in my "cave area" was a natural consequence of our recent explorations after so many months of inactivity.

On Monday afternoon I dragged myself to Dr. Silverberg for a real opinion. He took some blood, a urine sample, and a couple of swabs and left me to get dressed. I waited in his office for what I dreaded would be a lecture on getting more sleep or drinking more water (his two favourite health tips). I heard the door open and close behind me, and before I could sassily suggest, "I know, sleep more," I was interrupted:

"What in hell did he do?" he barked.

"Huh? He who? What are you talking about?"

"He, Harvey, that's who I'm talking about! What's going on Rachel? How did this happen?"

"You're scaring me, Dr. Silverberg. I don't know what you're talking about."

"I'm talking about that bastard husband of yours who gave you a venereal disease!"

"Oh my God! Oh my God! What is it? Please tell me it's a mistake. Please don't let it be fatal."

"It's not a mistake but it isn't fatal either. I'll give you some medicine that'll clear it up in a week or so. I have to give you a prescription for Harvey, although I wouldn't be upset if you lost it on the way home."

"Dr. Silverberg, he swore to me he wasn't seeing her anymore."

"Rachel, are you telling me you knew about Susie Black?"

I barely nodded before I realized what he had just asked.

"Dr. Silverberg, are you saying that you knew about my husband's affair?"

"My son lives in her building. I spotted them together once, but my son has seen them many times. Rachel, you can't live like this."

"What am I supposed to do? I'm scared to death."

"You can get him the hell out of your home for a start!"

"How? What about the kids? They don't have a clue about any of this. I can't just tell him to leave. It's not that simple."

"Rachel, it is that simple. You didn't survive death to live like this. At least speak to a lawyer, so you'll be prepared before it blows up in your face, okay?"

I gave him my word and left with Harvey's prescription burning into the palm of my hand.

When I got back to my office, Mimi was a little rattled.

"Oh, Rachel, I hope you're not going to be pissed with me but Harvey called and I told him that you went to see your doctor and then he kept calling back and he seemed really worried. I didn't know you hadn't told him you had an appointment. I hope you're not mad."

"No, Mimi, everything is fine so..." Before I finished my sentence Harvey was on the line again. I isolated myself in my office to take the call.

"What did he say you have?" he asked breathlessly.

"What a curious question, Harvey. What makes you think I have something?"

"Well... you ... uh...went to the doctor didn't you?"

"Let's not play games, you bastard. You know exactly what I've got...and you also know I got it from you and that pig you call your soul mate."

"Look, you don't have to be a Goddamn bitch about it. I didn't plan it you know. We thought it was all cleared up before she went away, but obviously it wasn't. Anyway it's not that big a deal. For God's sake, lots of people get it!"

"Not any people I know."

"Just take the medicine and it'll be gone in no time. Did you get a prescription for me?"

Harvey and I continued to reside apart, in our home, for several more gruelling months (he in the king-sized bed and me in the victim-sized tub). It's almost impossible to imagine, but we continued to steam along, adding more and more pressure to the advent of an inevitable implosion, which finally came on New Years Eve 1979. It was exactly one year after our volatile trip to Florida.

I had gone to the theatre that morning to conduct our first company read-through of a new play. I knew it wouldn't be a long day because the cast and crew were all looking forward to leaving early to get ready for New Year's Eve. Even Harvey and I were going out together to celebrate with our friends, in spite of the fact that we had been a counterfeit couple for close to a year.

I arrived home in plenty of time to dress for the party. I rushed inside the foyer to shake off the icy vestiges of a fresh winter storm. I was starting up the stairs when Sophie raced down to meet me halfway, offering an enthusiastic hug before quietly delivering her message:

"Daddy said that I was to tell you that he won't be going

to Auntie Madeleine's party with you tonight because he has to spend New Year's Eve with his friend."

The sparks of burnt emotion scalded my throat.

"Mommy, are you upset?" she queried with the sweet face of innocence.

"No, honey, I'm okay. But when did daddy tell you this?"

"Just a little while ago when he came home to change and get some wine and stuff. Mommy, who's daddy's friend? Is it that Susie person he always talks about?"

I mulled her words over in my head. *"Is it that Susie person?"*

Sophie's inflection told me all I needed to know about the success of our year-long charade. That night I moved from the bathtub to the basement and our world war began.

CHAPTER TEN

I always thought of Divorce as a devastating and insidious disease. When my own brother was stricken with the bug in the early seventies, I was certain that it was an isolated California virus. I never imagined that it could spread to Toronto and infect my family.

It took five months and a court order just to get Harvey to move out. For almost two years, I had lowered myself to accept any humiliation if it would keep our family together until we found a way to fix it. Then, just when I was sure that there was no lower level to which I could stoop, I discovered that no act of attrition can compare with the growing disrespect, distrust, and loathing that follows the evolutionary process that begins when you dial a divorce lawyer.

There was no turning back; war had been declared.

The first lawyer I ran to was an acquaintance who was willing to listen, then he recommended his buddy who also listened, and then he suggested three other pals, "who specialize in various issues related to this most complex and painful legal situation," and they too listened. And every second they were on my team the money meter kept ticking like a bomb. Naiveté and fear made me embarrassingly dependent on their counsel, calling on their advice whenever panic set in.

Somewhere, I am certain, there exists a husband's secret code of divorce. This was evident by my lawyer's response each time I called to inform him of my husband's latest bizarre assault. He would prologue each conversation with therapeutic logic such as:

"I know that you're upset, Rachel, but I want you to know that it's not uncommon for a husband to undertake every conceivable action that could make his wife's life a living hell. His goal is to force you to leave your home so that, among other preposterous accusations, he can claim you deserted your family. Of course they don't really want the responsibility of being the primary caregiver, but when you don't take the bait, they get even more pissed off and escalate the assault even further. It's kind of a competitive sport. They eradicate their guilt by engineering outrageous reactions in you. My advice to you is *just don't react."*

Oh sure, no problem, I pondered. I can just ignore the abuse like I could small pox.

I've often thought that the army of lawyers who marched us into war owed me a fee for providing their mundane battlefield with substantial comic relief. I sensed it when Harvey and I were in the transitional stages of acrimony, en route to divorce and my lawyer suggested with a fleeting but evident smirk that I call Harvey and try to get the VD conversation on tape, "because one day Rachel, it might prove to be useful." I think he really meant entertaining.

I thought about it for weeks but didn't feel quite right about it. I still prided myself on the fact that I had never even opened a piece of my husband's mail in all the years we were married. But on one particular day, when I discovered that Harvey had deceitfully shared his shameful version of the VD story with some old friends, I was finally inspired to call him at his office and press record. I gave the tapes to my lawyer, who took the liberty of having them transcribed, off the record and just in case.

Since neither Harvey nor I had ever skirmished through the onslaught of a divorce before, we weren't equipped with compatible weapons for the job. I belligerently stood my shaky ground, while he doggedly attacked from the rear, but it was our children who were mortally wounded in the crossfire. The bitter residue of that war has never completely left their psyches, or mine. Sometimes, when the mood is right, I can reminisce on those turbulent days with my oldest daughter Wendy, who has developed a wry wit over certain parts of the ordeal. But my other children still can't find any semblance of humour in our "War of the Roses".

About two weeks after I moved into our basement, I arose as usual to shower before heading for the rehearsal hall. I stepped out of my room and into a warm, moist pile of doggy-doo. Now in some homes that may not seem unique, but in my home it was damn near impossible because we didn't have a dog.

When I finally emerged from the shower, after scrubbing the manure from between my toes, I was met in the hallway by not one, but two yappy Sheltie puppies. They had just returned from a brief, brisk winter run with my two little sons, whom I soon discovered were their new masters. And since the infant canines had already eliminated their waste on my hall carpet, my boys had no need to linger outside in the cold for the unpleasant task of scooping their poopings. I presumed that my husband bought the two fluffy little creatures in the hope that they might take my place in our children's hearts.

With chairs and boxes, Harvey had cordoned off a small

section of our huge basement, so that the only place those furry little pooping machines could roam was directly outside of the room in which I now resided. He gave our housekeeper strict instructions not to clean up the doggy-doo under any circumstances. He intimated that it was some kind of new-age housebreaking technique. My lawyer gave me strict instructions not to clean up the doggy-doo under any circumstances, but to take close-up pictures of the manure pile for future evidence. No instructions were necessary to prevent my children from cleaning up anything at all, let alone doggy-doo. So for the worst part of a week those innocent little puppies continued to be the advance line of battle in my husband's war on me.

After several days and many dollars the court ordered that the innocent puppies be removed from the premises, but they failed to order Harvey to pay to have the carpets cleaned, the house fumigated, and my favourite pair of shoes replaced. The Shelties were partial to the rich flavour of Charles Jordan.

One more notch in Harvey's gun. One more black mark against me. I was the evil witch who had ripped those innocent puppies out of my children's arms just to get back at their daddy. Or as Aaron put it, "you're the meanest mommy in the whole world."

I tried explaining to him why it was not a good time to bring even one pet into the house let alone two. I threw in the fact that Brandon and Sophie were allergic to dogs and it might make them feel sick to have them in the house. I also promised him that one day when everyone is ready and all agree to take responsibility, we can decide together to choose and adopt a pet. But nothing would comfort him. All he would say was, "daddy says you just didn't want us to have them and you made the judge force daddy to take them away just to be mean!"

I tried to reassure him that the puppies were living on

a wonderful farm with other puppies just like them. I used the "they'll have open fields to run free" tactic. I suggested that we contact the lovely family that adopted them and see if we could go and visit, but Aaron was resolute: "I only want to go and visit them if we can bring them back home. Daddy says they're ours, and if you wouldn't have made the judge say he couldn't, then he would go and steal them right back for us!"

Aaron's painful separation from his brief but tender encounter with those pups brought back traumatic puppy memories from my own childhood. I truly understood his deep sense of betrayal.

It all began the day that my brother David and I were playing hopscotch on the gravel road beside the Colonial Inn where we were out of sight of the gas station and Adam's mocking eyes. I was suddenly stopped in mid-hop by David's powerful "sh-h-h!" He thought he heard a sound coming from the back of the inn, so of course he sent me to investigate. I scouted the area, and I beckoned David to come and have a look.

We watched in fascination as our father lowered a potato sack into our rain barrel, placed the lid on top, and headed back inside. The two of us raced to the barrel, but we were both too short to reach. David dragged a wooden crate over and climbed up. As he removed the lid, a faint squeaking sound startled us both. David reached his scrawny arms into the barrel and struggled to remove a soggy gyrating bag that he carefully placed on the ground. He untied the rope and peeked inside. His robust complexion faded to the colour of putty. I sidled over and dared to peer in. There, clumped together like fish in a barrel, were eight tiny, whimpering animals that bore more of a resemblance to a pack of waterlogged mice than they did a litter of cocker spaniel puppies. Thankfully we had arrived in time to rescue the still breathing creatures.

We were revelling in our own heroism until a wave of terror washed over us as we realized that our father could, at any moment, catch us with our hand in the barrel.

But we couldn't turn back now. These little lives were depending on us. What could he do to us anyway? Drown us?

David hoisted the dank, smelly bag over his shoulder, and we headed out to the backfield. We placed the puppies in an old abandoned sewer pipe and then ran to find Brownie.

We pushed and dragged the sleepy spaniel mom all the way across the field only to have her look at her offspring, sniff twice, and casually saunter away. We tried over and over again to get her to feed her babies, but she just wasn't interested.

Before dawn the next morning David and I sneaked out of our house to check on what might be left of our starving puppies. We made a detour by the Colonial's refrigerator first to steal some fresh milk for the babies. We raced across the field like the Keystone Cops, but before we reached the sewer pipe, the fear and dread of what we might discover halted us in our tracks. We bowed our heads in a moment of silence for any dearly departed we might find. Then we knelt down and held our breath as we peered inside the pipe.

There we saw those eight darling little animals voraciously suckling away on their drowsy mother's nipples. Our prayers were answered.

It was then and there, on that lazy hot summer morning, that David and I declared a cold war on our dad.

Days passed in silence as we tried to freeze out the cruel haunting image of our father's needless attack on those innocent victims. Day after day we conducted ourselves in a passive and obedient manner so as not to raise the suspicion that we had outwitted our enemy by our covert rescue operation.

The loathsome idea that my father "the puppy killer"

could return to business-as-usual festered into an oozing boil on my conscience.

As hours turned into weeks we began to fear that the day would come when those puppies could no longer be hidden in a sewer pipe, and our plot would be exposed, as would our tender bottoms. It became obvious that David and I had to talk to someone who could help answer two incredulous questions: "How could Brownie reject her own babies?" and "How could our father commit such a cruel and heartless act?"

We sat in farmer Morrow's parlour pouring out our hearts, while he listened attentively, punctuating the stronger points in our story with a nod or a sound that fell somewhere between a sigh and a grunt.

Finally, between his sips of strong black coffee, he unravelled the mystery of why Brownie had initially rejected her pups.

"She just wasn't sure who them little critters was," he defended. "Doggy mom's recognize their young 'uns by their smell and she couldn't smell 'em 'cause they were soakin' wet and musty from that old potata sack."

I pondered this revelation briefly: "Okay Mr. Morrow, some day I might forgive Brownie ... but I'll never, ever, forgive my daddy!"

By now my burgeoning resentment for my father's heartlessness had blossomed into hate in spite of the wise old farmer's clumsy attempt to explain away our father's cruel deed as an act of kindness.

"But, Mr. Morrow," David protested, "there's nothing crueller than drowning helpless little puppies that've barely been born."

"Sure there is... doin' it when they're fully grown. Nope, he did the right thing, yer daddy. Brownie's been dumpin' those litters o' pups for years now and yer daddy's gotta try to give 'em away. I woulda done the same thing if it were my old hound Sport droppin' all them pups year after year."

Well, that was easy for him to say since Sport was a male dog.

In the hope of tallying up necessary reward points for the day the puppies would be unveiled, David and I decided to behave like model children.

One stormy afternoon a few weeks later, we were amazed to discover all eight puppies romping around in the storage room off the restaurant's kitchen; odd as it may seem, no one ever mentioned how they got there, and we were smart enough not to ask.

A few weeks after our daring rescue, a busload of kids stopped at the Colonial Inn on their way back from summer camp in the Laurentians and my dad generously sent all eight puppies home with eight lucky children, for free.

I was the mother of four when, over a cup of Red Rose tea at my parents' kitchen table, my father finally owned up to the dreaded puppies episode.

"Just seconds after I left those puppies to drown, I headed back outside to rescue them. I stopped when I saw you and David pull them out of the rain barrel and schlep them out to the backfield. Then after you were both in bed, I went out there, cleaned them up, and cajoled Brownie into feeding them."

I asked the big unanswered question: "But, dad, what would have prompted you to do such an awful thing in the first place?"

"Well, I sought the advice of our local animal specialist. I told him every year Brownie has a huge litter of pups and I go all over the county looking for people who'll give them homes and now I've run out of people who want to take them and we just can't afford to feed them. So if no one wants them and no one takes them, they're going to starve to death. I honestly don't know what to do with them. Mr. Morrow's advice was short and simple: 'Ya just gotta drown the little critters.'"

"Mr. Morrow?" I gasped and my father continued.

"I pretended to laugh at first and then I asked him: Is that some kind of farmer's joke? 'It ain't a joke Mitchell. Its watcha gotta do,' he said in dead earnest. So I told him I could never do such a cruel thing, but he was pretty clear about it. 'Now you listen here Mitchell Morganstein,' he shouted at me. 'I can assure ya that slowly starvin' them pups ta death is a lot worse fate than puttin' 'em back ta sleep when they've barely been awake!'"

So, now here I was all these years later, responsible for my own kids' trauma over unwanted puppies that were forcibly taken from them. At least I didn't drown them.

During the long and acrimonious divorce proceedings that followed, Harvey threatened that he would see me destroyed. One of the most insidious reminders took place not on the witness stand, where emotions are as expendable as the empty verbiage that spews from the diviners of justice, but in a dark hallway of the courthouse.

The scene still haunts me like a ghostly tableau from a Fellini film: I am seated on a wooden chair at the end of a long, bleak hallway that's lit by a determined flick of sunlight spying through bevelled glass. Behind me stands my outraged daughter Wendy; on my left Sophie snuggles in closely; my sadly ambivalent son Brandon is leaning against my right arm staring at the floor; and cuddled up on my lap with his head resting on my shoulder is spunky little redheaded Aaron. The children have been called in to be questioned by the officers of the Court of Solomon, who will decide whether Harvey or I shall be the custodial parent.

The hollow rhythmic plodding of plastic soles on the icy polished floor chillingly interrupts our collective silence. The sound gets more ominous as a shadowy figure begins moving rapidly toward us. It comes to a dead stop about fifteen feet away and it speaks in the crude, familiar, and booming voice of my soon to be ex-husband: "You are going down, Rachel! All the way down! And I'm going to be there to watch you!"

He ventures closer, and I can see the smug grin on his face as he puts out his arms to Brandon who has been staring at the entire scene in mute terror. The boys barely glance at me before they both make a beeline toward their father and wrap themselves around him.

"Now don't you worry," he insists. "Just remember what I said, Brandon. Tell the judge that you want to live with me and everything will be just fine. Now you have to go back over there with her for now... okay?"

During the many months of legal fencing, it had become disturbingly clear to me and to my legal team that Harvey was aiming for sole custody of Brandon or, as he so "altruistically" resolved, "Brandon and Aaron if the court insists. But I believe that girls and small boys need to be with their mothers, while more mature ten-year-old boys should definitely be with their fathers!"

My day in court had all the abusive subtext of a cheap romance novel, right down to the final chapter.

After two years of suffering through bloody divorce battles, the outcome of the war now hinged on an unusual question posed by Mr. Fulbeck the Official Guardian, the O.G., who was the independent lawyer assigned by the court to mediate for the children.

"Mrs. Krup, what would you say if the court, on my recommendation, were to assign custody of the boys to your husband and the girls were to remain with you?"

The question gripped my heart like a massive clot. It confirmed my fear that Mr. Fulbeck, behind closed doors, had already recommended that the court separate our children. All along I had feared losing all my kids in this battle, but I never entertained the thought that our civilized justice system would actually consider splitting them up.

I mustered all my strength to suppress an imminent panic attack while I tried to figure out how to avoid a complete breakdown. My lawyer had warned me, "Rachel, listen carefully when I tell you that, *number one, you are not to speak directly to the judge; and number two, you are not to cry on the stand.* This judge hates it and if you do it, you risk losing your kids!"

I tried desperately to hang on to my vanishing composure: I bit the inside of my cheeks, I clenched my teeth, I even tried to think of funny images like Harvey's lawyer dressed up in drag. But not even red spike heels, a leather mini-skirt, nor a blonde Marilyn Monroe wig could distract me. The dam burst, and the flood surged out of control.

The colossal black-robed figure towering over me asked in a monotone voice, "Mrs. *Kerrup*, do you need a break to pull yourself together?"

I was afraid to raise my eyes toward him for fear he would hold me in contempt for crying. A valiant rescue attempt was made by my lawyer, who asked the judge if I could be allowed to sit down. It seemed like a reasonable request from my attorney, who was certain by my pallor and the waver in my deportment that I was about to hit the floor in a dead faint. He felt confident that the simple request would have been a sure thing, since we had all watched the day before as that same judge sent the wheezing little bailiff scurrying to "get a chair for Dr. Krup" when Harvey groused about having a bad back

The judge wasted no words in his candid reply: "No. She can stand." Then he gratuitously added, "unless Mrs. *Kerrup* wants to break now for the day, in which case I would point out that we would all have to come back to finish up tomorrow."

I felt certain that once I left the stand I would never have the strength to return, but I was also certain that the judge would be only too eager to sign a warrant for my arrest. So I shook my head and asked the O.G. to repeat the question.

I listened and proceeded with caution:

"Sir, I am completely unprepared to answer such a terrifying question," I whimpered.

"Prepared or not, it is a perfectly reasonable question, and you will have to answer it, Mrs. *Kerrup*," his Honour grumbled.

The judge had repeatedly uttered the name Krup as if it were a disparaging term, which was ironic because by now that's just how I felt about it.

In desperation I turned the question back at him.

"Mr. Fulbeck, how am I supposed to stand passively by and watch what's left of my family be dissected yet again?" I blurted.

"He is not here to answer questions Mrs. *Kerrup*. That is your job," snapped the judge.

"Sir, I believe it's crucial that my children stay together. I have three siblings myself, and I know how important that connection has been to each of us during the best and worst of times in our lives. But, Mr. Fulbeck, if you decide to recommend such a thing, I could never split them up. I would have to send all four of my children to live with their father, even though I know it would be an unstable and unhealthy environment for them. At least they could turn to each other for support."

I looked down at the widening mouth of the O.G. who was yawning without even trying to disguise it. I felt doomed. In desperation, defying my lawyer's advice, I turned to the judge and ad-libbed.

"Your Honour, may I say something?"

"If you have something worth saying Mrs. *Kerrup*, go ahead and speak. This is still a democratic country."

"Thank you, Your Honour. Well ... um... judge ... and Mr. Fulbeck, Harvey has charmed many into believing he's the victim here ... but it's our children who are being victimized. He's tried to make me out to be an unfit mother ... um ... a nut case ... and um ... maybe you're thinking that I'm proving his point now as I speak. I can only hope that someone will see through this charade. It's ... um ... true, I have bad-mouthed him to our children ... but I have a great deal of trouble keeping my bitterness toward him from showing when he's doing everything he can to provoke it and then lying about it. I know I have no way to convince you of that ... but I hope I can make you believe that I will make whatever sacrifices are necessary to raise our children properly ... But if you must order my children to live with him, then I would beg you to also order him to provide them with a top child psychiatrist or they'll never have a chance!"

At this point my deluged sobs were more articulate than my words, but I managed to babble one last plea:

"Your Honour, Harvey has stated that my concern over the damaging effect that this divorce is having on our children is completely unfounded. His answer to their pain is that 'they'll get over it. Kids are resilient. They bounce back.' Well I disagree. They don't bounce when the wind has been knocked out of them. Every single day I see the pain they have to endure from the trauma of this divorce. Our ugly war of words rages on and our children are continually being wounded by our ricocheting expletives. Those kids need some semblance of normalcy in their lives. They need to live on their street, go to their schools, and grow up with their friends. Unlike Harvey, I want the responsibility of all four of my children. I want them to grow up together in the only home they've ever known."

I waited in the thick, murky silence for a word, a grunt, anything that would weaken the unbearable tension I'd created in the room.

After a ponderous moment, all eyes were drawn to the judge as he sighed a dangerously weighty sigh. Then with a grating clearing of his throat, he announced his decree:

"All four children will remain together... and with their mother."

He turned toward me with softer eyes and a gentler voice than I ever thought he possessed and added, "Mrs. Krup, you are as courageous and determined a woman as I've seen in my years on the bench. I hope one day your kids will come to appreciate that fact."

Solomon had withdrawn the sword… and the children had remained more or less intact.

I left the stand, overwhelmed with relief, and headed toward my lawyer to express my gratitude but the O.G. intercepted me en route and grasped my hand in a firm but brief handshake. He then returned briskly to his desk and began to gather up his papers. I glanced over, just as he slid a document into his briefcase that was boldly titled, "Rachel Krup vs. Harvey Krup re: VD Telephone Transcript."

CHAPTER ELEVEN

The year of 1982 was the first in a series of most notably worst years of my life.

I'll always remember it because it was the year my divorce became final, my parents' store burned to the ground and my brother Adam had by-pass surgery. And it was the year that my oldest best friend had a swift coronary.

When I heard my mother's voice on the line at 2 a.m., I knew she wasn't calling me for a recipe. Her words were brief but desperate: "Please come, Rachel...I need you. It's dad. I think he's gone!"

I actually fixated on the crazy fantasy that he might be a double agent who up and left for the Soviet Union on a top-secret spy mission.

"Please meet me at the hospital, please ... I don't know what to do!" she pleaded.

I broke with my first rule of civility and left my house without a stitch of makeup. I didn't even take the time to put on underwear before I pulled on a sweat suit, jumped into my car, and drove 140 km an hour through the city.

During the excursion, I concocted this spiritual revelation that reassured me that my father would be standing there smiling. "*Honey,*" he would say, "*your mother's been devouring that bloody Readers Digest again and she just jumped to conclusions. I had some indigestion that's all. Now come on you two, let's go home!*"

Indigestion made perfect sense. He did tend to go off the junk wagon now and then, and nosh on items that barely resembled food, like pepperoni sticks, onion rings and hot cinnamon jelly beans.

I imagined how embarrassed my mother would be if I walked into the hospital just as they were walking out. Or maybe by the time I got there they would have already arrived back home and my dad would be relaxing at the piano. He always did that whenever he was stressed. He would just sit down and play until someone called him away. My mother always thought that he would have sat at that keyboard for days on end if she hadn't called him to the table for meals.

That first bleak night we spent in the Colonial Inn he discovered a broken down upright piano in the dance hall. To my dad it was an ebony concert Steinway. He couldn't do much to save the worn and brittle cabinetry of that wreck, but to him the soul of that old piano was still very much alive. That skeleton, with its dusty keys, hammers, and strings, buoyed our father's morale during the dreary winter months he spent in that wasteland. Whenever the cold and exhaustion threatened to overwhelm him, he would rush to the comfort of that ivory giant.

It often seemed that mere minutes after he would disappear into the dance hall, our mother would send one of us running after him: "Go tell your father that I need his help right away, if he can tear himself away from that broken down piano for five minutes!"

It was always something that could have waited, like bringing in coal for the stove, even though there were two full pails sitting right there. Or to finish shoveling the back stoop, even though it was Adam or David who had left it unfinished. My guess was that our mother may have been jealous of her husband's intimate affair with his old upright. We, on the other hand, were happy to know exactly where he was, so that we could get into mischief without worrying about getting caught. We also knew that after exhausting his repertoire of blues, boogie-woogie and jazz, he would exit that hall a lot happier than when he entered, which could only work in our favour. If my family could have gotten beyond our own individual agendas, we would have clearly seen that playing that piano gave him a sense of peace that nothing else ever could. That first winter, any few minutes he could spare, our dad would steal away to the frigid dance hall in his heavy coat, scarf, and gloves. He'd thunder away on those icy keys, heating them up until his fingers defrosted and traces of sweat glistened on his forehead. I think that solitary pleasure was Prozac for his soul.

Often times when my brothers and I were trekking through the snow on our way home from school, we'd hear his soulful music drifting for miles along the highway.

It was many years later when I came to realize how deeply that colourful image had been woven into my memory …

It happened one summer morning, just after I had been appointed artistic director of the Anna Freedman Theatre. My secretary Mimi received a call asking if a couple of people could come by to check out the auditorium for a possible off-season rental. I told her that it would be all right, but they would have to be there and gone by four because by four-thirty, the doors would be locked and I would be on my way to my cottage.

Within the hour, Mimi muttered through the intercom,

"Those guys are here, so I'm gonna take them backstage and then I'm gonna take a quick lunch break."

Two hours later, with Mimi still on her quick lunch break, I thought it wise to check up on our backstage guests.

Passing through the auditorium, I noticed that our Steinway had been pushed to centre stage and that there was a variety of technical equipment scattered about. As I entered the green room, I saw a scruffy looking character sprawled out on a chair with his shoeless feet propped up on the kitchen table wiggling his woolly toes over a plate of cookies. Being an average, normal clean freak, I was righteously incensed.

"Excuse me, sir! Would you put your feet on the dinner table in a friend's home or in a restaurant?" I crisply asked.

The man immediately bounced his feet off the table and slipped them into his shoes, apologizing profusely all the while. Taken aback by his spontaneous humility, I tried to compensate for my officious entrance by burbling over with small talk. We chatted about the beautiful trees that surrounded the theatre property, the convenient loading dock and the family of geese that hung around it waiting for pizza crumbs.

"You have superb acoustics and a fine concert Grand," he declared, "so if I decide to do a concert, I think I might just do it here!"

I politely ignored his pompous suggestion, but having noticed that the guy was wearing an overcoat, gloves, and a scarf in July, I figured we could find some common ground if I told him the story about my father and the fact that he too wore an overcoat, gloves, and a scarf when he played, although I thought it best not to point out the fact that my dad played in an unheated hall in twenty-below-zero weather.

The strange "hippy" with the fuzzy socks got a kick out of my story, which put the tension comfortably behind us. As I turned to head out the door he asked me if it would be okay if they brewed a pot of our coffee.

"You're welcome to use anything we have in this green room ... as long as you don't put your feet on it," I teased."

I returned to my office and busied myself, until Mimi, satiated from lunch, stuck her head in to show me the immense bubble she'd engineered from a wad of gum she'd been accumulating all week. As she peeled the remnants of the busted bubble from her face, she muttered, "You should come into the theatre to hear that guy play. He's pretty good."

I put down my pen and followed her and her bubble gum into the auditorium.

The music was beyond good, beyond perfect. I turned to Mimi and barely whispered the inevitable question that should have been so completely obvious to me from the start:

"Mimi, did you ever get the name of that guy?"

"Yeah, but I don't remember it."

Mimi continued to manipulate the wad until it was ready once again to be inflated.

"Mimi don't blow … think!"

"Okay, okay, just give me a minute ... It's uhm-m... Gould ... that's it ... Glenn … Gould."

✦ ✦ ✦

The car careened onto the driveway and halted abruptly in front of the hospital's emergency doors. I jumped out and raced toward the entrance leaving the car running. I didn't care much if they towed it or stole it.

As I entered the chamber of curtained cubicles, the smells and sounds jarred me into reality. My breathing became more and more shallow as I frantically peeked into every chamber in a most terrible game of hide-and-seek. Since I could not find my father, I could have continued to fantasize that it was all a mistake, but as I passed beyond the curtained maze, I stumbled into an orange vinyl seating area where I found my mother. She was alone and hunched over with her arms locked around her knees in a rather bizarre fetal position. As I approached I could hear her softly moaning over and over, "He's gone. He's gone ..."

My body drooped like limp fettuccine as I collapsed onto the stiff plastic sofa beside her. I sat there for several hour-like seconds, not quite knowing what to do. Physical demonstrations of affection between adults in public were so uncommon in my family that we needed brush-up courses for such occasions. I finally reached out and gently pulled her toward me. She yielded like a sorrowful child. I held her and rocked her, and for that moment I was the mother she needed me to be. My arms remained locked around her frail shuddering body while a tear-logged lump in my throat gathered enough girth to strangle me. I swallowed hard as I caught a glimpse of a matronly nurse rushing by. I left my mother in a daze and darted after her.

"Excuse me, nurse, could you please tell me what's happened to my father?"

"Who's your father?"

"He's Mitchell Morganstein, and he was brought in here less than an hour ago by Ambulance," I dutifully reported.

"Oh yeah, he was in cubicle three, but they needed the room so they moved him out 'cause he was already gone."

"Gone?" I asked as if I had never heard the word articulated before. "What does that mean?"

"Gone means he's dead!"

The sting of her horrific response fleetingly paralyzed my tongue. Reason and fury began to race around my brain like crazed hamsters. I could taste bitter bile seeping into my throat as this keeper of the lamp, this Florence Nightingale, turned on her stumpy legs and began to stalk away.

"Hold on a minute! Are you insane? What kind of damn nurse are you? How in Hell can you be so bloody insensitive?" I spat the words out like buckshot and she spat back.

"Look, we're all very tired and very busy nursing the living here. Now, you asked me a question and I gave you the answer. If you don't like my manners, take it up with Anne Landers!"

I could imagine my father saying, "Don't make a fuss *Rifkala*, you'll only upset your mother. You know she doesn't like confrontations. Besides, I hear that they have ways of punishing bad manners up here that you can't even imagine. So if Ms. Nightingale ever makes it up here, she'll either search out Emily Post or she'll spend eternity down below shovelling dung with Hitler and his pals."

"It had been a perfect evening," my mother whimpered. "We went out for dinner with Auntie Lil and Uncle Dave, we played gin rummy, we went to bed early, and then we ... you know ..." she disquietingly mumbled.

Of course I knew but it was impossible to imagine my mom and dad clutched in the kind of walloping lust that could stop a man's heart.

I admit it is somewhat of a comfort to know that my parents could still experience such passion. Hooray! We can all hope to revel in the great sex ahead for all of us baby boomers when we reach the trendy age of Geritol and Viagra.

The night before my dad died, my mother had returned from a trip with her sister to Las Vegas. Sending her off on this annual sisters junket made my dad a truly feminist guy in my mother's eyes. The truth was he was never a gambler, and he liked being independent, for a few days. Of course I liked it because my children and I got to spend a lot of quality time with him. So, for five days every summer she flew off to bond with her sister and a one armed bandit, while my dad took pleasure in his own hobbies. He busied himself gardening, writing poetry, and repairing stuff around the house, but his greatest achievement was in developing his own style of art, which he proudly labelled cloisonné. Although his colourful and engaging paintings were primitive, they seemed to breathe a spiritual component into his otherwise secular world.

One night he and I sat over a luxurious dinner in the Kmart cafeteria, and that's when he became "my oldest, newest, best friend." We talked about all aspects of the human life cycle, as we often did, but there was one area that had always remained taboo: We had never discussed death. It was a subject that had always made him uneasy. Throughout my father's life he had professed to be a devout atheist, but that night, he was actually leaking traces of serious thought about God and Heaven.

"I'm not afraid to go when my time comes," he announced. "I know that a creature that's as complicated as we humans are had to evolve to fulfil a more important purpose than we generally do. There has to be something greater than mankind or we would have annihilated our ilk back when we were bludgeoning each other with the hind leg of an ox."

When the truth finally invaded my psyche, and I had to accept that he was dead, I felt some peace just knowing that my dad would be up there debating the meaning of life with God and his Biblical cronies throughout eternity.

I called on Wendy to come and stay with my mother while I drove out to the country to gather up the three younger children from camp. That was where, thanks to the largesse of my father, the younger ones had been enjoying their summer vacation.

As I drove through the eerie pre-dawn fog, I tried to figure out what I could say that would make it possible for my children to bear the wretched burden of loss that was already consuming me.

Throughout the divorce wars, their grandfather had been a stabilizing force in their lives. He was their mentor, their cheerleader, their ever-faithful friend and social director. Given a choice, they would rather have spent time with him, sharing their dreams, listening to his stories, planting a garden or fishing for trout, than to be anywhere else on earth. An invitation to prowl the aisles of the local hardware store with Zaidah would elicit squeals of delight from his two eager grandsons. And a chance to raise perfect rhubarb or learn to carve exotic animals out of soap would keep the girls amused for hours. I took his presence for granted and never considered his absence and the vicious impact it could one day have on my family.

Later that awful day, a visiting rabbi tried to give us comfort by assuring us that God had taken my dad "with a gentle kiss."

If that was gentle then I guess a full lip lock would have been tantamount to Armageddon.

The funeral director advised me that a member of the family needed to identify the body in the casket before the funeral. I waited until all my siblings had arrived in Toronto and then I asked each in turn if they would like the honour. They unanimously declined.

I followed the funeral director into a screened-off area where the casket sat poised on a table-like apparatus. He made a dramatic choreographed exit, while I ventured forward with trepidation. I was about to gaze upon the second deceased body I had ever encountered in my lifetime.

It was a strange and inappropriate time for a vivid childhood experience to come flooding back, but it seems that we have no control over the insistence of our memories to appear at will.

It began one breezy spring morning when my brothers and I arrived at our schoolhouse all excited because Victoria Day was rapidly approaching, which meant that we would be planting copious flower and vegetable seeds in our school garden. Students planted and maintained the gardens throughout the summer and then reaped the rewards of the produce we grew when it was ready for picking.

The vegetable gardens took up most of the back yard, while the flower gardens bordered the entire periphery of the school. That may sound impressive by today's architectural standards, but ours was a one-room schoolhouse and not too much bigger than a modern prefab toolshed really. Behind our schoolhouse was a large white cottage surrounded by award-winning gardens. The Murphys who owned it were a kindly old couple whom I suspect had a lot to do with the fact that our student gardens never suffered the cruel deaths they should have when we were errant in our duties.

Our family didn't own a car, so we had to endure the three-mile hike to school every morning unless we could prove that we had a fever higher than 103 degrees or we were covered in seemingly contagious spots. Our dad was pretty strict about attendance, even for me, and I was only five years old.

On that particular spring day, we arrived at school hot and tired but elated by the idea that we would be spending the next few days outside in the fresh, sweet air rather than in our musty, dark classroom.

First we gathered inside by our desks and stood at attention to sing "God Save the King," which was our moral duty. Then, instead of telling us to line up and march outside to begin planting, our teacher, Mrs. Winston, told us that we were all to return immediately to our homes, change out of our dungarees and into our best dress-up clothes, and be back in our seats by noon.

No explanation was given and of course no one dared request one.

Obediently we trudged the three miles back to the Colonial Inn, where we were met by our very sceptical father who was ready to spank each of us in turn on his assumption that we had been suspended for bad behaviour. Thankfully our oldest brother Adam stepped forward to defend us. He did that whenever he was implicated in a crime. But if David and I were the only ones at risk, he would just stay mum. Anyway, he convinced our dad that we were all innocent of any wrongdoing, thus our tender bottoms were blessed with The Warden's reprieve.

We were twice blessed that day. The second blessing was on our return when our neighbour Mr. Morrow stopped to offer us a horse and buggy ride all the way back to our school. My two brothers scrambled into the back of the wagon but Mr. Morrow invited me to sit right up front with him. I was a little surprised by the honour at first, since I had been accustomed to sitting in the back with my brothers whenever we hitched a ride. But he made a suggestion that seemed to make perfect sense to me: "Any young lady wearin' such a beautiful dress should be sittin' pretty, right up front there, like yer at the head o' the parade."

I can still clearly remember what I was wearing that day because when I was five, I only owned one fancy dress. It was faded pink satin and very frilly. My mother had made it for me out of an old nightgown of hers, and I loved it. My entire wardrobe consisted of clothes that had been reconstituted from old housecoats, jackets, and bedspreads. Of course I always thought that my brothers had it worse. They had to wear my dad's old trousers that had been shortened to remove the frayed bottoms, but since our mom had never learned how to alter waistbands, they were always on the verge of losing their pants or at the very least facing that cursed plumber's butt. In addition to her magical sewing act, my mother spent cozy winter evenings by the radio, unravelling old sweaters so that she could recycle the wool to knit winter socks for 'the men' and scarves for the "women" in our family.

"Come on Missy, we gotta get goin' now, so climb on up!" he urged.

"Okay, sir, but I need to ask one question first, 'cause I am wearing my best dress today."

"Of course you are my dear. You just git on up here and ask away."

Wait, Mr. Morrow! Please? Before I climb up I need to ask my question, privately.

He lowered the reins and leaned toward me. "This is about as private as it gets out here missy, unless ya want me ta put a couple o' plugs o' tobacco in Old Red's ears?"

I leaned forward to whisper to the farmer, hoping with all hope that my brothers wouldn't hear.

"Mr. Morrow? Old Red wouldn't lift his tail and poop on me or anything, would he?"

"Now then, Missy, what kind o' manners do ya think I taught this old nag anyhow? You just climb up here and behave yourself, okay?"

And with that he reached out his giant hand and lifted me onto the worn velvet seat as if I were as light as a carton of eggs. I studied him as he raised the leather reins to set the horse in motion and then off we clip-clopped. We had only clipped and clopped a couple of yards before panic set in as I watched Old Red slowly lift his tail toward the heavens.

"Mr. Morrow," I squealed, "he's going to poop on me!"

The next sound we heard was the thundering boom of a horse fart as it barrelled through Old Red's rectum. The impact of that woeful breeze practically knocked me backward right onto my brothers.

"Ya see what happens when ya insult a sensitive horse like Old Red!" Mr. Morrow said as he tried to conceal a telltale smirk. He was kind enough to withhold his outright laughter, which is more than I can say for my two obnoxious brothers who, overjoyed by Old Red's defiance, laughed themselves into two major stomach-aches. As for me, I was relieved to discover that horse gas is colourless, even if it's not odourless.

Twenty-five minutes later, Mr. Morrow halted the wagon in front of the school, and we scrambled out, panting with excitement. All the way home we had pondered the possibilities: Perhaps it was a surprise birthday party for one of our classmates, or maybe we were going to have a celebrity guest like the Mayor of Johnstown, or maybe even the Princess of England!

We sat quietly in our seats, watching closely as the teacher strode to the front of the class. There was barely a breath heard as we waited for her to speak:

"Now children, we are going to go over to the Murphy's to visit Mr. Murphy. Afterwards, as we leave their home, Mrs. Murphy will give you each a treat. I want you all to mind your manners and say thank you to her and then continue to file out as I instruct you. Okay, now line up in order, as you do for recess. Thank you. Now, forward, march!"

We marched sprightly in single file across the velvety lawn, en route to our destination. We were all giddy with anticipation, but one sharp glance from Mrs. Winston reinstated decorum as we arrived at the front door. Mrs. Winston marched into the parlour and beckoned the oldest group of students to approach. Since I was the youngest, I remained outside with the last group, patiently waiting my turn. My five little classmates and I stood by quietly admiring each other's party outfits.

Finally it was our turn. I entered cautiously, waiting for sheer delight to envelop me. The teacher whispered, "Hurry along my dear, there are still other children waiting. Step lively now."

As I inched my way into the stately old parlour, I could see a long, brown, shiny trunk off to one corner that was partially hidden by a forest of gargantuan, pungent lilies. The chest sat nobly perched atop a flouncy, satin-skirted platform. I marvelled at the bizarre extravagance of that frilly blue fabric and secretly considered what a beautiful dress it would make for me.

Mrs. Winston impelled me toward the trunk and then lifted me onto a step stool that had been positioned there. With great anticipation I curled my tiny fingers around the edge of the trunk, raised myself onto my tippy-toes, and peered in only to find myself nose to chin with the stone cold apparition that was formerly known as Mr. Murphy.

His white hair and pasty skin were heavily contrasted by the shocking pink rouge circles that had been so meticulously painted on his cheeks. He was all decked out in a dark twill ensemble that was perfectly complete down to his shiny black shoes, their fashionable toe tips pointing appropriately skyward. In his hand he clutched the serpentine stem of an oversized calla lily a flower I have ever since despised.

I gawked at him in sheer wonderment until the familiar voice of Mrs. Winston invaded my macabre reverie. "My dear, do you have anything to say to Mr. Murphy?" she prompted.

I remained silent. I was utterly confused by the question. She tried again, more firmly this time.

"Say your good-bye to Mr. Murphy, dear." I remained riveted.

"Tell Mr. Murphy good-bye. Now!" she sputtered.

"Good-bye, Mr. Murphy," I barely whispered.

"Now you must lean over and give him a kiss... like a good girl."

What was I to do? She was standing within breathing distance of me. How could I escape this dreadful decree?

"Oh God," I murmured as I got a sour whiff of the formaldehyde that hovered over his lifeless carcass. "Please God, please don't ask me to kiss something that smells so bad," I prayed.

I needed to think. I needed a plan. I needed to figure out what my brothers would do in a situation like this, after all they were the mature ones, the crafty ones, the creative ones ... Then I remembered that they were also the first ones in line. What did they do?

I watched Mrs. Winston closely out of the corner of my eye until suddenly the moment revealed itself to me. As she turned her head to chastise one of my schoolmates, I puckered up tightly and smacked my lips to the air as loudly as I could. She turned back to me wearing a rather satisfied smile. "That was very good indeed, my dear. Now run along and see Mrs. Murphy for your treat."

A flock of goose bumps marched briskly up my back as the very pale and tearful widow gently placed her homemade treat in my palm.

A wave of nausea floated over me as I stared at the glistening brownie nestled in its frilly blue doily topped with a candied lily.

It looked just like Mr. Murphy's coffin.

The funeral director left me behind the opaque screen. I opened my eyes and looked at the smooth oaken casket that stood before me. This wasn't a stranger that I was about to gaze upon. This was my role model, my friend, my father. I shuffled forward. I could see him lying there in serene repose in his beautiful showcase, like a prince. His handsome presence and strong angular features were not diminished by death. I could feel his soft blue eyes smiling down on me from his new post. I knew he would be scoffing at the pomp and pageantry that was being lavished on him.

I saw no pain or fear on his face, only peace. And that

solitary vision brought abounding joy to my soul. I reached in, touched his strong smooth hands and whispered my good-bye. Then, gently, I kissed his soft cool cheek.

A dozen years after I said my last good-bye to my father, I wept again as I wished my mother her final bon voyage. Her heart and soul had died on impact twelve years earlier when her true love died in her bed. And from that very instant, her once curvaceous body began to devolve into a fragile dehydrated shell. From the day she lost her husband, she seemed to have unconsciously engineered her elaborate suicide, slowly killing herself with chocolate bars, French fries, maple syrup, and other poisons that her body couldn't process. She had, during her endless mourning period, managed to become the poster girl for a "Ripley's Believe It Or Not" list of senior ailments. She was the recipient of a thyroid condition, diabetes, eczema, asthma, heart disease, breast cancer, and multiple strokes which ultimately led to chronic depression and blindness. Gradually she was stripped of everything she had loved in her life. She was unable to knit her trademark cozy sweaters, bake fresh sour-cherry pies, embroider table linens, watch TV, or even read to her grandchildren. For the last five years of her life she vegetated in a seniors residence, unable to walk and barely able to talk. She hated having to be lifted onto the toilet, and couldn't bear to have her loved ones wipe her bottom. One of the few times she was able to string coherent words together was to beg me to "please, let the nurses do it."

I'd been preoccupied with my own embarrassment over the dreadful experience of diapering my mother, but it turned out that it wasn't about me after all.

Beyond the deep green tint of my mother's sad eyes one could glimpse the profound hopelessness that had settled there. It was plain to see that she didn't want to live, but it was equally clear she was terrified to die.

In the spring of 1994 she slipped silently and peacefully out of our world and into her beloved's.

CHAPTER TWELVE

Until my father's death I had always resisted any obligation to enter a cemetery, but I soon learned the power of the plot. And now whenever I feel untethered, I simply visit my parents.

It comforts me to see the fresh-faced pansies looking up at me from their double bed. The tombstone tells me things about my parents that they never said out loud in life, like how old they were or how much they loved us.

I always try to find the whitest pebbles (reminiscent of the white washed stones that encircled the Colonial Inn) to place on top of the headstone, so they'll know it's me that came to visit.

When I was a child I would tiptoe into their room, stand beside their bed and talk to them while they slept. I would quietly whisper my most intimate worries into the darkness and then leave, hopeful that they could magically resolve my problems. And many times they did. Now I do that each time I visit their graveside.

On one of those visits I stared at the pansies that blanketed their graves and soon found myself telling those smiley-faced flowers all about how and why I had hated those innocent blossoms for so many years.

Just five months after my mother passed away, the theatre that I had worked so tirelessly to create was forced to close down. The ever-capable and egotistical Mr. Sanders had been retired for a few years so the board of the YMHA had no one left to rein in their incompetence. In a flurry of progress, they implemented expansion programmes with no money in place, gambling that in no time they would easily collect the millions of dollars that were needed to pay for the elitist perks they were enjoying; but it never happened. The cadre of dirty politicians had struck once again. So, like the Titanic, when the bow sinks, the stern must follow.

Our theatre's "patron saint," Warren Freedman, offered to separate the theatre wing from the rest of the complex and take full responsibility for all future operations of that part of the centre, but he was flatly refused. The greedy Y politicians thought that leasing out the theatre to a well-heeled private school would roll in enough money to help drag their wing out of debt. That never happened either. We spent the next couple of years fighting for the life of the theatre in court, but in the end it was futile and the elegant theatre suffered an untimely and humiliating death.

So, after twenty-something years of hard work, compassion, and creativity, I was now an out-of-work director with pages of experience to list on a resume, a network of celebrities to sing my praises, an empty bubble in my heart, and an overwhelming sense of hopelessness.

Over the next three years I stayed ahead of bankruptcy by cashing in insurance policies and selling off whatever furniture and jewellery I had. Eventually I received a barebones settlement from the Y and a small inheritance from my mother that helped me get through another year. Within that time Wendy had wed, and she and her husband Noah had blessed us all with the birth of my first grandson Gabriel. Brandon had also gotten married, Sophie was in a serious relationship, and Aaron and Elaine seemed to be a regular item. Everyone was on the road to independence. The timing was remarkable given the fact that my meagre resources were almost depleted. So on yet another landmark day I gathered my children together to break the news that after nearly thirty years, our family home was going to have to be sold.

Silence infused the room as I explained why I could no longer afford to keep up our family home. Having been out of work for three years, one would hardly think it likely I would need to explain the economic facts to four adult children, but judging by their blank faces, I felt compelled to lay it all out for them. I acknowledged the crushing sadness we'd all feel over the pending loss of our venerable house. And when I was done, a chorus of voices offered commentary:

"Is that what this whole big meeting was about? Of course you're going to sell the house! We love this house but we never expected you to rattle around in this big old place all alone. That would be just plain depressing!"

During the gathering it was Aaron's weighty silence that bewildered me. His style is to be so vocal and blunt; a characteristic that he claims is laudable, while the recipients of his opinions would soundly disagree. The moment his siblings were out the door, however, he let me know exactly how he felt.

"I knew you'd sell the house before I was ready to move out. I've never had any of the opportunities everyone else had, so why should this be any different?"

"Hold on just a little minute there, Mister," I pleaded with a glint of confidence and humour. "All your siblings had the opportunity to live at home until they were ready to leave which was before retirement age, but after thirty, right? Well, you're only twenty-three. So like I told you, the plan is for me to get an apartment that's roomy enough for the two of us, so that you can also live at home until you feel you're ready to leave. So don't panic over the sale of the house. It was inevitable at some point. It just came sooner than we'd hoped."

"But," he continued, "I agree, it should be sold. In fact it should have been done years ago when dad's lawyer told you, you had to sell it. After all, dad paid for it. He did you a big favour you know, letting you stay here all these years."

"Letting me stay here?" I sputtered, munching once again on the bait. "I paid the entire mortgage, principal and interest, for eighteen years. For the ten years he lived here he paid interest only. I renovated and maintained this house. Your father wouldn't put a penny into repairs when he lived here. I raised all of you in this home while he was doing what he could to have us all thrown out, and then I was finally forced to borrow money to buy out his half or we could have ended up on the street. How can you even whisper the notion that he paid for it?"

He looked away as he wryly asked, "What are you planning to do with the money anyway?"

"Well, first of all, half of it goes to pay off the loan and then until I can rebuild my career, we'll need the rest to live on."

"What about your retirement fund? Why can't you live on that?"

"What are you talking about? I'm light years away from retirement and anyway, that fund is minuscule right now, but it's all I'll have when I do reach that age."

"You must be kidding! You're worried about your old age? You know, that's a disgusting insult to your kids. You don't think that we'd all look after you in your old age? You all did it for your parents didn't you, so why would you think that we wouldn't do it for you?"

"It's nice to hear that you would, but, Aaron, I've been an independent person since your father left eighteen years ago and I'm not about to start planning for a future where I become my children's responsibility. Besides you'll all have plenty of other financial responsibilities to take care of by then, believe me!"

"Well, all I know is that you're going to end up with a lot of money for a house that you wouldn't have had if it weren't for dad. But since the reality is what it is, I think that you should give each of your kids a share of it to make things easier. I've got student loans to pay off; and Wendy, with a kid and another one on the way, needs a house; Brandon and Sophie are each going to need one eventually too ... and maybe it's time you did something for yourself as well."

There was no point in trying to make sense of my son's jaundiced view of life in general. The possibility of any discussion between us that might include the mention of their father was compromised by the reality that we had no common ground on the subject.

I walked around in an altered state for days after, preoccupied by the disturbing clinical conversation I'd had with Aaron concerning the sale of our house. My mood darkened again a few days later when Wendy called to ask: "Hey, Mom, did Aaron and Elaine find a place yet?"

"What do you mean ... a place?"

"Didn't they tell you? Oh my God. Aaron didn't tell you they're moving in together? That's weird."

I tried to appear unruffled over this revelation by offering up logic in response.

"Well maybe he hasn't had a chance yet, what with the real estate agents coming in and out all week."

"Mom, they've been planning it for months, long before you told us about the house having to be sold."

It was another two weeks before I brought the subject up with Aaron. Finally, one evening as we were sitting in the den, I asked him how the apartment hunting was going and if there was anything that I could do to help.

"No, there isn't ... and who told you anyway?" he snarled.

"It doesn't matter and I don't know why you seem so upset about it. I just can't figure out why you wouldn't tell me yourself. You're an adult, Aaron, and I respect your right to make your own decision about moving in together. I'm not that old fashioned. I adore Elaine and I'm glad to hear that you're serious about her. Anyway, honey, if you feel I can help just let me know."

With that he turned up the volume on "Jeopardy" and ended any possibility of a conversation.

I left the den and headed up to my bedroom to lick my wounds in private. I knew by his tone that there would be no productive discussion that night. Like Pavlov's dog, this bitch was learning to respond to the warning bell.

The next evening it was oddly reassuring that over dinner, he voluntarily talked about the many apartments they had seen and the ones they were seriously considering. He didn't ask for an opinion so I didn't offer any. I just listened, offering o-ohs and a-ahs of approval and compliance, while Pavlov's bell continued to reverberate softly in my head.

It seemed that the closer it got to his moving day, the angrier and more hostile he became. He was transforming himself from a responsible and concerned son to a disrespectful and apathetic stranger. Garbage day was not his concern, tidying up after himself was not his concern, and showing up for dinner, or at least calling in, wasn't of any concern either.

One verbal skirmish ensued over my "inability to grasp even the most elementary of computer concepts," as he put it.

I had never learned to type so I was fortunate to have had a staff to do it for me and if they weren't around I had my trusty Dictaphone. But then came the time when that was no longer an option since there was no longer a theatre or a staff. Brandon encouraged me to leap the mammoth hurdle and attempt to master the computer. He guided me through the dark recesses of the computer jungle and taught me to tame the terrifying word processor. Since I am plainly technophobic it probably took me longer to absorb computer-speak than it would the average six-year-old.

When Brandon got married the teaching mantle was passed on to Aaron. Since Aaron was a real whiz kid, especially when it came to this new-age tech stuff, it was understandable that he would lose patience when he had to pull me out of the same mire more than once.

One night I called out in a panic. I needed his help to find pages of my novel that had disappeared from my screen. I was mortified when he planted himself in my bedroom doorway and declared, "Either get someone else to help you or stop using the computer 'cause I'm not doing it! When I give up my valuable time to help you, I expect you to pay attention. Maybe Brandon was idiot enough to show you the same kind of thing twice but I'm not."

As I pulled myself out of my seat to protest, I slipped and slammed my rib cage against the hard plastic arm of my chair. I was so embarrassed by my own clumsiness that I pretended it never happened, but by the next day the pain was so excruciating I had to drag myself to the doctor.

"You've got a couple of cracked ribs in there," he concluded. "Unfortunately there's not a darn thing you can do about them except stay away from stress, and I guess I don't need to tell you, no lifting."

When Aaron arrived home that night, I asked him if he would carry the cartons of left over garage sale stuff out to the driveway for the charity truck to pick up in the morning.

He snapped, "Do I look like a *grunt* to you? I come home to relax! You're up early in the morning. Tell those schleppers to carry that crap out of the garage themselves. You're giving them the damn stuff for nothing; it's the least they can do."

"I'm not up at four in the morning, Aaron!"

"Well, if you want the boxes gone then maybe you should make an exception."

I was in desperate need of a clue as to how my formerly compassionate and respectful son was morphing into this cold, rude, insensitive stranger. But I kept all queries to myself. Instead, I initiated the oldest trick in the Jewish Mother's book of rules: I tried guilt.

I told him all about my painfully cracked ribs and how it happened during our argument over the computer. (My own mother, in spite of her pure Russian Jewish lineage, would have been ashamed of me, since she had never resorted to such stereotypical tactics.)

Aaron, however, only wanted to know where I went for an X-ray. When I told him that the doctor didn't send me for one, he responded with, "So I guess he's Superman then, since he obviously has X-ray vision. Look, I've got friends who've cracked their ribs, so I know that there's no way that you've got 'em or you'd be in so much pain you wouldn't be able to move."

He stomped into his room while I limped truculently out to the garage to move those damn boxes myself.

I was about to pick up the smallest of the five boxes when I glimpsed the tall redhead out of the corner of my eye, charging in slow motion toward the garage. He watched sheepishly as I slowly moved toward the largest box and pulled the huge, broken down carton toward the edge of the rickety old table on which it sat. I didn't ask for his help and he didn't offer it. As he turned back toward the house, I inhaled as deeply as my cracked ribs would allow, spread my arms wide, grasped the bottom of the carton tightly and then prayed that momentum would carry me and the box to the finish line. I was managing alright until I heard a strange crackling sound which I was certain, was the snapping of my remaining ribs. Suddenly the seams on one side of the box split wide open and dozens upon dozens of books tumbled to the ground leaving me with a gross imbalance that sent me propelling forward like a runaway train headed down the wrong track. A sharp pain accelerated through my body. I dropped the box and fell to my knees groaning. I looked up in time to see Aaron heading back in my direction. He stood just inches away and seemed breathless for a second until I rose to my feet looking as if all parts were intact.

"Why didn't you ask me to take it?" he grumbled as he picked up the books and dragged the injured box down the driveway. "You saw me standing there. I go to the trouble of coming out here to help and you don't even appreciate it."

I shuffled back into the house while my son carried the rest of the boxes to the end of the driveway.

From that night forward, things got progressively worse between us.

Several weeks after my cold war with Aaron began, I was awakened at 2 a.m. by Sophie who sprinted into my room announcing that on the stroke of midnight, her prince had proposed to her. Like most everyone who knew my daughter, her fiancé had also been hypnotized by her exotic beauty, sharp mind, and infectious smile. Now Sophie would join her two siblings who were already members of the "wedding club," and since Aaron would be moving out as well, it was clear that the cozy, domestic era of my life was looming close to its end and it would soon be time for me to enter a new realm of the cosmos. I could either inhabit the dark lonely world of discarded mothers or the illuminated universe of reinvented matriarchs. With the iceberg that stood between Aaron and me still chilling our home, it was certain that I would find myself in the discarded category if I didn't find some help to thaw out our relationship.

I finally resorted to talking to a therapist to help me figure out why my son had suddenly evolved into a veritable stranger. He had all kinds of theories about what might be hovering over Aaron's karma and penetrating mine:

A. "Maybe he thought you would not approve of his 'living in sin'."

B. "He may conceivably feel he must cut you out of his life in order to feel like a man."

C. "Perhaps he feels guilty about leaving you after all you've given to him for so long… or he might be punishing you for everything he thinks you didn't give him." or

D. "Maybe he believes that turning away from you will finally prove his loyalty to his father and make him his favourite son for a change."

By then this was starting to sound like a really scary game show where any choice I made would have dire consequences; but if I chose the right one, it could open a door to a treasure.

I tearfully asked, "Is there another set of options to choose from?"

"Look, Rachel, we can conjecture about this for years and it will cost you a small fortune, not that I would object, but the reality is you have to talk to him to really know what's on his mind. You need to tell him how you feel and then listen to him in turn. Let him respond without interruption. Don't be adversarial; just lay it all out … Afterward you can both discuss your feelings openly. You must clear the air before he moves out. It's the only way."

Finally, the doctor had earned his fee. Now I had some practical advice to ponder, uninterrupted. He had opened the door to a treasure and I didn't even have to play the game.

All I needed was courage.

Our cold war had been raging for too long and I had now discovered the key to resolving it. Yet almost two weeks after my visit with the doctor, I was still searching for the grit to talk to my son about our growing hostilities.

Then one evening after sharing a pizza while watching Tom Brokaw on the "Nightly News," I cautiously forged ahead and asked Aaron if he would mind if I turned off the television so we could talk.

"Fine," he declared as a silent smirk edged its way across his lips.

I spent about twenty minutes telling him how bad I felt about the chasm that separated us and how anxious I was to get across it, particularly since he would be moving out soon. All the time I spoke he remained uncharacteristically quiet, but it was clear from his body language that his thoughts were noisy. He seemed to be gathering information for a lively response, but he didn't appear agitated or resentful as I feared he might be.

He sat forward on the sofa and cleared his throat. "I knew we were going to talk tonight, you know."

You did? Really? And I had no idea until the words came out of my mouth two seconds ago, were my first thoughts, but I responded with, "I've been wanting so much to do this for weeks, but in any case I'm glad we're finally talking."

Over the course of the odyssey that followed, I came to realize that Aaron's perspective on our history was written in a cultural language I clearly didn't understand. He appeared to have lost all recollection of any joyful, humorous, interesting, or loving times we'd shared through his evolution from embryo to manhood. And each time I offered an anecdote from his childhood, he would deny it or even worse turn every sweet innocent memory into a bleak, bitter flashback.

I told him the ring-bearer story hoping to trigger some light-hearted memories. He admitted to remembering the modeling experience but added, "I was just too young and innocent back then to realize how badly I was being exploited!"

There was no use in reminding him that his modeling debut was also his curtain call. Perhaps the designers weren't as impressed as the audience was when Aaron stopped at the end of the runway and explored the inside of his nose to the strains of "Every Thing I Have Is Yours."

I also lovingly recalled for him the time that our junior Dr. Doolittle dragged home a half dead tabby cat and demanded immediate medical attention: "Daddy, this pussycat has very pointy teeth and he's very sick ... and you said that people can get sick and die if they don't get their teeth fixed, so I want you to fix the pussycat's teeth 'so he won't die ... Okay?"

What had never been told was how Harvey planned to discreetly drop the cat off on some lone country road until I insisted that he whisk the cat away to a vet instead and try to save it. To his credit he agreed. But before proceeding, the animal doctor declared that his fee would be a hundred and fifty dollars and the odds on saving the cat were less than fifty percent. Harvey unilaterally decided to fast-forward through Kitty's nine lives and come home catless.

Since we had wisely chosen never to share that fact with the children, I didn't think that this was the time to set the record straight, so I just continued to relate the best of that experience:

"You were so confident that your dad could fix him up

that every night you put out a saucer of milk to celebrate the cat's hopeful return. Then one morning when you found a stray ginger cat lapping away at the dish instead of your tabby, you confidently declared, 'See I told you daddy would make him better … and he even coloured his hair to match mine!'"

"You don't remember that?"

"Yeah, sure I remember that. But I also remember when I was like eight or nine, dad finally told me the truth, that he could have fixed my tabby up just fine if you wouldn't have made him take the cat to some quack vet who made him put him to sleep!"

Aaron's memory bank had been burgled. His kindergarten graduation was a blank, a joyful three-day trip to a fishing resort with his grandfather, brother, and me … a blank. Picnics in the woods, monopoly games (which he generally won), swimming in the ocean, baking cakes and cookies, days at the zoo, toboggan rides, theatre outings, exotic vacations, birthday parties, merry-go-rounds … all a complete blank. A young life filled with rich experiences, wiped clean of all memory like a PC overrun with a lethal computer virus.

Even the more recent moments we shared were being rapidly expunged. I figured, if he was determined not to remember the most precious of long past memories, then I would try something less sentimental and more recent. I was desperate. I reminded him of a scenario that had happened just one year earlier when he was suffering through a crisis and I was still playing a featured sympathetic role in his drama. I knew I would be bordering on the manipulative but what other weapon does a Jewish Mother have when all else fails but to resort to the stereotypical guilt our ancestors created as maternal insurance?

After graduating from university Aaron had been fortunate to receive a position with a major corporation and was proving to be invaluable to them. He had a genius for all things computer and was being groomed for greatness. But after several months of developing programme concepts that amazed even his more senior coworkers, the top executives wanted him to prove himself by working the sales floor in one of their chain stores for a couple of months. They felt it would give him a better understanding of what kind of software advances the stores needed to operate more efficiently. Aaron had never had the experience of standing on his feet in ten-hour shifts, so by the end of his first week, he arrived home barely able to walk from the car to our front door. Once inside I helped him peel off his shoes and socks, which exposed his raw, chafed, and bleeding feet. Seeing your child suffering pain is a disturbing sight for any mother, no matter what age he is.

I quickly plied him with Tylenol and prepared a soothing foot bath. Then, once the pain had somewhat subsided, he slipped on a pair of sandals, and we headed to a shoe specialist to find a pair that would withstand the stress of his hundred and eighty pounds and six feet, three inches of stature.

The shoes seemed magical. From the minute he put them on, he mellowed right out. We even went out for dinner and talked and laughed until the waiter hinted that they were trying to close up for the night.

I asked him if he remembered the evening we got the shoes and he barked, "Big deal, you bought me a pair of shoes. You want a medal?"

He couldn't seem to remember even one heart-warming moment from the past unless it involved his father; but he was able to recall numerous perceived injustices levied on him by his mother.

"Like the time you stormed into my room and started smacking the crap out of me, for no reason. I wasn't doing anything, I was just a little kid sitting quietly on my bed and you completely flipped out. I did you a big favour that night you know, 'cause I could have had you thrown in jail for child abuse."

When I was a kid, Rebecca was always claiming victimhood and my father always believed her, which left me vulnerable to being wrongfully accused and unjustly punished. There were occasions, I suppose, when I may have been slightly mean to my little sister. Well, at least that's the way I used to remember it, but I never understood back then, how my dad could make so many cruel mistakes in his role as judge, jury, and executioner.

Then I became a parent.

The victimhood incident Aaron accused me of happened when he was around the age of fourteen. By then he had graduated from his relentless teasing of his siblings to outright verbal torture. He had particularly targeted Sophie, whose reaction to our divorce scenario had been to indulge her pain and emptiness with an abundance of food so that during her teen years she had grown from lithe to corpulent. Aaron turned every extra pound to his advantage.

On the night of the alleged "child abuse," he was mocking his twenty-year-old sister as she tried to get through her bedtime beauty ritual. He guffawed like a donkey and smacked her butt with a wet towel while she was leaning over the sink brushing her teeth. I could hear her gagging on toothpaste as she sputtered for him to stop. I tried to stay out of it. I had been referee, mediator, umpire, and warden, through a lifetime of childhood wars.

She has to handle it herself now; she's a grown woman, I told myself. *She's a smart, beautiful, capable person … she'll deal with it.*

My stomach swirled and my head throbbed as each vulgar epithet struck my ear. I tried to ignore the broo-ha-ha so that they could work it out on their own, but Aaron's attacks grew crueller until Sophie dissolved into a storm of tears. I headed him off in the hallway and demanded that he stop. He stifled himself but only until I returned to my room and closed my door. A heartbeat later Sophie was shouting and pleading hysterically with him to leave her alone, but Aaron doggedly continued, 'Poor, fat horse-meat' never has any dates. Ya know why? It's 'cause guys are afraid that the restaurant bill will bankrupt them."

Staying out of it was no longer an option. I stomped into his room to deliver a red alert:

"Aaron, I've had it! You'd better stop bullying your sister right this minute or you're gonna be bloody sorry!"

He sat on his bed with a supercilious grin and asked, "Why will I be sorry? What are you gonna do, call the fat police?"

"I don't think you want to test me, young man. I've listened to just about enough of your disgusting harangue for one night."

"So what are you gonna do, send me to bed without supper? Maybe if you did that to my 'pig' sister once in a while she'd lose a couple o' hundred pounds. Anyhow, I don't care what you do 'cause dad says I should go and live with him anyway! I don't have to live with all your rules. He says if I live with him I'll never have to hear 'Clean your room, Aaron' or 'Take out the garbage Aaron,' ever again! He says I'm not your slave!"

As his taunts increased I could feel the frustration burning red hot in my ears.

I darted toward him as he instantly pulled the quilt over his head. I tried to pull it off but he held on with vice-like strength. My frustration now blended with rage as I began frantically slapping at the quilt, striking anywhere I thought I might make contact. With each slap he continued to mock me.

I guess he must have felt it at some point because after four or five swipes, he became silent … and I stopped slapping. The quilt slowly cascaded onto the bed revealing the tears welling up in his eyes. Aaron had finally stopped taunting and baiting. I stood there holding my breath, waiting ... as if something monumental was about to happen, but he just glared at me defiantly.

A cartoonist might have sketched the scene as sadly comical: The agitated and dour hausfrau being badgered by a terrible over-sized, over-age toddler.

Rallying his defences, Aaron belligerently bellowed, "It didn't even hurt!"

I silently brushed passed Sophie and retreated to my bed. Seconds later, Sophie peeked in my door and blew me a goodnight kiss. I got up and gave her a mutually comforting hug as she tearfully whispered her thanks, and for the rest of the night, silence reigned.

Over the weeks that followed that incident, I developed both a sleeping and breathing disorder. Since I was wholly adverse to mind-altering drugs, I was certain the only possible cure was through therapy.

I told the doctor about the dreadful thing I had done that awful night and waited for him to call in the Children's Aid Society or the white coats. Instead he placed a hand on my shoulder, smiled, and told me that the incident had probably hurt me more than it hurt my strapping six-foot son.

The therapist couldn't have been more wrong. Just weeks after things had apparently improved between us, Aaron announced that he was moving in with his father. I knew I couldn't forbid him, but I pleaded with him to reconsider. I reminded him, "You'll be leaving your siblings, your friends on the street, and maybe even your school, not to mention the fact that I will miss you terribly."

He told me that he had had a long talk with his father, who really wanted him to move in with him.

A month later he was gone.

Harvey had already divorced his second wife, the 'real'

soul mate after they'd shared one year of marriage that yielded two kids. So now he was between wives and living in a penthouse with his third and newest soul mate and Aaron.

Earlier that year, Aaron had begun to work at my theatre as an usher. I was delighted he had stuck to the job in spite of his move because it gave me a chance to see him regularly and know for myself that he was okay. I would often hang around my office at night until the show let out, just so I could offer him a lift back to his father's penthouse. On the way, he would fill me in on some selected history he cared to share about his present school days or social life.

Our relationship appeared to be cool and polite, but I sensed that warmth continued to percolate in his heart as it did in mine.

From time to time his siblings would suggest that they didn't think Aaron was very happy at his father's and I would remind them that it was his choice to leave and that he could always come home as long as he was prepared to live by the rules.

During Aaron's filibuster, I tried to defend my version of the victimhood slapping incident to no avail; but when I heard Sophie's key in the door and her footsteps on the stairs, I felt a breeze of relief.

"Sophie," I beseeched, "do you remember the time I blew up and started smacking Aaron across the head?"

"It's after midnight," she announced. "I left here at six o'clock and you two were sharing a pizza. What happened between then and now?"

"Come on, Sophie, cut the crap, do you remember or not?" Aaron demanded.

"I'm getting married in five months, and I really don't want to get into the middle of a war. It was about ten dress sizes and a thousand years ago, but yeah, I remember it vividly. As a matter of fact I'll probably never forget it, since I was the real victim!"

"Oh, so now I slapped the hell out of you too?" I sighed.

Sophie chuckled, "Hardly. And who said you slapped the hell out of anyone?"

"Your brother is adamant."

"Oh please," she protested, "are we going to go through all that dreck again? Aaron, you were just asking for it that night. You tortured the hell out of me and then hid under piles of blankets when mom came to the rescue. Anyway it's like ten years ago or something. Get over it already!" And with that she marched into her bedroom and closed the door.

While his filibuster continued my memory wandered back to the quasi-jubilant moment my fourteen-year-old prodigal son returned from his father's wilderness.

It was a cool spring day when I came home from work to find five over-stuffed green garbage bags and fourteen-year-old Aaron sitting on our front veranda.

Evidently after just three months of responsibility, his father had packed him up and virtually dumped him, like a Good Will drop-off, on my doorstep.

I unlocked the door and helped him carry his bags up to his room. I didn't want to press too hard, so I just asked if he was home to stay.

"Forever," was all he said. That was good enough for me.

Those first days back he was picture perfect. Without my prodding, he helped around the house, did his homework, and treated everyone with respect. It was a wish granted.

On the first Saturday after his return, I gave Aaron permission to go out with his friends, providing he promised to adhere to an eleven p.m. curfew.

That Saturday night I sweated over every minute that ticked away after the clock struck eleven. Aaron finally arrived home thirty-five minutes late. I met him at the top of the stairs and calmly asked, "Where were you?"

"I was over at Derek's with the guys."

"I see, well you're thirty-five minutes late, so I hope you know that you're grounded?"

"Uh-huh I know," he said as a grin spread across his face.

"Am I missing something here, Aaron? You did hear me, didn't you?"

"Yup, I heard you. I came in late and I'm grounded, right?

I nodded and then, dizzy with bewilderment, I said good-night and headed for my room.

A couple of minutes later Aaron walked in and sat down on the edge of my bed.

"Wanna know why I'm not mad?" he asked rhetorically. I didn't dare breathe as he continued without a pause.

"I almost never ate dinner with dad and we never did anything together. If he wasn't out with her, they were in the bed-room, doing it all night long. The worst of it was that their bed was against my wall so I couldn't get any sleep. And if I turned my ghetto blaster up, dad would run into my room yelling and threatening to cut off my allowance, which is basically what I used to buy my own food. The final straw was a couple of weeks ago when I went downtown to a junior political rally with a bunch of kids. Only one of them was old enough to drive, and he ditched me at one in the morning. I had no way of getting home so I called dad and I kept calling 'til two o'clock, but he wouldn't answer the phone because he was probably too busy doing it. I was so scared; I even accepted a ride home with a stranger.

"I didn't get home 'til almost three in the morning, and Dad never even noticed.

"So I came in late tonight... just 'cause I wanted to see if you'd be waiting and worrying like you used too. And you know what? It was worth a grounding!"

CHAPTER THIRTEEN

A couple of weeks after Aaron's return to us, I arrived home from work to find an ominous looking envelope propped on the banister. The lawyer's letter stated clearly that I had thirty days to put the house up for sale and evacuate the premises or action would be taken to have me forcibly removed. Harvey had left the missive there when he picked the boys up for their Wednesday night outing. Until that night, all legal correspondence had been sent to my office. In hindsight I realized that Harvey had intended for me to find this eviction notice before he dropped the boys off after dinner. It was a wonderfully effective plan. By the time they bounded through the door, they found me sputtering and steaming like water on a coal fire.

Where would we go? What could we do? Two of the three kids who were still living at home were probably old enough to be on their own but they weren't ready. Since they were both struggling to get through university on our shared shoestring, they needed to live at home for another couple of years and I didn't have the money to buy Harvey out. As we all huddled together sharing our mutual fears, the phone rang. It was a familiar ring. It was the melodious sound of long distance. It was Adam.

After hearing my hysterical reading of Harvey's eviction notice, he told me to stay by the phone. Within the hour David called to tell me that he and Adam were committed to loaning me whatever financing it would take to finally be free of Harvey and his remaining hold over me.

As my children and I sat together rejoicing in our hopeful solution, Aaron added a dash of spice when he explained why he had moved in with his father just months before.

It seems that Harvey had promised to help the other three kids through university but only if the house was sold. Aaron told us how Harvey had clearly set the parameters. "Dad said, 'you should've all been outta there years ago. It's your fault she hasn't sold yet and as far as I'm concerned I'm not spending one cent on any of you kids until that God Damn house is sold! No tuition, nothing! It's as simple as that.'"

"I tried to tell dad that he was being unfair but he got furious. 'Ya know, you have a really short memory Aaron,' he yelled. 'Just a few weeks ago she beat the shit out of you for no reason, so why would you want to live there anyway. Are you a sicko? Anyway Brandon's moving in with me, so I figured you'd want to come too. The bottom line is that if you both move in with me, she has no choice but to sell.' After I found out that Brandon never had any intention of moving in, dad took me aside and told me, 'It's up to you Aaron. Do they go to university or not?'"

"I didn't know what to do. I thought it would be a great opportunity to spend the kind of time with dad I'd never had and ... I didn't want to let Brandon and everybody down."

My therapist-inspired talk with Aaron continued for almost seven hours while he led me through a gruelling ritual killing of my psyche. By the time the night was over I was no longer sure who I was, and I couldn't recognize my son at all.

During the course of those torturous hours of confrontation, I was accused of a series of offences, the worst being the sin of trying to turn him and his brother against their father after the divorce.

"You just despised him for leaving you and you wanted us to hate him too."

If they only knew how much I despised Harvey in the year or so before he left, while I was stoically smiling through a myriad of humiliations, like during our legendary Mother's Day dinner or soon after our Father's Day brunch.

Aaron praised his father's virtues to the heavens, insisting that Harvey had never once lied to them about anything, ever, leaving me to conclude that he believed I had.

"I never got to have all the happy memories that Wendy, Sophie and Brandon had 'cause as far back as my memory goes you two were splitting up. I never got all the things that the others got 'cause you claimed you didn't have the money. I never got the attention 'cause you were always working. All I ever got from you was, 'Clean up your room Aaron! Take out the garbage Aaron! Do your homework Aaron! If you want spending money then you'll have to have a part-time job Aaron.'"

"That's called parenting, Aaron. That's what responsible parents do. They make rules and teach their children how to function in a tough world. And they work so that they can look after their children's needs. I was home more than most parents because I had no social life, period. I never had the time or the courage to find one. I worked because it was crucial for our family. How else could we have survived? I did the best I could with no help from your father."

"Oh here we go again! When dad left all you ever did was badmouth him. Well let me tell you ... I got nothing from you, but I always had fun on the weekends I was with dad. He took Brandon and me away on vacation every summer and he took us to ball games and everything and we didn't have to do one thing around his place. And by the way, dad told us that you don't need to be out two or three nights a week because first of all, professional actors rehearse during the day and second of all, he knows all about how businesses are run and he said that nobody has board meetings at night. He says you're just looking for excuses to cover up that you were fooling around."

There was no point in trying to explain that my board members worked at their careers during the day and volunteered on our board at night. There was no point in reminding him that plays do require evening rehearsals and production meetings and costume fittings and a myriad of other time-consuming activities that need to fit into a twenty-four hour day. And there was no point in explaining the fact that, since I was a single woman, I didn't need to look for excuses to go out whenever I wanted. If only I'd had the time, opportunity, and courage I might have found someone who would have liked to spend time with my children as well as fool around with me. I also saw no point in telling him that his father had used every mean, unfair tactic in the book of unethical behaviour to hurt me. He just didn't want to hear it.

"The fact is mom, dad told Brandon and me a lot of stuff about you that we've never mentioned 'cause dad made us promise not to 'cause he knew it would complicate our lives if we were to bring these sick things up while we were still living with you."

"Sick things?" I queried.

"Yeah, like VD maybe?"

"What are you talking about?"

A sardonic grin smeared across his face as he continued.

"Oh please, don't act so innocent. Dad told Brandon and me over a Big Mac when I was barely nine years old. He figured you must have gotten the clap or whatever it was from some low-life actor you were fooling around with. Uch-h it grosses me out to even think about it."

I was completely speechless. Was it possible, even for Harvey, to have vomited up such a horrendous lie and feed it to our children? I gathered myself together and relented.

"It's true, Aaron. I did have it."

"Oh God, I knew it. Ugh, how can you just sit there so casually and admit …"

"… But it was your father who gave me the disease."

"Oh, this is just getting pathetic! Look, dad swore to us that he never in his life had such a gross disease and we believe him. I know you'd love for us to believe he lied to us but it's never gonna happen!"

I stared at my twenty-three-year-old son with incredulity and asked:

"Are you telling me that you believe everything your father tells you and nothing I do? Are you saying that unless you've heard it from him it isn't true?"

"Yes, that's exactly what I'm saying. He has never lied to us!"

"Aaron, just give me a couple of minutes, okay? I'll be right back."

I raced up the stairs and rifled through my file drawer. God was with me. I found what I was looking for. In my hand was the cassette tape that my lawyer had shared with the O.G. before our day in court. I popped the cassette into my little portable gismo, fast forwarded to the appropriate section, and raced down the stairs with the evidence behind my back. I asked once again before I revealed Exhibit "A".

"I want to understand, Aaron. You say that only if you heard something in your father's own voice would you believe it, right?"

He nodded emphatically. I placed the cassette player on the coffee table and let it roll. He fidgeted as he listened.

"Rachel, why in hell do you have to keep talking about that VD shit? It's over God Dammit! Why can't you just forget about it, for Christ sake?"

"I'll tell you why, Harvey. Why, is because it's caused me unbelievable pain and humiliation, but most of all it's because you looked me right in the eye that night and vowed that you and that slut were finished. That's why I slept with you, Harvey. I thought that maybe it was an opportunity for us to start over. It was Father's Day for God's sake."

"Yeah, so it was Father's Day. She and I took a break from each other so she could go away for a while to recuperate and think things over. But at the time I slept with you, I was sure I was all cleared up. It wasn't like I planned to give you that disease ya know, but God dammit you can't let it go, can you? It's not like it was syphilis or something. We both took the medicine and we were both cured ... so get over it already!"

After a few minutes, I asked Aaron if he wanted to hear more. He shook his head. I stopped the tape and turned to him. "That was your father's own words admitting that he gave me that dreadful disease that he vowed to you he had never had ... and never gave me."

Aaron's face had become crimson with rage.

"That is the most disgusting, despicable thing I have ever heard in my life. It makes me want to puke."

I could feel the cool relief of vindication wash over me as my son's words of indignation reached out to me. I listened intently as he continued.

"It's inconceivable to me that you could stoop so low as to tape-record a private conversation with my father!"

✦ ✦ ✦

Planning Sophie's eighteenth century-styled wedding with her was one of the happiest indulgences of my motherhood memoirs. Her wedding day would have been a thing of complete bliss and beauty, except for the fact that Aaron and I had not spoken a word to each other in five months, and I hadn't even seen him since he moved out four months before the wedding. During that time there were a variety of dinners, brunches, and cocktail parties held in our house for the engaged couple, but Aaron was always noticeably absent.

On the morning of Sophie's wedding, I was in the hotel reception area waiting for the photo session to begin. I spotted Aaron standing near the snack table all decked out in his formal wear and munching on a bagel. I gathered my courage, walked over to him, placed my hand on his arm, and softly uttered, "Mazel Tov, Aaron." He looked down at me from his lofty six-foot-three vantage point, threw off my hand, grunted in utter disgust, and stalked away.

It was the most profound rejection of my life. The weight of that solitary moment impacted on my heart with the ferocity of a Mac truck.

My righteous paranoia led me to ask myself this question: Could Harvey, on the threshold of our daughter's wedding day, have somehow provoked this vengeful scene?

As I slunk away to lick my wounds, haunting images of past confrontations began to stalk through my memory. Snippets of scenes rushed through my head like a videocassette on rewind until it stopped abruptly on Aaron at age eight.

I was packing up my sons' duffel bags for their bi-monthly weekend with their father. Harvey and I had been separated for a couple of years and my ex-husband's initial animosity had matured into an insidious hatred that he demonstrated by his untiring quest to affect my sanity. I on the other hand had focused my respective anger toward him on the more intimate dynamics of mere gut-wrenching angst and periodic outbursts of verbal annihilation. On that particular day, Aaron and I had a falling-out over what clothes he needed for the chilly mid-winter weekend. He insisted on taking summer cotton t-shirts and I insisted that he take cozy long-sleeved sweaters. I continued to insist and he continued to refuse. The basis of his argument was that if he needed anything his father would go out and buy it for him. That was a shock to me since their father left all the selecting and paying to me.

"Dad would buy us anything we needed if he didn't have to give you all his money. Dad told us how he gives you loads of money, but you always tell us you don't have any money for 'extras.' He says you have just as much money as he does and that you must blow it on yourself, 'cause otherwise we'd have everything we could ever want!"

Harvey's finances and mine were curiously relative: he grossed a little less than four hundred thousand dollars a year and I grossed a little less than ten per cent of that. He always maintained that women were only worth ten percent of anything men had anyway, so he was doubly blessed to have kept us in the courts until he found a judge who agreed. The absurdly low three-figure cheques I received from Harvey each month were more like a nominal grudge tax than a responsible contribution to our children's welfare.

My young son continued to proclaim his father's virtues until I wanted to holler ... and of course eventually I did. Aaron was a young master at the game of "Can I ever push your buttons!" For this achievement, Harvey had been a true role model, the "master baiter," and I was an easy fish to hook. But on that frigid winter's day my eight-year-old left our house wearing a thick, double-knit sweater and a very angry face. It wasn't unusual for us to have a verbal war over his father, but I especially hated when it happened just before he left for one of their male bonding weekends.

When Aaron returned on Sunday evening, he made no mention of our previous tug of war. He even finished his homework without a fuss.

Sometime during the wee hours of the morning I was awakened by a soul-wrenching scream. I rushed into Aaron's room to find him crying out and thrashing about in his bed. I tried to calm him down, but he pulled away from me, insisting that he was fine and that it was just a bad dream. I asked if he wanted to talk about it.

"No!" he snapped.

I tried again and again to comfort him, but he consistently refused. I reluctantly returned to my room where I lay in the dark, feeling bewildered and frightened by his reaction. Only a few minutes had passed when my door flew open and my little redheaded scrapper scurried to my bedside sobbing. I wiped his eyes, blew his nose, and then slowly wrapped my arms around his shuddering little body. After a couple of minutes, I heard his soft, tentative voice gasping through his tears, "Why are you hugging me? You don't care about me, so how come, huh?"

I was stunned.

"You don't have to pretend, mommy." he tearfully implored. "I know the truth!"

"What are you talking about?" I sputtered.

He poured out his story through sobbing gasps. "Daddy

told me everything! He said that you have a problem with me 'cause you almost died because of me. He told me that you'll never get over it and you'll never be able to love me the same as the others, so I better get used to it!"

I was in utter shock. Aaron was my baby. My adorable, spunky, feisty little redhead who never failed to make every day an interesting adventure for us all. How could his father have stooped so low?

I drew my fingers through Aaron's silky curls and listened while his breathing finally settled into a soft rhythmic hum. I realized that, somehow, I had to tell my devastated child about the strange and wonderful event of his birth so that he would know the truth for himself. I also knew that I had to walk a very fragile line or I might weaken our connection forever. I had to tell him why he had a special place in my heart that would always be reserved for him.

I guided Aaron through our great adventure step by step, taking care to tiptoe around the grisly aspects of the journey and to concentrate instead on the miracle of our ultimate triumph. I told him that when I got to the end of the story, I would share a very important secret with him that I had told only one other person … and that was Dr. Silverberg.

Thinking back, I wonder if the overtly gruesome details that surrounded his actual birth might have been more gripping to that eight-year-old than the pure magical fact of his being born at all. After all, he had been conditioned to the ugly side of reality ever since the divorce, when Harvey began to entertain our five- and nine-year-old sons by sneaking them into such enlightening "children's" films as *Damien* and *Scarface.*

Now that Aaron had heard the complete story of his miracle birth from me, I hoped that he would never again have any serious need to question the depth of my love and commitment to him. When I finished, he asked, "Mommy, is that why you send Dr. Silverberg roses every year on my birthday?"

"Uh-huh," I murmured. "I want him to always remember what a miracle he brought into our world."

"So, is that the secret that nobody knows about, except Dr. Silverberg? He asked with wide-eyed innocence."

"No, honey, that isn't the secret." I took a deep breath, held him even closer… and continued:

"Remember I told you that just before the doctor had to put me to sleep, my heart stopped beating? Well, this is going to be a little difficult to explain, but I'm going to try my best. Aaron, I'm going to tell you a wonderful story about something called a near death experience.

CHAPTER FORTEEN

Memory is the peculiar human device by which our individual histories are recorded involuntarily by each living person. The conundrum is that two people who witness the same incident will later recall it as two completely different events.

With little effort, I am able to evoke bygone images, recall voices, and even recollect scents from years long past, but my meager recollections are diminished by Shirley McLaine's blinding light. She can regurgitate centuries of vibrant past lives and astounding adventures while I struggle to remember mere decades of patently commonplace events. I even have the luxury of baby books and photos to aid in my quest, while poor Shirley has to make do with meditation and hypno-gurus. Strange as it may seem, the closer I move toward my present history the more nebulous my memories become.

I do remember, however, with complete clarity, how and when I heard the news of Aaron's engagement.

It was a clear, cold Canadian winter's morning and since

I was leaving the next day to direct a workshop in Los Angeles, I had been invited to Wendy and Noah's for a bon voyage breakfast. When I arrived, my daughter was scurrying about the kitchen preparing an overly hospitable buffet and I couldn't help but notice from the minute I stepped inside that I was being handled with a hint of excessive politeness. Noah declined my offer to help them in the kitchen and insisted that I was to move into the sitting area where my two grandchildren were anxiously waiting to play with me.

While I was belting out songs and exchanging tall tales with the little people, a powerful argument seemed to be building between my hosts even though not an angry word had been uttered. Instead they exchanged a series of animated scowls and grunts, which clearly raised my suspicion that something important needed to be said out loud.

My attention was soon diverted to a more pressing agenda when Gabriel and Olivia asked if I would play a game of "what animal am I" with them. Three-year-old Olivia was up first. I think it was the "meow, meow" that gave her away so quickly. But she did manage to lick her hands and my cheeks before accepting defeat. Five-year-old Gabriel changed the rules by insisting that we imitate the animal that we most closely resemble. He chose a lion. He said that everyone tells him that with his thick mane of blonde hair and long, muscular legs, he looks just like the young lion in the "Lion King." So a lion it was.

Then it was my turn.

"Saftah, what animal do people think you look like?"

"Well, I've never really thought about it, Gabriel … but someone once told me I looked like a water buffalo."

"I've never seen one in my whole life, Saftah," Gabriel confessed.

"Are they pretty? Are they purple?" Olivia purred. It was

evident from her shirt to her shoes that, to Olivia, everything pretty was purple.

"Can you show me a picture sometime?" Gabriel pleaded.

"You know what kids, after I return from L.A., I'll try to find a picture of a water buffalo at the library, but only if you remind me. That'll be your job, okay?"

There was a simultaneous nod of intent.

While deals were being forged in our area of the room, Wendy and Noah were still working on a détente.

Finally, my courageous son-in-law pulled me aside and cleared his throat in a most commanding way before proceeding.

"We all heard days ago, and we were all told not to tell you. But I refused to agree. In fact I emphatically stated that I would not agree and that I would tell you. So now I've told you and I'm not sorry I did either."

It's fair to assume that I was bewildered but I sensed that patience would bring me the answers to the questions that were suffocating in my brain.

As Wendy raised her bowed head, I saw a path of tears trickle down her dimpled cheeks and then I heard her barely whispered words as clearly as if she had screamed them from the top of Mount Zion.

"Mom, Aaron's engaged."

Those three words pierced my heart as deftly as a carving knife.

During Aaron's years at university he often regaled me with stories of the infamous philosopher Machiavelli, but I never suspected that my son would become a follower.

In my head I could hear Alex Trebeck leading me in a game of "Jeopardy".

The answer: "When I heard my son was engaged."

The question: "When did you last experience complete and utter rejection?"

There were many unfortunate times in my childhood when I felt snubbed, ignored, or forgotten and strange as it seems, sometimes I was the architect of my own shunning.

Because I spent so much of my young life repressing issues that I was sure my parents would either dismiss or misread, I evolved into a lonely child with a voracious appetite for books. It comforted me to read about other children who were worse off than I. Some of my favourite characters grew up in orphanages, had wicked stepmothers, or were oppressed by cold calculating elves that made their lives sad and hopeless. As for my parents, they had all the qualities required to do the job well. It was just that they were too busy struggling to survive to notice how desperately I craved their attention. I was, however, determined to take full advantage of any opportunity to divert their attention away from any of the other kids and on to me. So I was on drama queen standby the stormy summer night my brother David suffered a life-threatening asthma attack.

The doctor had been attending to him for hours, and it seemed that everyone was allowed to be in the room with him, except me. I surreptitiously tiptoed in to have a peek and was daunted by the dark unbridled sense of foreboding I felt as I peered into the pasty face of Adam standing vigil by our brother's sick bed. A paralyzing fear gripped me when I saw my father brush a mysterious tear from his cheek. Since I had never seen my father cry before, I felt overwhelmed by the pain I saw etched in his face. But rather than retreat quietly and allow him to focus his attention on David where it belonged, I instead began to whine, "I have a tummy ache! I think there's a monster under my bed! My socks are itchy."

My father's pale blue eyes darkened like the storm clouds

that now encased our cottage. A threatening bolt of lightning and a crash of thunder shook the entire house at the very instant my father hollered, "Stop that whining and get out of this room ... now!"

I ran out of the room and out of the house and I didn't stop running until I reached the Morrows' back yard.

The rain had thickened into hailstones the size of pigeon-droppings. I plunked myself down on the rope swing under the big old elm tree and I sobbed. I wanted my parents to notice that I was gone. Maybe I would get asthma too and then they'd heap all their rapt attention on me.

I sat there drenched and cold and waiting to be discovered. But Mr. Morrow didn't come out. I cried louder. There was still no movement from the farmhouse. I called out his name... but there was absolutely no response.

After what seemed like hours, Mr. Morrow finally stepped outside. He called me into the tool shed, handed me a rain slicker, and ordered me to go home.

"How dare you do such an irresponsible thing, young lady? Now ya know full well that yer mommy and daddy are worried sick about yer big brother tonight, so how could ya run off like that? Shame on you, Rachel Morganstein! And I always thought you were a smart little girl. I hope I wasn't wrong about you. Now you been sittin' out there in that weather for over five minutes, so it's past time for you to skiddadle on home and dry off before they find you missin'. And don't ya go actin' like a spoiled brat again, ya hear me?"

I stood outside David's room dripping wet and grateful, just this one time, that no one noticed me.

... *Aaron is engaged*! Those three words had caught us all in a grotesque tableau, so after an eternally lengthy silence, I swallowed a persistent sob and gathered the chutzpah to quip, "So,

Wendy, what was it that you weren't supposed to tell me?"

Up until that morning, the Krup family tragedy read like a fragmented Bible story: *Prodigal son leaves home in anger and travels the world seeking his muse while his mother waits by the pigeon coop awaiting word of their much anticipated reunion.*

So, the word had been reluctantly delivered: the prodigal son wanted no part of a reunion.

The wedding planning machine raced along the fast track while I remained tied to the rails waiting for a rescue. Even after surviving all my gruesome experiences with Harvey, I still found it impossible to believe that he could throw our last child a wedding that would not include his mother, especially since our primary battle over the other three weddings was always about money.

To meet my half of those commitments, I had to stoop to cashing in insurance policies and selling anything of value I could find around the house. I was even desperate enough on one occasion to successfully interview for a weekend "mansion-cleaning" job, which I wisely declined for fear I might get spotted by one of my elite board members while scrubbing a guest toilet. It was kind of gratifying to know I was worthy though.

Harvey had refused to pay one cent more than me for any of the other weddings but now it seemed that the biggest and most expensive of all celebrations was to be freely bestowed on Aaron as a gift; perhaps for his willingness to leave me out of the wedding album.

I desperately wanted my other children to stand up to their father and brother; to tell them that the wedding shouldn't go ahead until our problem was resolved. But they didn't. They wanted to, but they weren't willing to alienate their brother or defy their father to do it. It was a difficult position for three children who had suffered through all those turbulent years of our divorce war.

In spite of Harvey's irresponsible behaviour, all four children had hung on through his many relationships, even when the new women in Harvey's life rejected them. They supported him when he decided to give up dentistry and go into the insurance game. Everyone talked around the issues but no one dove right into the centre of them. No one was brave enough to face the indignant accusations of betrayal that Aaron would reveal whenever the subject of reconciliation with me was even hinted at.

My children admittedly knew that if the roles had been reversed, I would never have allowed the wedding to proceed. I wouldn't have stopped Aaron from getting married, but I would never have paid for a public wedding celebration that did not include his father. This would not be a decision of preference but of conscience. I can admit that the very idea of Harvey being ostracized conjures up a vivid picture in my mind of delicious revenge. My conscience, however, recognizes that malicious vengeance can only be that sweet in a fantasy because in reality, everyone gets hurt.

As the months passed and the date drew nearer, the word "wedding" was all but deleted from our family vocabulary. Bridesmaid dresses, rehearsal dinners, orchestras, photographers, and the like were subjects that were never mentioned in my presence. Perhaps the idea was that if they didn't share any of the details, then they wouldn't have to take any responsibility for not taking any responsibility. Or perhaps they thought if I wasn't told anything, then the reality wouldn't exist for me and I therefore couldn't be hurt by it. What they failed to comprehend is how many of Aaron's weddings I had attended over the months in my mind. He was married inside the waterfall cave in Kauai, on the Serengeti at sunrise in Africa, atop of Masada in Israel, and in the cozy parlour of our grand old home. At every one of those weddings, I stood proudly under the canopy, admiring the exquisite bride and groom.

It was natural that tensions rose as the date drew nearer. Everyone was hoping for a miracle that would quietly end the war. I had made overtures early in the battle, but my wounds were so deep, I was left shell-shocked. If I were to try to make another attempt, I needed a sign that I wouldn't be jumping into a minefield. I listened closely for any hint that Aaron wanted this to stop, but it never came… until one day in a phone call, Brandon, perhaps inadvertently, said something that shook me to the core.

"Look mom, we don't see things the way Aaron does. For some reason, he sees his whole childhood as a miserable experience and no matter how we try to remind him of all the good times, he just doesn't acknowledge them. He either says they're figments of our imagination or else he gets even more angry and yells at us that those great memories were ours and it only reminds him how miserable his life really was. And, mom, we don't know why he says it; we know it's crazy but he says he doesn't believe you ever loved him."

In that Dr. Strangelove moment, Brandon was straddling an atomic bomb headed directly towards me and he didn't have any inkling that he was steering it blindly.

The wedding was fast approaching, and I had little time left to do something.

Finally, several days before the big day, I made a decision. I got up and exercised, showered, and dressed, all before seven in the morning. Then I spent the bulk of the day talking myself in and out of calling my son. At least twenty times I lifted the phone and replaced it until my wrist hurt. The sun was going down and my mood was darkening along with it. I knew it was now or… perhaps tomorrow.

The next day I went through the same routine until dusk, when finally I picked up the phone and dialled the number the operator had given me, which turned out to be a very nice Pakistani man who sounded nothing like Aaron.

On day three I tried again. As the electronic signal bleeped again and again without a response, I bit down on my lip as hard as I could to keep a grip on reality. Sobs rumbled through my body like a rolling earthquake while Gulliver sized tears soaked everything in sight. I was now caught in a new dilemma. If I hang up and he has caller I.D. what terrible things will he make of that? If he doesn't answer and I leave a message, will he even listen to it?

"... So, leave your name and a short message and either Elaine or I will be sure to call you back...

"Beep ..."

"Hi Aaron ... it's Mom ... I guess this call will come as a shock to you ... I'm sorry you're not there ... but I wanted to uh ... wish you and Elaine a Mazel Tov ... And I wanted to tell you that uh ... I, uh ... a couple of days ago ... uh ... Brandon told me something that took my breath away ... He said that you believe I don't love you and never did! ... Well, I called 'cause I didn't want you to stand under the wedding canopy on the most important day of your life, doubting that you lived all those years with a mother who never loved you ... Whether it matters to you now or not Aaron, I want you to know that I've always loved you and I always will ... and you'll always have a special place in my heart ... And no matter what ever happens ... I'll never give up on us ... I'll just pray that one day you'll have a light bulb moment when you'll start to recall all the good things we shared over those twenty-three years. I wish you every gift life has to offer ... be well ... be happy and ... even if you choose to doubt any other words in this message ... please believe that I love you."

After two days of hearing nothing about the call from any of the kids, I decided to ask if they knew that I had called their brother. They knew, but they had been reluctant to share Aaron's reaction to my call. By the end of the day, empathy for my need to know finally convinced Wendy to tell me the truth.

"Oh sure," Aaron had scoffed, "she calls when she knows I'm not there so she can leave a message. How weak, stupid, and pathetic is that?"

Well, maybe he was right. Maybe unconsciously I had hoped he wouldn't answer so that I'd have a chance to say what I wanted to say without being decimated.

The next day, I attempted to fill my time and senses with anything that could distract me from thoughts of Aaron's imminent wedding. I drove to a local mall to wander the corridors in search of thought polluters like pitchmen hawking kitchen aids or Muzac or bawling babies, anything that would prevent me from thinking.

I wandered aimlessly along the neon corridors until I crashed headlong into Harvey's current soul mate. The calamity of my being struck speechless was Zelda's good fortune. She smiled condescendingly.

"Oh, it's so good to see you," she gushed. "You'll have to excuse my appearance, I've just come from having a facial and a pedicure which was really so dumb because I still have to rush around trying to find another pair of shoes 'cause the ones I bought hurt like hell and... oh crap, I think my God-damn toenails are still wet, well there's thirty bucks down the toilet. There's just so much wedding shit left to do before Sunday. I need to go for a final fitting on my bloody gown and I have to pick up Cornish hens for our out-of-towners dinner tomorrow. So, I really better get going. It was great seeing you. You look terrific. Have a nice day. Bye-bye now."

I remained immobilized, flash frozen in her icy quagmire. I'm not sure how I made it back to my condo, but I'll bet I was a far more dangerous weapon in the car than is a cell phone.

I climbed into my bed where I've remained ever since.

✦ ✦ ✦

Today my mind is like a VCR that has short-circuited mid film. Now I'm left with a jigsaw puzzle of graphic snippets that crowd out the complete pictures to which I'm clinging. This hard reality has drained all hope from my psyche.

As the hours tick by, I sit here doing my nails and clinging to the feint hope that my phone will ring and Aaron will beg me to get a good night's sleep, throw on a gown and get myself under that wedding canopy for five o'clock tomorrow.

If he doesn't call in the next twenty minutes, then it's not meant to be… Well perhaps twenty is a little rigid. I'll give him a full hour… or I can actually give him until morning, now that I know my nails are done and the gown still fits. I could make it to the chapel with time to spare. I already told Madeleine that she shouldn't bank on my being at the impromptu dinner party she has scheduled to coincide with Aaron's ceremony. It was very thoughtful of my friends to want to lend me their support, but I needed them to understand that I may very well be standing under the wedding canopy at that time.

The night has passed too quickly and now the unwelcome dawn is attempting to ooze into my bedroom and dab a golden glow on all my dark thoughts. I used to welcome such vibrant rays of sunlight during the bleak days of November but today it will take more than this "Stepford Sun" to lift my black mood.

The ritual phone calls that started earlier in the week have grown more frequent and frantic. My entire L.A. family has logged hours of long distance minutes and an elegant cavalcade of faithful friends has followed suit.

It's mid morning and I have heard from each of the three children who are still in my life. They called to say hi as if it were any other Sunday of any other month. One at a time they struggled to share the tiniest of small talk they could improvise. For example; Brandon's take on the weather: "It sure is cold out there today, huh?" Sophie's position on her newborn's status: "I feel so bad 'cause he's got a really bad diaper rash. I hope he'll be okay." But then came Wendy who mustered the courage to make a reference to the actual event: "Mom, I'm really not looking forward to this wedding and you wouldn't either if you had to wear puke green."

Finally, the wedding subject is on the table and I am in the loop.

At five o'clock my sister picked me up to take me to Madeleine's special dinner party for "uninvited wedding guests." There were over thirty people there and lots of food. I think they told jokes or maybe it was war stories about divorce or estrangement. Perhaps it was just an evening rife with familial myths. I simply don't remember.

The morning after the wedding there was a traffic jam of phone calls. Three in particular from my children who were struck dumb by the enormity of the history we had all encountered. It seemed as if they were filled with frustration, sadness, and perhaps even guilt, but they just didn't know what to say about the event. So they said nothing.

That afternoon, however, I got a phone call from six-year-old Gabriel who wanted to tell me that he was very upset about a bunch of things. I encouraged him to tell me all about the things that were bugging him, but I feared the worst. After all, wasn't that the way it all began with Aaron?

My gutsy little six-year-old grandson heaved a big sigh before proceeding.

"Saftah, I was really upset that you didn't come to Uncle Aaron's wedding yesterday 'cause I wanted to dance with you. Why didn't you come?"

"It's kind of hard to explain, sweetie, but I'll dance with you the next time you come to visit okay?"

"Saftah, I asked Uncle Aaron where you were, and he said that you were too busy to come. When I asked mommy, she said, 'You'll understand everything when you grow up,' but I don't want to wait that long. Anyway, last night I heard Grandpa Krup telling people that Uncle Aaron didn't want you to come. Is that true?"

"Oh, I would hope it's not, sweetheart. But, Gabriel, I think it would be best to ask Uncle Aaron about that."

"You know what, Saftah? Uncle Aaron better be nice to you before he has kids 'cause they're gonna be really mad at him if they can't have play dates with you like the rest of us. And you know what else, Saftah?"

"What?"

"You forgot a long time ago to show me and Olivia a picture of a water buffalo."

"Oh, you're right. I'm so sorry, honey … But hey, wait a minute here, weren't you supposed to remind me?"

"Uh-huh we were, but its okay, Saftah, mommy looked it up on the Internet this morning and you know what? Whoever told you that you look like one of those yucky, smelly beasts is very, very mean and I don't think you should ever talk to them again. Mommy thinks so too."

I dared not to tell him that I couldn't agree more. Instead I brought the subject back to the game.

"So, Gabriel, what kind of animal did you guys finally

decide I'm like?"

"Well, Olivia thinks you look like a fluffy, purple puppy but mommy thinks you're more like a gazelle."

"And what about you, Gabriel?" What kind of animal do you think I'm like?"

"I think you're like a perfect people animal, Saftah, and maybe someday I'll tell Uncle Aaron that and maybe he'll think so too."

There was no need for me to speak. His words were like a shot of morphine for my pain.

"Saftah?"

"Yes, Gabriel?"

"Can I come and sleep over at your house tonight? 'Cause then I can get to dance with you … or maybe we can bake some more sugar cookies … or if Olivia comes too, we could all put on another play … or …"

ABOUT THE AUTHOR

In 1977, Reva Stern became Artistic Director of the Leah Posluns Theatre in Toronto, where she maintained her position until 1994. Ms. Stern has been the Guest Director at the Coconut Grove Playhouse in Miami as well as major Theatres in Kansas City, Chicago, New York City and Los Angeles. Passionate about collaborating on new scripts, Ms. Stern found herself in creative company with such notable writers as Isaac Bashevis Singer, Richard Baer, Arthur Marx, Rubin Carson, William Gibson and Elizabeth Forsythe Hailey, while she has also written and produced several original stage plays.

Director, writer and dramaturge for almost thirty years, Reva retained the position of Regional Casting Director for the American Academy of Dramatic Arts for New York City and Los Angeles for almost twenty years, while still at the helm of the Leah Posluns Theatre and Theatre School. Ms. Stern has been bestowed with several awards of merit in theatre and has been a guest speaker at esteemed venues such as The University of Miami, the Actor's Workshop, the New Play Festival in New York City, and the Playwright's Conference at the University of Pittsburgh.

In recent years, Reva Stern has brought her love of writing to the forefront as her primary career. Writing and editing professionally for the past decade, she has been encouraged by several writing award nominations. Additionally, her manuscript "The Prescott Journals" was optioned for the screen prior to publication, and is slated to become her second published novel. But stage plays, screenwriting, and novels aren't nearly enough pen-to-paper action for the impassioned Reva. She has compiled a collection of short stories and a series of Children's books titled "Tales from Grandma's Cupboard". Her additional publishing credits include extensive freelance writing for periodicals, magazines and newspapers including the National Post, and several years as an editor for Wellness Way Publications.

Ms. Stern is the proud mother of four amazing people.

ACKNOWLEDGEMENTS

On Passover, we Jews measure our good fortune by listing the many ways in which a divine hand spared us from defeat as we crossed the Red Sea; and with each crisis, all who are gathered around the Seder table respond in unison with gratitude and humility vowing ... *"It would have been enough"*.

In looking back over the odyssey that led me to complete this novel, I have felt that Passover gratitude ... that freedom to continue on when defeat seemed the easier road to travel. It was the support and encouragement of family and friends that kept me on the path.

Early on, it was my mentor, Rabbi Avraham Feder who challenged me to write for the stage. Later, I was encouraged to write this novel by my brother Sandor who as a successful screen-writer knows a thing or two about writing. I was motivated by my brother Steven who as an experienced film director thought my first manuscript was worthy of optioning for the screen and sent it to an LA producer who agreed. And so I was optioned before I was published.

I was inspired to write in the first person by humorist Rubin Carson and urged to be brave by my late loving friend and fellow writer Richard Baer.

If it had turned out that only one of these wonderful people would have had a hand in nudging me forward ... *"It would have been enough"*... but there they all were along with so many others:

My remarkable children Paula, Tirzah, Josh and Asher who gave me the courage to define love.

Text Editor Stacey Balakofsky for her pain-staking effort to keep on top of my often slovenly punctuation and grammar.

My agent Jasmine D'Costa who led me into and through the awesome halls of publishing.

My publisher Robert Morgan who took a chance on a first time novelist.

The brilliant artist Kandy Stern who created the charming and insightful "Water Buffalo" illustration.

Photographer Jim Allen for his skill and ingenuity.

Lawyer Michael Levine who always took the time to edge me along the right path.

My entrepreneurial sister Ruth who was steady and serious in her determination to see me launched.

My friend Andrea who managed to nudge me forward whenever I lost the will.

To Eva, Denny, Larry, Maggi, Maureen, Sarah, Shiny, Wilfred and so many other friends and family members … "*it was enough.*" It was your gift of support and encouragement that helped me to stay on course.

I am grateful and humbled by the enthusiastic endorsements of Elaine Dembe, Syd Field, Elizabeth Forsythe Hailey and Andrew Neiderman.